COURT

OF

DREAMS

A Young Coach Thrust Into
High Profile Obstacles

FRANK MICHAEL STALLONE

A man's quest is for his grasp to stretch beyond his reach.

~ Frank Michael Stallone

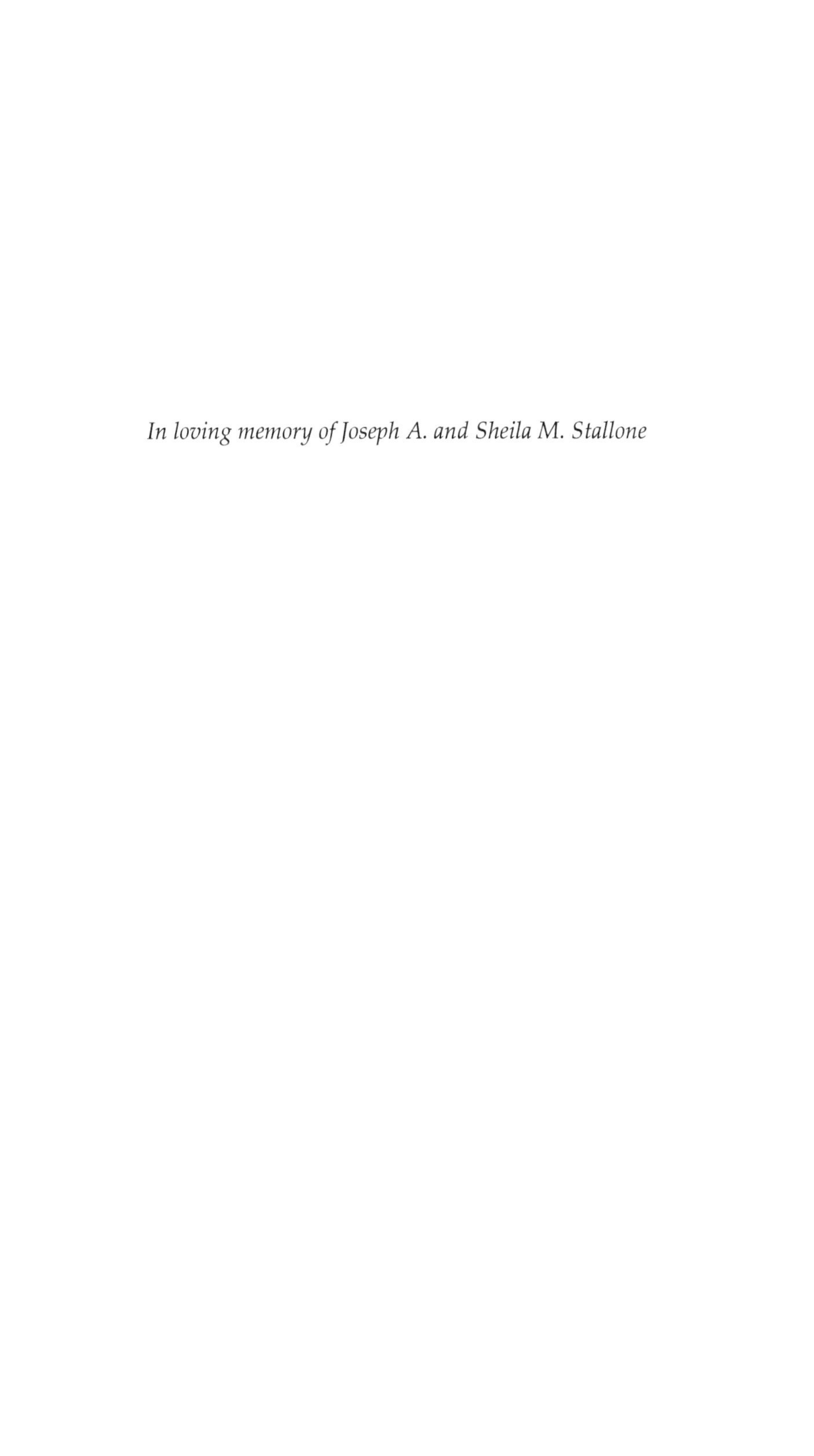

In loving memory of Joseph A. and Sheila M. Stallone

PART ONE

CHAPTER

ONE

The elongated, black, four-door Lincoln Continental hooked a right onto Clay Pitts Road in the southern part of the suburb of Taffin. The doctor's name was Richard Rosen, and he was the only driver traveling this maze of a roadway that was outlined like oversized twisted spaghetti.

The night was persistently miserable–rainy, cold, and very dark. He couldn't have imagined a more dreary setting, and the environment that he found himself contained in was bringing the birth of what would be termed in modern-day language as an Excedrin. If it did develop itself into a full-scale monster of a migraine, he felt secure that he knew exactly how to supply the antidote that would douse the flaming inferno within his cerebral cortex. After all, that is what he did for a living. He was a specialist, a professional doctor, and had been one for nearly thirty-five years. Remedy complaints of the physical nature, with respect to one's body. Only about a third of the time, the problem could be deemed as purely mental, and for that, he had no cure. Just a recommendation, and it wasn't to take two aspirin and call me in the morning and thus hand over a business card.

The clock flashed 7:19 p.m. in green illuminated light according to the digital display in the computerized dashboard.

He was already twenty minutes late, but that didn't worry him any. This wasn't a pre-arranged confirmed appointment back at the medical center. It was simply an early evening house call to a long-time friend. Thank God this wasn't one of those psychological cases. He knew that he wasn't going to have to think about his facetiously created recommendation to this particular patient. Though later on he wished he could because he would soon find out that the patient to be examined was, unfortunately, practically brain dead already. Comatose.

As he pulled into the circular driveway of the destined residence, he could see the faint yet congested density of the light rain dancing with up and down movement in the exposure introduced by the halogen headlights. This was made possible by the up-weaving gusts of ever changing winds and their fluctuating velocities. After all, this was the windy city of Chicago.

After the black Lincoln had come to its temporary resting place and upon the good doctor's exiting his automobile, he skipped up the front steps, which was weird, as well as unduly recognizable, for a man of his age. The doctor wasn't in a rush to examine his good friend's wife. He was impatient and found it physically rebellious to be subjected to this type of climate. The moment he got under the porch's ceiling, which prohibited any further wetness falling upon his head, he was still protected by one of those typical black fedoras that only visiting doctors wore. The big, brown stoic-looking door stood ajar, and a man the same age as the doc, sixty-three years old John Connors, let him in and closed the door on the evil storm.

John Connors was about six foot three, two hundred and ten pounds. He appeared strong, handsome, intelligent, and refined, which he was. He was wearing dark blue pants that were the other half of a suit, slippers, and a very smart-looking housecoat covering his dress shirt. Both men exchanged hellos.

John said, "Let me take your coat, Richard."

The doctor responded with a "Thank you. It sure is a nasty night out there."

John continued, "Sorry to make you come out all this way on such a night, Richard, but Priscilla seems to be out of it."

"Don't apologize to me, John. Let's just tend to Priscilla."

"This way," John said.

They crept up a staircase single-file to the second-floor bedroom. John was on the point and the good doctor anchored up the rear. They walked quietly as if it mattered. Just before they entered the master bedroom, the doctor's imagination began to play tricks on him. His migraine, which never fully matured, was replaced by a morbid, imaginative flow. It just popped in there. He was hoping, upon entering the room, that they wouldn't witness Priscilla's entire body levitating six feet or so off the ground, or perhaps her head spinning completely around, or talking and cursing in a multitude of changing voices. If the good doctor did experience one of these visions, he would surely turn to John and request a swap, a trade. The priest for the good doctor and then order two straight jackets; one for the possessed, and one for the obsessed. Naturally, as soon as they rounded the corner and entered the master bedroom, his wildly gross scenario vanished and was again replaced by the simple, sweet scene of Priscilla sleeping ever so peacefully. His crazed imagination had fled, but it did not leave him bankrupt of the spirit he had as a doctor who would determine the problem and resolve it if he could. He wasn't going to be satisfied with Priscilla's condition after his immediate look over. Needless to say, neither would John. The doc certainly could diagnose the condition, but he would have no remedy. No cure tonight.

John was standing at the foot of the bed, simply observing his friend administering his knowledge. John pretty much knew Priscilla's current condition. He didn't need to be a physician to see that the end was near for his sixty-six year old wife. All John could remember was the moment on the day of their wedding ceremony (until death do us part). He could sense, feel, and see it coming.

The doctor was seated on the bed close to her head, looking, searching intently for signs. Signs that would signal good or bad. There was none.

While the doctor was conducting his routine analysis, John asked, "Is she in any pain, Richard?"

The doc responded, "No, absolutely not."

John countered immediately, "Good."

The doctor stood and walked over to John.

John said, "Come on, Richard, let's go down into the parlor."

They then exited the room. John closed the door, and they headed for the staircase. This time the doctor led the way while John pulled up the rear. Once in the parlor, John immediately positioned himself by the liquor cabinet, clutched a bottle of brandy, drew two glasses, and poured some in both in silence.

The doctor witnessed the pouring, and said, "Ah, brandy."

As John handed over a full shot glass, he said, "Priscilla's condition is deteriorating, isn't it?"

The doctor looked at the floor, his eyes searching for an escape hatch, but there was none. This was the hard part. It always was and always would be. After taking a good wallop of his alcoholic beverage, he said, "Yes, John, she's declining rather quickly. She's beginning to lose her vital signs."

John sat down in the chair next to him. After thinking for a moment or two and staring into space, he asked, "Do you think we should have her taken to Mercy Hospital?"

The doctor looked at John and said, "No, John. In this case, that won't be necessary. She's not in any pain at all. She's simply sleeping. If Priscilla had a very strong heart, I would suggest it. But the fact is that her heart is very weak, and they won't be able to do anything for her now." Richard crossed over to John, put his hand on his shoulder, and said, "John, she has a week to ten days at the most, maybe not even."

John felt the kiss of death through the touch of the doc's hand and heard it through his ears at the doctor's words, simultaneously. He sniffed as a tear started to surface and crawled slowly down his cheek. John looked up at the good doctor and said, "Thanks for coming all the way out here tonight."

The doctor reciprocated instantaneously. "Don't mention it, John. I'm here as a friend tonight. Do you want me to stay with you for a while?"

John answered, "No, Richard, that won't be necessary. You have another half hour or forty minutes to drive in this weather. Besides, your wife is waiting for you."

The doctor said, "You're right, John. Thank you, that sounds like a good idea. She's probably very worried."

John handed the doctor his raincoat, and he swung it over himself. He then proceeded to see the doctor out. When John opened the door, the doctor repeated what he had said when he entered John's dwelling forty-five minutes earlier. "What a nasty night out there. Good night, John."

"Goodnight, Richard, and be careful."

"Thank you," said the doctor and left in a slight jog back to his Lincoln Continental. John closed the door and stood there long after the dark vehicle pulled off his property.

He saw rain, wind, coldness, and darkness. It looked like an abyss out there, and he felt the imaginable intangible commodity. He whispered to himself. "Jesus, God, it's such a dark night." Then he took a long-lasting slug from his shot glass as if it was the last drop of water in a canteen shared by a platoon of men in the hot Sahara desert where the sun set fire to your mind. He turned slowly and began to walk back up the staircase with a very slow, shuffling gait.

CHAPTER

TWO

It was an extremely cold morning on the campus of Western Chicago University. It didn't help matters that the heat in the athletic building decided not to show up for work that day. If the seventeen people who were employed in the department knew that the heat would be on the blink, at least half of them would have joined the inconsistent system of calling in sick for the day.

The athletic building lay on the east wing of the university, on a corner of the campus, which left it quite secluded. There were nineteen buildings plotted on the twenty-five acre property. Like all college campuses with great acreage, there were wide open gaps that stretched as long as three or four city blocks, ostracizing one building from another. Also like all other college campuses that experience winter semester in the true sense of the word, Western Chicago University seemed to be the coldest place on the planet. Each morning, afternoon, and night during the hard winter months every student of the 22,000 making up the student body would pledge an accord on that account. There were many moments that seemed like hours where students would shuffle from building to building, in between classes, feeling like paper dolls as the cutting gusts of unrelenting wind seared their bodies like thin tissue paper.

The campus tundra simply was a wind tunnel far from a magic carpet ride from early November clear until mid-April, converting each day's walk into a hell of a pilgrimage.

It was a busy morning in the Athletic Department this December day. Al Perkins, who was the athletic director of the entire university, was quite oblivious to the heat being bumped for the day. He was breaking a shallow beaded sweat between his eyebrows and where his hairline met. Al was thirty-six years old and stood six foot one, weighing about one hundred and ninety pounds. The attire he wore was half uniform and half not. He could always wear slacks of his own choice, but he had to wear an alligator-type shirt with a collar that had the college logo embroidered on the shirt pocket. Naturally, the shirt had to be the university's college colors, which were red with yellow trim, and sneakers of his own choosing. He always wore white sneakers, either Adidas or Nike.

When problems arose, Al was only merely concerned about them. He had been employed by Western Chicago University for six years now and had trained himself to be just concerned, not overly worried, when situations cropped up. Fortunately, working for the Athletic Department for a college program was a great deal less stressful than working for a stock brokerage house with the Dow Jones on a downward streak in a depressed market. One's aptitude for stress was not determined by the kind of work people do for a living but how much each individual deals with their specific problem. Al learned that a long time ago. A relatively trivial development could cause a major nervous breakdown for one, while a truly incredible, drastic situation could be treated with much less anxiety by another. To each his own. The current day's problem was not a devastating one, yet this particular one was not easy by any stretch. He was worried as he had no solution in the broadest of horizons.

He had heard the bad news of what was going to happen today the night before. But only this morning, he learned additional information that he would soon relay to the others. It was the kind of news that stigmatized the phrase, "Out of the frying pan, into the fire." He would divulge the ever-important, surprising news in a meeting he had called to take place in just ten minutes time. This news would cause havoc in the minds of the university decision-makers.

They were all standing just outside a small conference room adjacent to the front counter area. They seemed to be standing there waiting to go in. The office area was quite congested. There were two female students who were acting receptionists, and the phones were ringing off the hook. There were several different small groups of on-going conversations taking place. Standing to the side were John Connors, Bob Saunders, Sam Hastings, Melvin Thompson, and Al Perkins' personal secretary, who was holding her notepad close to her bosom. They all seemed to be in a close huddled formation. Strangely enough, none of them were speaking.

Bob Saunders was John Connors' first assistant, as was Sam Hastings to Al Perkins. Melvin Thompson, a short, stocky man, was the dean of Western Chicago University. Al Perkins came over to join the group and addressed them. "Okay, everyone. Let's all go into the conference room."

They proceeded to do exactly that. Upon entering the room, each one took a seat except for Al, who shut the door behind them and chose to stand.

"Well, gentlemen, we have a situation here that has developed into something that's not quite tragic, but pretty well desperate. The tragedy here is the state of health of John Connors' wife, Priscilla, who is very ill. Because of this, John must take a leave of absence from coaching Western Chicago's basketball team. In all likelihood, this will probably be for the remainder of the season."

Dean Thompson quickly interjected before Al could continue. "I'm sorry to hear that. John. You do whatever you have to do. Take the time you need. If and when you're ready to return is entirely up to you." John reciprocated by thanking Mel. The dean then asked John if he had to leave since he didn't feel what-ever plan they were about to discuss was of concern to him. Actually it was. John was naturally interested to hear what options they had and which alternative they'd choose, but not at this particular moment. He was genuinely worried about his wife's condition.

John stated, "Yes, I do, if you don't mind. I need to hire a part-time nurse to assist me with Priscilla."

"Of course. Go ahead, John. This is trivial in comparison to Priscilla's health. I'll call you tonight. And give Priscilla my best."

John nodded his head. He knew that none of them were aware of how bad off his wife was, and he chose to keep it that way. John stood up with his raincoat on his arm and his hat in his hand and left the room. As he did, each one of them said simultaneously, "Take it easy, John."

John's last words before he departed were, "You, too," addressing only one of them, but meaning each of them indi-vidually.

After the door was closed, Al began again. "That's not all, folks. Now, for the real crux of the matter. This morning, Bob here informed me that last night he signed a contract to become the new head coach at the University of Idaho effective imme-diately."

Dean Thompson's eyebrow climbed upward, perhaps even one full inch. This was a shock.

Sam Hastings contributed his first words to the group. "Wow! Talk about bad timing."

The dean stated, "Now we've got ourselves a problem."

Bob Saunders was eyeballing Dean Thompson. He said, "I'm sorry, Mel. I've been here for nine years as an assistant, learning and waiting for something to come my way. Now that it finally has, and on the very day it does, he decides to pack it in after I sign a contract."

The dean seized the moment and diffused his apparent anger.

"Don't worry about it, Bob. Everyone deserves an opportunity one time or another. You shouldn't hate John for the irony of timing. Things happen. Now, if you don't mind, Bob, I think you can excuse yourself. I don't see how you can assist us any further. Good luck in Idaho."

Bob Saunders was still irate at John Connors as he exited the room. He couldn't believe it. If he'd known about John considering resignation, he would probably have assumed the head coaching ranks right where he was currently employed. But John Connors did not so much as whisper a syllable about his wife's illness to anyone. Saunders was totally in the dark as to why John suddenly had relinquished his helm. Because his adrenalin was so pumped from signing a contract less than twenty-four hours ago, he didn't give much credence to the sincere reason as to why John Connors was resigning. He was ignorant of Connors' wife's condition and pretty much discounted its validity completely. Bob Saunders left the room quietly but distinctly pissed off.

The dean sighed and said, "Now, gentlemen, we have a problem. Al, what's your proposal?"

Al, still standing, took his hands from his pockets and began again. "Well, taking it from the top, let's be logical. First off, we all know this is Division One basketball. This is not some high school Mickey Mouse operation. Now, even though the season is already more than half over, we have to hire a guy from the outside. And we don't wanna pick someone within forty-eight hours and then find out three days later that we could have had such and such. But facing the facts, we're not going to get an Ivy League guy overnight. Getting someone overnight means at least ten days, maybe even more. To compound matters, we have three games in the next seven days."

The dean's face showed alarm at this last statement. "Well, what are we going to do?"

Al answered, "The two remaining assistants are Phil Conig and Andy Trella. Phil's been here for four years and Andrew for three. They're both knowledgeable, but they're both very green and young."

Dean Thompson asked, "How old are they?"

Sam, butting in, gave their ages. "Twenty-eight and twenty-seven."

The dean voiced his instant opinion. "They're too young for this."

Al addressed the dean by his first name, showing he was lacking a truly confident plan. "Mel, we know that. But listen. Of the next three games, two are against easy opponents, and the third is here at home."

The dean bellowed disgust. "Damn it."

Al cut him off. "Mel, we could let the two assistants take it for a week or two and have Sam with them since he knows Round Ball pretty well. But we'll have to hire a guy to finish up the season, especially for the Tournament."

The dean asked, "How many games the following week?"

Sam spelled out the answer. "Just one."

The dean stood up and spoke out, "So that's the scenario. Doesn't look too promising. I'll tell ya that."

Al said, "That's all we can do."

Mel insisted, "Well, you two guys better get on the horn and start calling all over the country and find out who's available. Do whatever you have to. But just make sure we don't find a way to lose that national bid. The television contracts are worth almost one million dollars in revenue to this university. That's our bread and butter. We lose too many remaining games and the committee eliminates us, we'll all be on welfare by the summer. I also strongly suggest you call those two juggernaut assistants in here and get their asses in gear. Start mapping out strategies." He paused and continued. "Oh, what about this Davis guy who was canned in Idaho. Maybe he'll finish up for us."

Al shook his head negatively. "No way! He's washed up, Mel. He's terrible."

Dean Thompson concluded, "Alright, men, good luck!" and

ambled out of the room. Al and Sam remained, looking at each other, stumped and in silence.

Sam then said, "Time to hit the drawing board," and they pressed on out of the conference room. Al's secretary followed them like a lost puppy dog.

CHAPTER

THREE

Andy Trella stood in the living room of his apartment. He was five feet, ten inches tall, slim, one hundred and seventy-five pounds and had dark brown hair and and hazel eyes. Wearing black slacks and a white tee shirt, Andy was currently engaged in feeding his pet parrots, Moses and Spartacus. The parrots were quite voluminous. Andy had named them after the two epic characters in the legendary major film classics. Symbolism was the criteria. Spartacus, after the great movie and character played by star actor, Kirk Douglas. The analogy being that Spartacus was a slave who became free when he died. The parrots lived in a cage, confined as slaves, and would not be free until they died. Moses, in the epic extravaganza *The Ten Commandments*, played by legendary actor, Charlton Heston, whose only concern was to free the people from their bondage. Like his fine feathered friend, he, too, would not be free from bondage until he passed on.

Andrew Trella was highly impressed by the great portrayal of these two characters. What they stood for, how they conducted their lives, sacrificing themselves, only to perpetually help others. That's how Andy wanted to model his life and why he named the parrots as he did. It didn't particularly matter if he became a leader of men or not. But in the world these days, most people deprecated others, stepped on one another, were rude and cold, and were only interested in their own self-gain. Andy wanted to be moral, ethical, and considerate to others. It was the only way he could truly be proud and live with himself.

As Andy fed the crackers to the green-colored birds, he fixed his eyes upon their stomachs and said, "Keep eating. Keep eating. Your stomachs look like 747s. Fat shits."

The parrots retaliated by saying in unison, "Screw you. Screw You. Screw You." Andrew smiled and passed more crackers through the cage to the green birds.

He then turned on the television set and moseyed on over to the huge portable blackboard, which he kept in his living room. He was looking over the diagrams he had drawn. The board displayed many Xs and Os, about twenty in all, with chalk lines signaling directions of specific plays. Andy picked up a piece of chalk from the ledge and started to scratch out something in the maze of the diagram, and it wasn't Tic-Tac-Toe.

The parrots bellowed out, "More grub. More grub."

Andy smiled to himself and sarcastically went on, "Sure, what do you care. More grub means more shit for me to clean up."

Suddenly, the phone rang. Andy picked up the receiver. It was his coaching colleague, Phil. Phil sounded exuberant. Exuberant to the point of being out of control. Andy asked, "What's the matter, Phil?"

Through the receiver he heard, "I just got a phone call from Al Perkins at the university. He said you and I should get down there right away."

"Why? What's wrong?"

Phil was still very excited. "You're not going to believe this, but both Coach Connors and Bob Saunders have resigned their coaching positions effective immediately!"

Andy refused to believe what he had heard and responded, "Get the hell out of here. You're cracked."

Phil blurted out. "I'm not kidding, Andy! Get ready. I'll pick you up in five minutes."

Andy heard the phone slam down on the other end with a thud. He replaced his receiver much more gently than his counterpart had. Just as Phil was shocked, so was Andy. Only Andy *thought about it* intensely. Phil *reacted* intensely. He was thinking about the information that had just been disclosed to him. Andy said to himself, *He's not kidding. It really happened!* He then went into his bedroom to change his clothes.

Andy was throwing his leather jacket over his upper torso when he heard the signal, a beep from a car horn. Phil was outside waiting for him. He darted out, but just as the front door slammed shut, Spartacus and Moses squeaked out, "TV's on. TV's on."

Andy re-entered and turned the switch to the left, canceling any further transmission. He looked at them and instructed the fruitless parrots, "Don't forget to do the laundry and vacuum this place while I'm gone." He swiftly left and again slammed the door.

The parrots leaked out, "Screw you, Meatball. Screw you!"

As Andy walked down the inclined blacktop pavement, Phil was waiting rather impatiently in his four-door Chevrolet sedan. Andy opened the passenger side door and slid inside.

Andy said, "Phil, what is happening?"

Phil instantly replied, "This is our big chance, kid" and put his foot to the metal to the floor. Andy's and Phil's upper bodies jerked backward, as if someone tied a string around their necks and started to run.

Andy replied, sincerely acting like he didn't understand, "What is?"

Phil countered abruptly, "No time to waste."

Andy insisted, "Will you please calm down and fill me in?"

"The Athletic Department is going to ask us both to take dual coaching control of the team."

Andy asked, "What happened to J.C. and Bob Saunders?"

Phil answered, "Last night, Coach Connors took a leave of absence due to his wife's serious illness, and our friend and buddy Saunders signed a contract to be the new head coach of Idaho University. That leaves us in charge of the full operation."

Andy insisted to Phil, "Will you please slow down? You're driving too fast."

Phil ignored Andy's advice and kept full throttle as the huge four-door vehicle barreled down the road. Subconsciously, Phil was working up to ramming speed.

Andrew uncovered, "Phil, did it ever occur to you that they're going to bring in someone else from the outside?"

Phil instantly defended, "Naw, no way, man. The season's more than half over.

Andy came back with, "Yes, I know that. But, we're talking Division One."

Phil, still very confident, said, "Doesn't matter. There's only eight games left; three in the next week. The school is not going to make any long-term commitment with anyone for a handful of games. Besides, what if Coach Connors is only taking a leave of absence until his wife dies."

Andy quickly got mad at Phil for revealing aloud such a morbid thought. He said, "Phil, what's the matter with you?" Andy quickly noticed they were traveling much too fast. The speed limit was thirty miles per hour. The four-wheeled machine was traveling forty-eight miles per hour and naturally climbing steadily. Andy remarked. "Will you please slow down before you..."

Phil screamed out, "Look out!!"

A huge, Greenline bus decided to enter the upcoming intersection very late, going through a red light, like a blind, drunken dinosaur. The bus was traveling perpendicular to the Chevy's position on Glory Road. Thus, a major traffic accident occurred as Phil's driver's side smashed into the indestructible Greenline. The disparity between the vehicles caused all the damage to be assigned to the automobile. The Greenline dinosaur didn't wear so much as a dent.

The smoke began to clear. There was not one single solitary person in sight. There was complete silence for nearly eight seconds. All that could be witnessed was smoke rising from under the front hood of the car. The radiator had been opened up from the hit it took, like a ship at sea that had taken torpedoes into the teeth of its own hull. The steam was escaping with a flourish, rising up like a soul to heaven. Glory Road was clearly named erroneously.

Andy managed to exit through the passenger side window. He was unable to use the door and climbed out until his feet firmly hit the street. He was walking gingerly, quivering around the front end of the vehicle, which had been beached. Grounded. Permanently out of service. The front end looked like a magnified beer can that had a great white shark's bite taken from it. Dazed, Andy made his way to the driver's side window. Before checking on Phil's condition, he touched his head and saw a good amount of blood on his hand. It started to drip down the side of his face and onto the street and was the only injury he suffered that would require stitches later on, five, to be precise. He had received a bump and a small gash on the side of his head where his eyebrow ended when his head kissed the front windshield unnaturally. Even though he was hurt, he was quite fortunate for only sustaining a head cut, especially since he hadn't been wearing his seat belt.

Andy finally looked over at Philip, who was clearly unconscious, knocked out cold. For a brief second, he thought Phil was dead. Then he took a closer look and could hear him breathing along as if he were just sleeping. Andy began to stand upright from his crouched position for the first time since he had left his house. For a moment, he wished he could go back in time to the point where he told Phil to slow down and prevent the doom that had now fallen upon them. Normally, he would have been persistent in insisting that Phil alter his driving antics. But the subject matter they had been discussing was so unbelievably intriguing, since its development was so uncommon, it controlled their minds enough to make them unconsciously vulnerable and thus jeopardize their safety.

Just then, he heard a voice. He didn't know where it came from. But it sure as hell did. "Are you guys out of your Goddamn minds?" He said it in a tone that led Andy to believe he was definitely irate. He was a fat, short, burly-looking man. A typical-looking bus driver. He had just rounded the front of the bus, saw what resulted from the collision, and bellowed out his phrase.

Andrew yelled back with blood still dripping from the side of his head, "Call an ambulance; he's hurt badly." The contentious fellow changed his disposition dramatically and his position, as well, immediately swiveling about-face. Once pointed in a different direction, he started to run off through the intersection in an attempt to call for help. He ran like a turtle, since his arms moved faster than any other part of his body.

Andy dropped back down into his original crouched position in his attempt to get through to Phil. As he stuck his head through the driver's side window, he did a double take. He noticed Phil's leg was twisted in a quite unnatural position. Not just a single twist, but a very abnormal one that looked so unconventionally forced, he knew it was a multiple fracture. And it was.

CHAPTER

FOUR

Andy sat upright on a medical examining bed in the Emergency Room. A doctor, a young one at that in his late twenties, was patching up the side of his head, applying a bandage parallel to his eye, just below the temple. Andy seemed to opt for silence, patiently permitting the intern to administer his treatment.

Finally, Andy said, "Just a scratch, right, Doc?"

The young doctor, working in an indulgent manner, said, "It's nothing at all. This will be completely healed within a week's time."

"How come it was bleeding so much, Doc?"

"That's because when the skin was cut, you suffered a short, but sharp incision. It penetrated maybe an eighth of an inch deep. If I was to scratch your face with my fingernail, it would hardly be deep and probably wouldn't bleed at all. This injury will heal so quickly, you'll never know that you had stitches inserted because it's so small. It's just that it was pretty deep. Several layers of skin were severed, causing the excessive bleeding."

The way the young intern was working so diligently, affixing the bandage, Andy wondered if he was fitting him for a Tampon in his head.

Suddenly, entering the room was Al Perkins. Al asked, "You O.K.?

Andrew shook his head affirmatively.

The medical doctor issued the statement, "You're done."

Andy immediately hopped off the bed like a jack rabbit and asked Al, "How's Phil doing?"

Al elaborated, "He's in pretty sad shape. Fractured leg in two places. Broken ribs, three of them. And a concussion. He's lucky he didn't get killed, and so are you!"

Andy whispered, then continued on by broadcasting loudly, "Asshole, three times I told him to slow down. He was hysterical."

Al repeated it as if it were important, "Hysterical about what?"

Andy ignored Al's question and chose to ask one instead. "Can I ask a question? What's happening all of a sudden?"

Al began to answer when Andy twisted a half turn and yelled to the doctor across the room, "Hey, thanks, Doc!" The intern simply waved, acknowledging Andy's appreciation.

Al put his hand around Andy's shoulder and said, "Come on, let's walk. I'll brief you on everything."

Andy reciprocated, "Yeah, let's get outta here." The two men started walking down the hospital corridor.

Al began, "Andy, for some strange reason, a weird epidemic or cancer has ripped itself right through our coaching staff at a rapid rate of speed."

Andy interjected, "Al, you're not making me feel better."

Al continued, "In less than six hours, I've lost three coaches, all of whom for the same team."

Andy recoiled, "Al, they're not dead, ya know!"

Al fashioned his next statement, mindfully being tactful. "They might as well be. Ya know how my day is going?"

Andy looked at him, paying intent attention to him.

Al went on, "It's like someone I don't know owns Boardwalk

with a shitload of hotels and houses on it, and all I do is keep landing on it."

Andy looked at Al and asked, "Can we see Phil?"

Al responded, "Sure, he's right down here on the left, Room 294."

When they reached the appropriate room that contained Phil's badly bruised, sore, and unconscious body, Andy peered inside through the small glass window in the door. And that's exactly what his eyes saw–a badly bruised and sore, unconscious body, that was surely drugged up with pain killers. Andy asked Al if he knew what they'd given him, and Al informed him it was ten milligrams of Percodan. That did the trick nicely and would every time.

Andy instantly thought back to his own personal experience with the powerful pain killer. He had had two wisdom teeth pulled on the same day when he was in college. It was a lost weekend. He remembered a friend calling him on the phone and how he could hardly talk for two different reasons. First, due to the two ounces of gauze pads that were embedded in his mouth, and second, he was under the influence of a temporary mind-altering drug. He was laughing on the telephone ecstatically for almost a full twenty minutes, seriously and convincingly. He thought it so unbelievable that no matter how he tried, he couldn't complete a single sentence. He couldn't hold on to a single thought for three seconds. It would drift away as fast as it came. He was so high, so completely out of it. So drugged up. Not making sense at all. He remembered having sudden memory lapses. That was Andy's experience with Percodan. A weekend on a sofa. No food, only medication and drink and bleeding gums.

But it also brought back another memory. That was also the weekend of the Boston Massacre. Not the Tea Party that was two hundred years ago. This Massacre was when the New York Yankee baseball team invaded Fenway Park in Boston for four games with the Red Sox. Andy watched all four games on television that weekend. One Friday night, one Saturday, and two on Sunday from the sofa in his father's house, which was also his at the time, with nothing but liquid nutrition. The Yankees had tied the Sox for first place that Sunday afternoon, sweeping all four games, having pummeled the Red Sox into submission, out-scoring them sixty-five runs to six in three days. Those Yankees eventually went on to win it all. Andy couldn't remember what year it was–either '78 or '79–he wasn't sure. But that's what his memory bank eclipsed when he rarely heard the term Percodan.

Phil appeared to be sleeping soundly and comfortably. This was ironic. How could he possibly be comfortable when he looked anything but. Leg hung up in the air, bound by a cast like a cannon. Head wrapped up, looking like a mummy and very much out of it. However, he was comfortable. It was the Percodan.

Andy looked at Al and said, "He's definitely out of commission."

Al nudged Andy in the ribs and said, "Come on, I have to talk to you."

CHAPTER
FIVE

"How the hell am I going to do this by myself?" Andy said, rather forcefully. The three of them were in the conference room discussing the critical status of who was going to assume the head coaching duties of the university's proud college basketball program.

Actually, Al and Sam were discussing. Andrew was shouting. He first thought they were kidding with him. In this initial phase, he discounted their offer at the outset, originally thinking they were joking. Then he suddenly caught their drift and abruptly realized they were, in fact, not jesting. Then came the second phase in which he declined to regard their offering as legitimate. He simply didn't believe what he was hearing. The third phase that his emotions revealed to him was he had gotten surprisingly and strongly irate. He was mad at them now. He thought them very foolish to actually attempt to offer him such a prestigious opportunity that he didn't feel deserving of. He would even experience a fourth and final emotion, but that would come later.

This basketball program at the University of Western Chicago was a major Division One college program. Geographically located in the mid-western region of the United States, they'd play competition of all their sports programs against the likes of Notre Dame, Indiana, DePaul, Dayton, Illinois, and many others. At least six of their thirty games were televised by major network television: ABC, NBC and CBS would each televise two broadcasts apiece. These few telecasts would bring exposure to the college of Western Chicago. Naturally, each time a broadcast was seen on network television, the school received dollars for it. Revenue was earned: income generated to come back to the school in a supplementary method.

Whenever they'd play contests versus Notre Dame, Ohio State, and other top-notch caliber schools, the University of Western Chicago got financial compensation for it. The bigger school received seventy-five percent of the proceeds, which would still leave the university with the flip side of twenty-five percent profit. Twenty-five percent of say, some three to four hundred thousand dollars was a lot better than one hundred percent of nothing.

This was the plan of attack by Western Chicago's Athletic Department. To upgrade the quality of this college's sports program, handing out more scholarships, recruiting better basketball players, bringing in better coaches, improving the team's win-loss percentage each year, consequently elevating the school's status and becoming competitive within the top gun schools.

Sooner or later, a cable network would come in and offer to pay the school in order to televise the Western Chicago Eagles complete thirty-game season. This would bring in several million dollars worth of revenue to the university every season. That time would still be a couple of years away. But it would be better than the normal one hundred thousand it was currently bringing in, as a result of getting to play the top echelon core of schools.

Naturally, by becoming a very good basketball team and winning more games per year against the big schools, other name universities would want to engage in having contests versus Western Chicago. Perhaps then, schools from the west and east coasts would want to play Western Chicago. That would give the university some expanded national exposure. Of course, the players and coaches would benefit by receiving the opportunity to travel by plane to various additional parts of the country a couple of times during the season: instead of being confined strictly to bussing to central sites of the states where the opponents home town could be connected to theirs by the shortest distance of two destinations, a straight line bus ride.

These other elite college programs would play twenty-five of their thirty games against the same schools every year. That left five openings for different newer, upcoming colleges. That's what the University of Western Chicago was at present day. What UWC wanted was tougher schools, tougher teams, tougher games, and tougher schedules, leading to big time money. The elite college programs would basically plan to play against schools that had a lock on televising complete seasons campaigns. They naturally would then receive half of the proceeds by playing a school that had their entire season pipelined in on a cable T.V. network.

John Connors' abdication from his head coaching status put a serious blockade on their campaign to lift the college basketball program. While Bob Saunders' departure and Philip Conig's accident could only succeed in impeding their expected progress, it left the university, the Athletic Department, the students, the booster club supporters, as well as Dean Thompson all reeling. The Athletic Department had to do something, and that something was Andy Trella's appointment.

Of course, the major stipulation was that it was only a temporary solution. A week to ten days, tops, until they could find and then sign someone else. It was to be completely understood by Andrew to completely take the team over as acting head coach for a definite short interim period. There was no way in hell he would maintain this newly acclaimed status for more than two weeks. Perhaps by then, even John Connors would have a change of heart and get back into the swing of teaching and instructing young athletes. At least Andrew knew he couldn't get fired. He would coach, or try to coach, three to four games the most, and then quietly be relegated back to his regular assistant coaching status.

Astonishingly in actuality, they weren't offering this position to Andy. They were instructing him without letting him know it. They had wanted him to feel some sense of confidence and esteem, for the next two weeks would surely be extremely burdensome and tough. Andy was an employee of the college. Al was his supervising boss and could simply tell him to do it or fire him. No quips. No qualms. However, Al had a bit of a predicament himself. It would be pretty ignorant for him to let developments come to that. especially since he just had three coaches of the same sport team get knocked right out of the line-up faster than you could say, "Supercalifragilisticexpialidocious."

Al was smart, though, and wanted Andy to feel as good as possible in undertaking this task. So he had it sound like he was offering a great opportunity to the young man. Instead of shortly telling him to do what he wanted, in plain, old-fashioned English.

The amazing thing of all is that the university's top echelon decision-makers had been working for years to get a major cable network to extend a big time deal to carry the Eagles' full Fall schedule of games. They'd been working for that for the past three years and calculated it would take a minimum of two more years with hard campaigning, assuming first that the team would be on the upswing. Without that, they'd all be drawing at straws. They would attain that goal through the incredible fame that would follow Andrew Trella. He would be able to get several cable companies bidding against one another, jacking up the price considerably for the university's auspicious benefit. Astonishingly, he would accomplish that without even campaigning for it. Not for an iota of a moment would he solicit for that achievement. The fame he was about to acquire would run rampant, not only through the ivory of the campus, it would spread like radiation fallout. Marketing and advertising firms would come in throughout all of Chicago and ask to sign the young chap to do commercials, promotions, interviews and photographs to display their products. But this would all not come that easily. He'd first feel relentless deprecation.

Al stood up from his seated position, approached Andy, and said, "We're going to help you. Sam will be your full-time assistant, and we'll get another volunteer student assistant for you right away."

Andy retaliated, "How come you don't do it?"

"Andy, the university has thirty-seven sports, not including the fraternities and sororities who are very demanding. Without Sam, that leaves me with thirty-six different activities to run." Andy paced the room in a slow gait, rather perplexed by the developments. He turned around, facing them.

"Do you know how much preparation goes into... "

Al interrupted him sharply, "Hey, I don't care! We have a real dilemma on our hands. I know this program requires three to four guys putting in fifty hours a week. I'm not asking you to make up everyone' work load.

Andy shook his head and said, "Guys, this is a major university college basketball program here."

Sam finally contributed, "You're not telling us anything we don't know."

Andy replied, "Oh, no. This is the biggest sports town in the whole Goddamn country. Around the corner you've got the Chicago Bears, the Bulls, the Black Hawks. Across the street, we have the Cubs, White Sox and the DePaul Blue Demons; and down the road we've got Northeastern, Notre Dame, Indiana and Illinois. There are a dozen sports magazines in this town. Next month, my picture will be on the front cover of all of them, saying 'Joke of the City'." He would, in one month's time, be on the cover of three of the magazines in question. No one could ever completely knock Michael Jordan off the newsstand. The reason for his sudden exposure would be for glorified, unpredictable resourcefulness, which supplied great success to a basketball program that was in dire need of leadership that was immensely volatile.

Sam said, "You don't have to remind us that you're from the streets of New York." He was referring to his analogy of Andy's street talk he had used while informing them of his opinion.

Andy said, "I wasn't trying to be facetious."

Al again took the floor as they all seemed to jockey for position in this power struggle. "Isn't that why you came here to begin with? Opportunity. You sure as hell weren't going to get a chance like this in New York."

Sam unified Al's contention. "Tremendous scrutiny and competition in that town."

Andy regretfully agreed. "Yes, but this is too soon for me. I'm skipping right over serving my apprenticeship. I'm still learning. I'm not prepared for this."

"This is the wrong attitude, son. A lot of people would kill for this opportunity," Sam said.

"You're wrong," Al said, assuming control. "You've been serving your apprenticeship for three years here, and five before that. Besides, it's just for a short ten days or so. Of course, it's not the most ideal situation, but at least you can't get fired, and it'll be quite an experience for you."

"I'll say." Andy instantly agreed.

Al desperately grasped for a solvent balloon that would entice Andy. "Listen, we'll give you a raise and a considerable bonus."

Sam's face was flushed with surprise. He was sincerely perturbed with the mention of a financial increase. Al drew closer to Andy's position within the room. He placed his hand on his shoulder, and said, "You'll do fine. I want you to come back here at 7:00 tonight. Sam will line up a few candidates for an immediate student assistant."

Sam felt like saying distinctly, "I will not," but he refrained from divulging his true feelings.

Al continued on, "Select one to help you run the practices. Now, I think you better get over to the gymnasium. I suspect that the brothers are getting restless.

Sam jumped in, "And don't forget, you have just about, seventy-two hours before you make your head coaching debut."

Andy took special note to the word "debut" and manufactured a long, hard stare directed at Sam for a few strong seconds.

Andy started to depart the room, when Al said, "Oh, Andy. One more bit of advice!"

Andy didn't seem to mind. In the state he was in, nothing could surprise him now. He was done with his fight. They could have put handcuffs on him and asked him to single-handedly row across the Potomac. He would have attempted it as if he were brushing his teeth.

"Andy, don't think in terms of what's happening. The entire picture boggles you. Just think basketball. It's what you know," Al said.

"Okay, Al, I'll try," Andy said, submissively.

"Good boy!" Sam stated. "Good luck, Andy.

He bookended all further discussion by saying, "Thanks," and then left the room.

Andy was thinking if he were one of his pet parrots, he would have relentlessly repeated to both of them, "Screw You. Screw You. Screw You." Like his pets, he ostensibly felt like a bird in a cage. For he wished he was one of his fine feathered friends so he could spring out and fly off. He would be the slave of Western Chicago's University in the next coming weeks. Then he realized which one of Spartacus and Moses he would really like to have been. The selection wouldn't be his little green friends. There was something much nobler emulating the other beings. Like the real Moses and Spartacus, he would attempt to leap up and lead this team, and free the school of its depths of despair, its reputation, and its bondage, capturing the elite status everyone wanted to achieve. Andy was simply doing what most people would do in his position: fantasize.

Once Andy left the room, Al and Sam continued the conversation. Sam was looking up to Al. "I think we're in trouble."

Things could get really hairy around here," Al said astonishingly. "What do you mean," Sam asked, intrigued.

"Come on, you must have thought about it!"

"Thought what?" Sam was nonplussed.

"There's a better than fair chance that this team is going to flunk out big time." Al said.

Sam was shocked. His countenance would reveal that expression a multitude of times inside of a month's time. He would be amazed countless times before the end of the month. The days and weeks to follow would not be regular ones at all. Things at WCU would not settle down until after Christmas and the beginning of the new year as far as the Athletic Department was concerned. For now, he was sincerely curious for Al's next sentence. "What do you mean, Al?"

"Yep, big time. And we're not going to get accepted to that Tournament. He's too green. Mel's gonna have a shit fit. The school's not going to get $800,000 or so this year."

Sam was fearful and said, "You don't think he can win?" referring to Andrew Trella's capability.

"We'll try, but it's very unlikely. There's going to be a lot of heat and pressure around here, and now we have a fall guy. And he's it!"

Sam instantly and unwillingly felt like he was an accomplice to a super sting operation. Without hesitating, Sam decided to put Al on the spot even further. He couldn't help it. He had to know more. "What are you talking about, Al?"

"See, that's why I'm the director, and you're the assistant. You think because he's gotten a raise and bonus that he's been promoted. Reality is we're desperate, and to me, Andy Trella is our only alternative. Don't get me wrong, I hope to God he pulls it off; that would be great. But unfortunately, we're dealing with reality. And then we'll have an automatic scapegoat when the bricks come tumbling down."

Al was playing devil's advocate. Not that he wanted to. He really wanted to be successful at the services he provided for the university's ultimate benefit. He just suddenly gave his own personal estimation on what he honestly believed was going to occur. He surely was rooting for Andy and would help assist him in any way that he possibly could. He simply came down with an emotional wave of insecurity of the insurmountable tasks at hand. Great difficulty. Too much to deal with simultaneously. So he projected his confession to his assistant quite credibly.

There was another reason. Al was very sharp in regard to intelligence. He knew Sam was kind of jealous of Andy's new found position. The salary increase, the opportunity, at such a young man's age. Al didn't want Sam to be argumentative and controversial with Andy. He deserved more than that. He deserved a fighting chance. Sam could easily be more destructive since he had reason not to like Andy. Sam was now to be Andrew's full time first assistant for the next couple of weeks.

The last thing in the world Al wanted was to have these two guys at one another's throats. So, he painted a picture. A *very* vivid one, intangibly inserted in Sam's mind. This, naturally, would cause Sam to feel sentimental toward Andy. Not only would he not give Andy a hard time, but he would sincerely assist Andy like a true colleague would. Unification by subtraction. Al also knew that Sam would not dare repeat these words to Andy. For that would cause a helluva scene.

Sam was unequivocally baffled and said, "You mean that the cards have been shuffled and we've got a rigged game?"

Al replied, "Stacked. The odds have been stacked heavily to one side, I might add."

Al thought to himself, *They're stacked in a huge way. Like Niagara Falls coming down in a toddler's summertime pool.* Al continued on his roll.

"Are you kidding?

First he's got to win over the respect of all the players, and that's not going to be easy on an all black team, especially for an exceptionally young amateur head coach. Problem Number Two: the students, the booster club, the fans. There'll be screaming for his head by this time tomorrow.

Sam looked at Al like he received words of wisdom from the Lord, Himself.

CHAPTER
SIX

Ah, but Andy Trella would fool them all. He'd move the mountain, but only after he'd initially been buried by it. There would be gold in this imaginary majestic mountain that would be disguised as kryptonite. He was about to become Western Chicago's Superman, but first he'd be hung out to dry. A hangman's dream, guilty before proven innocent. In the wild, wild old west, sentencing came first. This was the midwest, some two hundred years later, but the old precedent held the same *shoot first, ask questions later.*

The cards would be shuffled many times, and hopefully, the last time would be in his favor. But for now, there were many dealers in town who stacked the deck against the amateur coach. There would be many hands to play with: the athletic department, the booster club, the student body, and the players, themselves. Andy would go many rounds, and he'd get decked time and time again, literally and figuratively. But for now, Al was going to be right. They'd come. They'd come to lobby and protest in massive numbers.

The hallway was quite congested; it must have been in between classes. It was three minutes to two o'clock. Students were leaving the gymnasium, and students were entering it.

They were either carrying duffle bags containing their gym attire or books and clipboards with pads of paper.

Andy was totally unaware of what was happening around him. There may have been forty students walking crisply in both east and west directions. If the hallway were completely empty, he wouldn't have noticed. His mind was racing. Actually, he was talking to himself, without permitting his mouth to move; his mind's subconsciousness was talking a mile a minute. *I know what's going on here. They need a fall guy. Well, they have another thing coming.*

Andy walked fashionably quick paced, en route to the practicing gymnasium. Hugging the left-side wall, he prepared to make a sharp left at the hallway intersection. As he did so, he collided with her. She had been walking close to the wall in the opposite direction. The collision took place exactly where the two perpendicular walls met. Her briefcase flew out of her hand like it was indispensable garbage. They actually came within inches of bumping heads. That was all Andy needed. He already owned one bump on his head that required stitches to mend the wound. She clutched her chest above her breasts with her beautifully polished white nails, proving she was caught off guard. Andy apologized immediately by saying, "I'm sorry…," as he backed off quicker than a cat. He then went over, picked up the leather briefcase from the marble floor but did not assist in gathering up a slew of papers that fell out of the briefcase. Several students scramble about and proceeded to hand them back to her. She stood there silently for a moment, taken aback by the unpremeditated incident.

They had made eye contact for maybe just a hundredth of a second, but that would be enough. She had beautiful, dark hair that was loftily shaped, and she stood approximately five feet four inches tall. She wore a light lavender-colored lipstick and some blush. She wasn't wearing any eye make up at all, she didn't need to, for she possessed big, beautiful brown eyes. She was wearing a gray woman's executive-type suit with a white blouse. Her semblance was professional, intelligent, and sophisticated.

Andy hadn't noticed any of these details about her. He really was in another orbit, which was understandable. He already had one accident this morning. He praised the fact that he wasn't driving a car presently, for this accident would have been his own fault. Head-on collisions are usually fatal. This one was going to turn on the dime. But not now. The time was not yet right. After he released the suitcase into her hand, he stepped to her right and walked away from her as if the incident hadn't even occurred.

Her name was Sheila, and she simply watched him walk on in amazement. She finally called out to him as he was close to thirty feet south of her position. "Hey! Have a nice day!" She took special notice that he didn't even have the decency to turn back toward her, acknowledging her cliche of a statement. This made her curiously upset. From her point of view, this fellow had gaul. She decided to try again. "You shouldn't speed; that's how accidents happen, you know!"

Andy halted his walk and touched the bandage that was framed on the side of his forehead. A smirk began to surface as he turned around and prepared to remark. His mouth opened and automatically froze as if he had been shot by a phaser set on stun. Gone. She was gone. Either that or she was invisible. Unless ... perhaps she was standing directly behind him, where he couldn't see her. But that was impossible. This was not *Star Trek* where you could beam yourself to any location at any time.

The main conclusion was, she disappeared like a phantom, and obviously upset, getting to where she was going. Andy registered a smile that seemed foolish, then reconvened with his business.

CHAPTER

SEVEN

Andrew entered the practice gymnasium. This was the school's practice gym in the athletic building. Not the one where full-scale inter-collegiate competitions took place. These events, and that's what they were, were held in downtown Chicago at the Rosemont Horizon. The Horizon was built strictly for big time college ball exhibitions to be held. Western Chicago shared the huge facility with the DePaul Blue Demons and Northeastern University. The three schools only played their host games at this location.

The gymnasium's seating facility was naturally empty, except for maybe ten to fifteen students who were sporadically set in the bleacher-type benches at this mid-time part of the day. About a dozen or so students showed up each day to watch the team work out. What Andy saw and heard was just what Al spoke of. The brothers were surely very restless. They were playing wild, wide open, flamboyant basketball. A full court contest between ten team players was evident. They were playing five on five, street style ball. Andy noticed they were playing starters versus the substitutes. At least that was good. Coach Connors always had it that way. The more they played together, they'd get to know each other's moves and styles. This would help to achieve the best possible results.

What took greater precedence was the gregarious loud-mouthing. They were naturally revving it up. Yelling and screaming, and carrying on like animals in a circus. None of them would or could behave in that fashion during inter-collegiate affairs. This gave them a chance to be the real African Americans that they were. Andrew didn't mind, he knew they'd been waiting for the better part of an hour. Besides, there wasn't anyone to oversee them, what could he expect? So, all they could do was what they did best. Play pick-up street-ball. It was either that or do some studying. They were not even curious as to why there was no enforcer governing over their physical activity. That passed in less than ten minutes. Andy heard one of them yelling at another, "Hey, Honky! You lost it, bro!"

They stopped playing suddenly and saw Andy standing underneath the basketball hoop on the complete opposite end of where they were playing. The loud-mouthing and hotdogging subsided. Even the pounding of the ball hitting against the glossed-over wooden court stopped, like the ticking of a time bomb that had just been disarmed. They all began to walk from their distant positions toward him.

Andy just stood there, plain and simple, not moving a fragment of an inch. It began. He felt an aura of this moment. It would be the first moment of feeling uninhibited autonomy. So, he remained still and strong and awaited their gathering around him as if he were Jesus Christ. From a distance, the group appeared like separate stars in a nighttime galaxy constellation. As they came closer to their destination, they seemed to be unifying like the nucleus of a meteor about to land right before his feet. They were all there now, and they remained silent, awaiting Andy's words, whether they be words of wisdom, or not.

There were eleven of them on the squad. Their height ranged

from five feet eight, to six feet seven inches tall. Amazingly, five of the eleven had last names that were equal to the surnames of past United States presidents. There was: Alan Jefferson, Chris Washington, Calvin Kennedy, Glen Johnson, and Cory Jackson. The others were Willie Jones, Jarvis Williams, Travis Bennett and Eric Turner. The remaining two were brothers, actually they all were known as the brothers to one another and everyone else included, except Skin Head and Skin Brain, who were biologically related. Their real names were Don and David Brunson, twins, who both sported shaved heads. They were referred to by anyone and everyone by their nicknames, and that's what they not only preferred, but insisted on, for some strange, God-forsaken reason. Even on their game and scrimmage jerseys above their designated number was stenciled in the nicknames: Skin Head and Skin Brain.

One of them finally said, "Hey, Coach, what's happening?" Usually, that comment can be taken in a jovial manner. However, it was stated in a truly sincere fashion.

Andy looked at a couple of them eye to eye and said, "Have you guys heard anything of what's happened today?"

Kennedy volunteered. "Naw, man, we ain't heard nothin from nobody!"

Washington interjected, "What's happened, Coach?"

Andy's eyes fell to the floor for a moment of disgust, since they were not informed of anything by anyone. As his head rose up, he said, "Coach Connors, Bob Saunders, and Phil are not going to be with us the next couple of days." The return Andy heard back came like a tennis ball that had been rocketed by a seasoned pro. He heard a chorus of, "Say What?" They started to unravel, bringing on a commotion. They were so surprised, they resorted to their jive talk.

Willie Jones said, "You must be joking, man. No team loses three coaches the same day unless they were arrested or killed."

Turner continued on, on Jones' path. "Yeah, man, and those three guys wouldn't be caught dead together to begin with."

Like a foreman of a working crew, Andy said, "Guys, I want everybody outside on the grass in three minutes."

They were widely curious but responded receptively. For they were used to that kind of talk. Andy made it sound like he was a policeman about to frisk them all. Almost half of them had suffered that kind of experience at one time or another. So they were relaxed. Andy yelled out, "Now! Let's go, fellas. We have to talk." They continued to move out.

The one named Williams said, "Hey, Coach, what happened to your head?"

Andrew ignored his question for the present, then said, "When you get outside, you'll find out. Let's go, everybody! Outside on the lawn. Jefferson, leave the basketball here."

Perplexed, Jefferson said, "Don't we need this outside?"

"Drop it, Jeff,"

Jefferson said emphatically, "I'm going, boss, I'm going."

The one named Smith said to the others, "What's on this Honky Boy's mind?"

Andy remained standing still for half a minute as he watched them leave the gym bewildered.

EIGHT

They were all sitting on the green campus grounds under a single banyan tree. The group did not advocate this formation. It was like a class session, with the speaker, usually a teacher or professor, about to serve up a lecture. They had been in this type of setting all day long and didn't care to be within it again. The only refreshing part was the environment. It was taking place outside and not within a four-wall instructional facility.

Andrew was standing before them and said, "So, there you have it. It doesn't matter one bit whether you like it or not. That's how it is."

A player raised his hand. Andy asked, "Bennett, what's on your mind?"

"If they're gonna replace you in two weeks or less, then why should we listen to you at all?" The teammates all laughed, singling out the thought that put their mentor on the spot. Andy smiled as he was momentarily embarrassed since Bennett's question seemed to be very pertinent.

Willie Jones added, "In your face, Coach."

The group laughed loudly. They seemed to think that they had the upper hand and he was now on the ropes. "Good question, Bennett. When you're all done laughing, I'll answer it,"

Andy replied assertively. Collectively, they did not want to stop their anything but affable behavior, but they all suddenly selected to shut up. They were curious as to how he'd attempt to diffuse the verbal attack. After all, he was their temporary proxy. They wanted to know if he was going to be a pushover or a hard ass. Strangely enough, he wasn't going to be either.

"Gentlemen, there are two kinds of coaches in this game. A frequently mad, frustrated, yelling, screaming coach, and his practices consist of two hundred sit-ups, two hundred push-ups, twenty laps around the track, jogging, sprints, and, lastly, suicide drills." Their faces revealed terror and a timorous distaste. "Then, there's the coach who respects his players and they respect him. Those practices consist of shooting a basketball, passing, rebounding, foul shooting, and practices that finish up with one hour of full court, wide open basketball. You all will decide what kind of practices we'll have, not me."

Their eyes had ballooned. He said the magic words, wide open streetball is what they lived for. For them, it was like an ecstatic orgasm. Washington smiled and said, "All right!." The teammates were clapping and moving around with joy. Most of them could not suppress their emotion and gave the signature of approval with the expressions on their faces, except for Jackson, Turner, and Willie Jones. They disagreed, electing not to voice it presently. There would be time later, and plenty of it to be adamant. They just remained silent for the moment. They wanted to witness first hand what Andy was really selling them before they'd purchase it or commence dissension tactics.

Andy went on commandingly, "One more thing, fellas. I want each one of you to really think about what I'm about to tell you. There are close to 12,000 college basketball players in this country. And only ten to fifteen at each college. There's 22,000 students attending this university. Only ten play on this school's basketball team. So, I ask you, what separates each one of you from the rest?"

They were all looking amused, wondering where he was

going with this. He did manage to have their complete, undivided attention. Andy continued, "You all can play ball with the best of them, right?"

They shook their heads affirmatively and several of them said, "Hell, yeah!"

Andy was walking around among them. He was pontificating and gesturing with his arms and hands as he spoke. "Jefferson, you can score with anybody, right?"

"Hell, yeah!"

"Washington, you can jump and rebound with anybody, right?"

"Yep!"

"Bennett, you can dribble your ass off, right?"

Bennett replied, "With the best, Coach."

Andy countered with, "Right. But you all have to be a better team than the next. Not just the Western Chicago Eagles. A real team. A truly real team uses each other to make the other players better than they really are. Expose each other's talent. Bring out the best in one another. And, remember the best team always wins. Now, let's play some ball!"

The players all jumped up and were rather excited to get back into the gymnasium and do what they do best. Andy wasn't sure what their motivation was. Was it that his sermon came to a conclusion, or they were going to play ball. One thing he did know, there would be battles with his players, a struggle for power, and respect yet to come. He still had more to prove to them, much more. Speeches wear off, they always do.

CHAPTER

NINE

It was dark and cold outside the athletic building. It was 9:00 at night. Inside the building, Andy was in the athletic department's office. He was sitting at a desk, shuffling papers and drinking coffee, when he suddenly spewed out a long, tedious yawn. He was conducting interviews with a handful of voluntary students.

Andy solely decided he was going to hire two temporary assistants. He was told he could have one and that Sam was going to assist him on a full-time basis. He decided on his own that he was going to tell Al to keep Sam for himself. Thirty something sports to govern over along with two dozen fraternities and sororities that also required a great deal of time with respect to their athletic competitions with one another was quite demanding.

Andy knew it was a serious disadvantage that the coaching crew had been diminished by leaps and bounds. But he only was expected to run this squad for a very short term, so he decided he was going to do it his way. Since the coaching forces were depleted by seventy five percent, he did not see a reason to let the athletic department also incur a drop off in its ranks.

Al would have the final word, which would be that Sam would still help out with the team, but only on a part-time basis.

He was only interviewing five students, but he was changing the rules. He was taking two, not one. Andy would still be able to keep two assistants, mostly because they were free. No costs to the university, they'd be temporary anyway. Andrew did not want just one. Since it would be such a new experience with all new people, he wanted that person to be at least comfortable. Whomever it might be probably wouldn't be that productive in a contributory way. He would possibly be intimidated by the extremely tall, uninhibited black players. So, if he hired two of them, at least they could pal around together, thus, being some-what secure in their new-found roles. Perhaps together they could be an asset in a very meager way. So that's what he'd do. He'd hire based on the old adage, two heads are better than one.

He got up from the desk, went to the door, shook hands with the door knob, and pulled it. Standing right there was a roly, pudgy looking fellow, who greeted Andy by fabricating a huge grin. His semblance forecasted a feeling of exuberance. His mouth opened wide like a sail that was inhaling a gale of wind. Andy shook his hand and told him to come in and sit down. The fellow was definitely in a classy upbeat mood. He displayed a great attitude. Great experience with respect to his accumulation of poundage.

Andy asked, "What's your name?"

The student replied, "Winthrop."

"Okay, Winthrop, tell me why I should select you for this position?"

Winny responded, "Well, sir, I know this is kind of temporary from what I was told. So I won't be coaching to any degree. I figure you just need someone to make sure the players complete their assigned drills. Chart their foul shooting percentages, stuff like that."

Andrew knew from the get go that he wasn't hiring for the FBI or CIA. The nominees did not need Senate approval, nor did the candidates have to stand before a committee and give a persuasive speech. Since it was only temporary, the position did not require great qualifications. Andy had only two criteria in making the selection. First, the student would have to be easy going and understand his role; secondly, Andy would need to like the person.

Andrew immediately liked Winthrop, particularly for how he carried himself, physical properties, included. Andy impressively said, "Pretty good, Winthrop. You've just described precisely what our need is. I'm impressed with your vision and foresight. You've got yourself a position."

"Really, sir?" Winthrop was extremely enthusiastic.

"You bet. Tomorrow, be in the gymnasium at 2:00 sharp. I'll introduce you to the team."

"Will do."

"And pick yourself up a couple of university shirts in the book store and don't pay for them. They'll be for free."

"Thank you, sir."

Winthrop jumped up from his chair like a mountain volcano erupting with passion. Andy grinned at Winny and told him never to call him sir. He did not feel the need to be power hungry or egotistical, preferrig to be addressed by his first name. Anything else would infer that he had some elevated prestigious status that was impregnable.

Winthrop, about to depart, said, "Okay, Andy, are you hiring any other assistants?"

This drew a curious expression from Andrew. "Yes, I am. Why?"

"Well, there's a couple of guys outside. One of them is named Bart. I just wanted to give my recommendation of taking him on. He also understands what you're looking for and has an idea of what your situation is. Like me, he's not the type of guy who would rock the boat."

Andy temporarily acquired the sarcastic thought, *No, but with your weight, we could pretty well sink it.*

Winthrop then said, "He's a real good X's and O's guy."

Andy considered the important increments supplied by

Winthrop. The last thing Andrew needed was two volunteer assistants who thought they were the reincarnation of Napoleon Bonaparte. He knew that wasn't the case and looked forward to interviewing Bartholomew. When Winny mentioned X's and O's, Andy became curiously intrigued. He thought maybe this would be a real blessing in disguise. Andy said, "Send him in."

"Okay, see you tomorrow, Andy."

"Good night, Winthrop. Hey, Winthrop?"

"Yeah?"

"Keep your fingers crossed, and wish us luck. We're gonna need it."

Winthrop said, "I'll even say nightly prayers." Winthrop then left the room.

Andy thought he should have told him to include a whole Goddamn rosary and that if Winthrop had the will power, he should try to keep his hands off the Twinkies. Andy then went over to a file cabinet, placed some papers in the drawer, closed it, and said to himself. *He's pretty good.*

Andrew crossed to the office door, answering the knock he heard. A rather thin, squiggly person entered. He said, "My name is Bart." They shook hands and the interview began.

It was Andy's last interview. He had found and hired his two sidekicks.

CHAPTER

TEN

His Chevrolet Camaro pulled into the parking lot of the prestigious downtown Chicago Diner. Andy often stopped at this specific diner two to three nights a week, picking up his dinner to go. The check would be somewhere in the neighborhood of eight bucks and change. He couldn't afford to spend that kind of money each night, especially since he also had to buy his lunch each day. Lunch would consist of a cheaper check, since it was usually comprised of your basic hot dogs, pizza, hamburgers, and of course, America's greatest food of all, French fries. He'd spend approximately five dollars a day on lunch. Therefore, it seemed reasonable that he couldn't spend eight to nine bucks each night. The other nights he'd resort to tuna fish without mayo, or perhaps simple cold cuts with salad dressing over the lettuce and tomato. Andrew made it a religious practice of treating himself to a good, hot meal twice a week.

Surprisingly, he knew how to cook, but it had been at least two years since he last immersed himself in that endeavor. Basically, it took too much time. An hour to cook, and ten minutes to eat, and that didn't even take into account cleaning up, washing the dishes, wiping down and throwing out the garbage. This was simple—eat and dispose.

There he was, addictively summoned to the Wishbone Diner, getting his usually late night dinner. As he began climbing the steps to the entrance, he was thinking that tonight would be souvlaki. Souvlaki was fried veal over a bed of rice, served on pita bread with a huge garden salad and plenty of dressing. That would satiate him and give him some much-needed nourishment.

Upon entering the diner, he approached the obvious designated counter where he ordered his feast-to-be. After ordering, he slapped down a crisp ten dollar bill. Andy always preferred to pay for it and get his change while he waited. He always played it that way. The same with filling up his automobile with a high test. Since he wasn't doing anything but waiting for services to be rendered, he always looked to pay while he waited. It saved time that way. He couldn't stand waiting for ten minutes to pay after services had been completed or tediously wait for change. Retail and service stores always seemed to be out of some denomination: fives, ones, dimes, pennies, whatever. It could always be taken care of beforehand, as long as a fixed amount of compensation was understood.

As Andy paced and looked around the diner, he suddenly saw her. There she was sitting in a booth against the window all by herself. It was the young woman whom he practically knocked down in the hallway corridor at the university. However, she hadn't seen him yet. She seemed to be very busy. It appeared to him that she was engrossed in correcting papers. Andrew didn't know whether she was a teacher or a student. In fact, he did not even know her name. He thought for a second of how stupid of himself not to even have asked for her name when he collided with her this afternoon. What he failed to recognize for the moment was that his state of mind at that time had been completely elsewhere, perhaps a million miles away. Such a simple task of asking her her name was an astonishing oversight.

Andy turned to the waitress behind the counter and asked for a glass of water. She obliged him, and he drank the full glass right then and there. He placed the empty glass back on the counter and started for the booth.

Earlier in the day, it was Andy who had been much too busy to even take part in the briefest of conversations after their unintentional collision. Amazingly, at this particular moment, it was Sheila who was very preoccupied with her work. She had a deadline to meet. She was in no mood to meet someone or have the slightest of conversations. Especially since two different guys had already tried hitting on her in the past hour while she worked intently in her booth that was temporarily converted into her own private desk. The tables had been sharply and perfectly reversed at this, their second encounter with one another. She was now much too busy for him.

Andy decided to sit down opposite her in the booth. He instantly tried to promote conversation. "Excuse me, but aren't you from the university?"

Sheila never even looked up to acknowledge his presence. She continued her writing crisply. "Nope, and bug off."

Andrew was quite taken aback and let down. It was the first moment since 9:00 this morning that he felt loose, calm, and in a good mood. Andy was quite embarrassed that he was shot down in such a cruel manner. He looked at her and really took it to heart that she never even picked up her head to acknowledge him courteously.

The waitress from the counter yelled out, "Sir, your dinner is ready."

As Andy slid from the booth, he said, "That's the reason why I left New York," and walked away from her. If she had been drowning, Andy would not have touched her with a ten foot pole.

Sheila raised her head now that he was gone to get a glimpse of what the culprit looked like. When she looked up, all she saw was a buttocks moving along with a sexy, swaggering gait. Then she looked up further to catch a configuration of what he looked like. Sheila was quite surprised as her mouth gaped. She instantly recognized him and congruently felt bad. She watched him as he grabbed his brown paper bag, said thanks to the waitress, and adroitly headed for the exit doors, all in an apparent fluid motion.

Outside the diner, Andy strode along the sidewalk that juxtaposed the huge bay windows of the booths inside the restaurant. He was now walking past her booth without knowing it.

Sheila was watching him all the way, just as a jungle animal would watch its prey. She thought for a moment and suddenly burst out of the booth like it was a starting gate. Within seconds, she was outside the diner, without her coat, chasing Andrew down. She called out, "Wait a minute. Sir, excuse me!"

Andy never looked back. He was like a thoroughbred with tunnel vision as he inserted the key to unlock his car door. Again she said, "Sir, excuse me!"

Andy turned around toward her as he opened the car door. "Are you talking to me?" he asked.

Sheila came toward him with her arms folded, as if it were keeping the cold off of her. "Yes, I'm talking to you, I hope. I want to apologize for being extremely rude inside! That's not like me. It's just that I have so many papers to correct, and two different guys tried hitting on me in there."

Andy said, "No doubt they were unsuccessful, which probably was a blessing." He really took the opportunity to send in a verbal zinger, which she deserved. Sheila just smiled. She had it coming and took it in stride.

Andy held his package, still sporting the swath over his eye, waiting for her next words.

She then said, "Didn't we meet this morning?"

Andy replied, "Sort of."

"What's your name?"

"Andy. What's yours?"

"Sheila, Sheila Clarke. Andy, would you like to come back inside and have dinner with me?"

Andy walked over to the window where her booth was situated in the restaurant. Sheila was watching him curiously.

"Will I be eating with the girl who was in that booth or the girl who's out here?"

"Not that girl, this one!"

Andy began to feel comfortable and decided to tantalize her a bit, especially since it was so cold and windy out. He said, "Are you sure? Cause if I'm eating with her, I'll need a gun and whip and perhaps brass knuckles just to feed her."

Sheila played along. All she wanted to do was to get back in the building as quickly as possible. "I know she was a monster, but she's gone now. I killed her."

Andy immediately became very positive, acting like her remorse made such a big difference. "Well, in that case, I think I'll be safe."

Sheila said, "Good. Thank you. Finally."

Andy continued to rake her over the coals a bit more when he said, "Sheila, ya know, it's pretty cold out here. Maybe we should go inside."

She had pursued him without her coat. Emphatically, she replied, "Yes. Yes. Let's go now."

They turned and started walking back together toward the diner. Sheila slid her arm under his as they walked on, mostly to keep warm. She couldn't wait to get back inside. She also wanted him to know that she was truly sorry for being such a bitch initially. She wasn't coming on to him at all, but she did give him her arm to let him know she appreciated his forgiveness and that her attempt to lure him back in was successful.

Sarcastically, Andrew said, "So, Sheila, how many different personalities can you manifest?"

She smiled and said with a serious, structured countenance, "About a hundred."

Andy smiled and said aloud, "This will be interesting." They were at the top of the steps about to open the doors to re-enter the restaurant.

"What happened to your eye," she asked. The doors closed behind them. They were back inside the building. They continued conversing with one another, without so much as a pause. What was to happen between them was very rare. She was completely interested in him. He was completely interested in her.

Andy and Sheila had met twice in one day by accident, and this was after he had already been in one. When they originally met, Andy was more than preoccupied. Now it had been her turn of the wheel. Both times they had met, it was not premeditated. It had been by chance. At each instance, one of them would not even be willing to pass the time of day. But both times one of them suspected curiously, unusual naturalness. Even though their initial contact was so unconventional, they both experienced brief fleeting moments of mystique that pleasantly interrupted the business of their days.

CHAPTER
ELEVEN

The athletic building was under siege. It resembled a fort in hostile territory. This was the third straight day the employees had seen this kind of turnout. It happened at approximately 2:30 in the afternoon, when eighty percent of the students had completed their last classes of the day. They gathered and assembled at the athletic building in force, obviously rebelling. Somewhere in the neighborhood of 100 students who were die hard Rock of Gibraltar fans of the university's college basketball athletic program were in attendance.

The growth rate of these turnouts was multiplying each day. That meant if this kept up, by late next week the unruly membership would mount upward and over 1,000 participants. By that time, Andrew's replacement would surely have been found, preventing the thousand-man regiment from ever coming into existence. Thus, the athletic department would be off the hook. But for now, they were dangling hook, line, and sinker.

The students were picketing inside the building, as well as on the outside. About fifty or so were inside, while over one hundred students were on the exterior. All this revolting had one factor behind it. They did not give their stamp of approval on the current selection of the newly appointed coach. There were countless signs and posters strewn all over the place. They were even pinned to the walls, as if they were permanent fixtures. Many were held up by hand. Some were: "Coachless Eagles, We Want a Real Coach," "Get on with it! We Need a Coach, and We Need it Yesterday," "Save the Season, The Ship is Sinking," "Get Rid of the Amateur and Hire a Pro," and "Andrew the Asshole."

There was yelling and screaming inside the building. Al Perkins was on the phone talking into the receiver in a very excitable manner.

"This place is crazy; it's getting out of hand. Send the campus police and some security guards down here right away."

Just as Al hung up the phone he noticed a tall, fairly big, intense-looking college student leaning over the countertop of the front desk area.

The student said to Al, "You're gonna get us a real coach, and a good one, or I'm personally gonna cut you a new asshole."

Al did not take it personally, even though he was taken aback by the man's aggressiveness.

The unfolding scene still maintained an ever-present aura of constant commotion. Phones were ringing. Employees behind the counter area were running back and forth in an abrupt fashion.

Sam Hastings exclaimed, "Al, it's getting out of control!"

Al responded, "Tell me about it, Sam. Get me Dean Thompson on the phone right away!"

Sam instantly said, "I'm on it." As Sam was dialing the telephone, he looked over the front counter area and saw nearly 100 people on the other side. Sam said to Al while he was waiting for someone to pick up on the other end, "Al, look how many people are out here now!"

Al said, "It's not a picket anymore. It's turning into a riot."

A security guard whose hat just fell off his head, overheard Al and Sam's conversation and said, "You should see how many are outside trying to get in here. About twice as many as you have here."

Just as Sam said hello to the apparent secretary on the other end of the phone, a fist fight broke out about five feet in front of the counter. The security guard struggled greatly just to get near the fight in order to attempt to break it up.

Suddenly, Dean Thompson marched in through the heavily congested crowd, but his presence went unnoticed. The rebelling students were preoccupied, engrossed with their activity, ignoring the fact that Dean Thompson brought in ten security guards and campus police to alleviate the ruckus.

Outside the building, there were still about 250 students holding their positions, posters and signs, as well. Now they began to set fire to about a dozen garbage cans that would help keep them warm from the Chicago cold as they prepared to stand their vigil.

CHAPTER

TWELVE

The team was already in the gymnasium, revving up for their daily workout.

Willie Jones was the last one to leave the locker room. It was common for him to be the last one out of the locker room on practice days. He was suited up in the special scrimmage uniform when he turned abruptly, went back to his locker, opened the combination lock, and grabbed a substance from within. Then he proceeded to take a hefty nasal whiff. Willie religiously did this activity before practice sessions. Every team seemed to have one or several along the line. Those who needed a dependent to get through the tedious, boring, laborious practices. On the Eagle team, Willie was the only one who used cocaine. Willie took it as if it were vitamins, thus transforming hard practice into easy ones. All players loved game time and hated practice. Competitive games were fun. Practices were a pain. Willie was now ready to join the team for he had his essential boost, enabling him to survive the bootcamp-like practices.

CHAPTER

THIRTEEN

They were shouting and yelling at one another in obvious disagreement. The two sides seemed to be balanced. Six of them were in favor of the newborn boss. Five of them were not. The speech that Andy had given them three days ago had worn off like old nail polish. The message he tried to convey to them faded from their hearts and minds. There were a few bad apples in the basket, and they were speaking out. These were young, black men, and they always seemed to have minds of their own, as well as a low opinion of authority figures. You'd rarely see an adolescent black man who was an athlete inhibit his emotions. Much like young kids up until the age of fifteen and sixteen, they just react to situations without thinking about them, claiming they knew it all and couldn't be told a thing without throwing a tantrum.

The confrontation between the players was still quite apparent, when Andrew entered the gymnasium. He was instantly appalled at what he saw and perceived it to be a very serious violation. He knew, beyond a shadow of a doubt, that he was their subject matter. Andy reacted. One thing he knew, if he knew anything at all, was that he had to win the ballplayers over by first getting their respect. If he couldn't do that much, he might as well give up and pack it in. Andy would not be able to accomplish one damn thing successfully with them unless he proved that he was going to be their leader whether they liked it or not. This was a tall order because he'd have to attain their respect, and he would have to respect each of them, individually and collectively. There was one generalization he knew was universal. They perceived him as an amateur like everyone else. After all, he had just read it all over the corridor only half a minute ago when he entered the congested edifice. He had read it many times, in many different ways. The point was, Andy Trella was an untested novice who suddenly had this thrown at him. He also decided that the only way to harness this deep-rooted discontent and disrespect of his knowledge and integrity of the game of basketball was not going to be attained through conventional means. He would have to embark on a campaign, resort to a series of events, not only to gain their respect but to claim a strong foothold in the nucleus of this group of uninhibited young men.

From across the gymnasium, Andrew bellowed out, "What kind of bullshit is this? We've got rebellion all over this campus, but we're not gonna have it in this gym. Is that Goddamn clear?"

They all simply stood in silence. Andrew was now standing right in front of them. "I want every one of you to stretch your feet apart and grab your socks."

One of the players responded, "Or what?"

Andrew repeated, "Your socks. Grab your socks, now! Do it!" Andy began walking around them, inspecting them to make sure they were doing the assigned punishment correctly. "Let's go! Spread those feet out; spread 'em out!"

Off to the side were Winthrop and Bart, just observing the current situation.

Winny said to Bart, "Jesus, he's tougher than I thought!"

They followed his direction to the tee. Once they heard the words "spread 'em," they immediately responded, categorizing the instruction to that of a shakedown, or frisk, by policemen of the old neighborhood's city streets.

They all knew that type of scenario so they responded like a unit in a platoon. They each dropped their upper torsos and grabbed their socks on both legs with both hands.

Andy paced around the court, checking on each one of them individually, making sure they were holding the tops of their socks. Then, he began to address them while they were in this unnatural position, introducing the two new assistants.

"Guys, these two gentlemen here are our new assistants, Bart and Winthrop. I want to make this perfectly clear. So listen up! They are not your coaches! Last week, you had Coach Connors, currently there's me, and next week, they'll be hiring someone else. The last thing you guys need as a team is 101 different coaches telling you what to do. These guys are merely my helpers and report to me. If they tell you to do something, it's only because I told them to tell you. Anything they say comes directly from me. So, don't give them a hard time. This way, I don't have to make jackasses out of the brothers like I'm doing right now. All right! Get up!"

As soon as they got up into a natural standing position, Washington, who was the tallest, biggest, and strongest guy on the squad, walked over to Winthrop and Bart, shook their hands, and introduced himself to them, saying as he towered over them, "Congratulations. Welcome aboard!"

The one named Williams suddenly yelled, "You don't know shit about basketball!"

Andrew looked straight at Williams, not believing that one of them was standing up to him, especially since he just got done demonstrating some sense of authority over them. Everyone's eyes strained to witness what would now become of this confrontation.

Andy said, "Is that so?"

Williams responded, "Yeah, man, that's what I'm saying. You don't know shit about this game."

Andy yelled out Winthrop's name. Winthrop came running over to him. Andy said, "Go to my office. In my top desk drawer is a key to my locker. Bring me the sneakers and gym shorts."

Winthrop ran off like Winnie the Pooh. He galloped his wide body over to the exit sign that led to the men's locker room.

Williams smiled and so did the rest of the players, for they were about to witness a short one-on-one contest between Williams and Andrew. Williams approached the novice coach and said, "You can't be this stupid."

Andy began loosening his tie and proceeded to take it off. "Well, I'll tell ya, Williams, you've got four inches on me, more talent, you're younger and stronger. You should destroy me, but you're gonna lose." The players laughed loudly, smiling in disbelief of Andrew's conviction and confidence.

Williams laid out a big smile and said, "This will be like slippin' stereos from a department store."

Winthrop finally came bouncing back from the locker room with the attire he had been requested to get. Andy began to take off his shirt and put the gym clothes on.

Bart, who was standing next to Andy said, "Are you sure you know what you're doing?"

Andy replied, "Are you kidding? Of course, I'm sure. Prediction. Final score: Good Guy: 11–Bad Guy: 6."

Winthrop and Bart were both shocked at Andy's boldly stated prediction.

Winthrop said, "Go get 'em, boss."

Andrew walked onto the court. Williams was waiting impatiently at the free throw line.

Bart said to Winthrop, "I think he might have guessed the right score, wrong winner, though." Winthrop simply shook his head in agreement.

One of the players yelled out, "Jeffrey, blow this honky away!"

Williams, impatiently confident, replied, "You know it!"

Williams gave the coach the opportunity to hit or miss for the first possession of the ball offensively. He felt some sense of sentimentality for Andrew, since he thought Andy was at a serious disadvantage, as did everyone else. Andy hit the shot from the top of the key, thus claiming the ball. Then he drove around Williams quickly to score the first point of the game. Immediately, he took the same jump shot at the top of the key and now led, 2–0.

The one-on-one contest between them went just like a professor teaching a student. It left anyone who witnessed this exhibition by the young coach in complete awe. Andy whipped Williams and did it in a completely decisive way. He outplayed him with his speed and superb outside shooting. He also had stolen the ball from Williams on four separate occasions, which befuddled the entire team.

The players on the sidelines displayed expressions of astonishment. They sincerely could not believe that this young white coach had annihilated one of the players so decisively.

Williams was cursing aloud to himself, "Son of a bitch!"

Jefferson said to a couple of the players, "He's a Goddamn iceman."

Skin Head agreed, "The man is a Goddamn ringer. Don't mess with him."

Kennedy asked, "Where'd he play his college ball?"

"Don't know, man," Jefferson replied. "I think it was somewhere in the Ivy League." They were all in disbelief when Jefferson said Ivy League, which was a high profile status conference of universities in the northeastern part of the country (Yale, Harvard, Cornell, and the like). The team was quite impressed that their co-player had just gotten fried by the smaller, smarter, quicker neophyte coach. Winthrop and Bart were smiling affably.

Andrew made an incredible twisting, turning shot to conclude the obvious mismatch of a one-on-one contest. Williams grabbed the basketball in obvious disgust and bounced it so hard with both hands against the floor that when it shot back up at him like a rocket missile, he misjudged its speed and missed catching it, resulting in a shot to his head hitting him so squarely that it sent his head and body reeling away. The players saw this occur and were jiving it up big time, laughing hard at the shocking conclusion of the contest that ended so appropriately, with Williams, personally embarrassed.

Andy walked back over to the side, approaching Winthrop and Bart. He was breathing heavily, panting, and gasping for air, and was holding his side with his arm. Fortunately, there wasn't anything wrong with him, but the victory over Williams took everything he had. It took all the energy within him to pull off this stunning little miracle of an upset. He was now quite fatigued.

However, Andy knew he had to win this one-on-one contest, and in a conquering fashion, otherwise he would never be able to secure respect from the players. He had to have their respect or everything else would be for naught. He still knew this was not enough to achieve that goal. It would have to be a series of six or seven impressive conquests of major confrontations. Not only would he have to survive these showdowns, but he'd have to be outstanding and successful in order to truly impress them. As of today, he was on his way. He had passed this test with flying colors.

The speech he originally gave them was step number one. It was good, but it wore off in a couple of days, as he expected. This was step number two, and he was impressive. There would be several more personal campaigns he'd have to use in order to claim their souls. He would have to be amazingly resourceful, and he was. He already had his grab bag of tricks that he'd use to stay on top of this team. Andy was just waiting for the proper events to occur before he'd unfold his plan of attack. When they put his back to the wall, he'd not only want to escape, but attempt to reverse it so completely, they'd have to be severely affected.

Even though he was their coach, they could easily make him

their prisoner, and he was not about to permit that to happen. Besides, the entire student body and fans and booster club were accomplishing that trick with signs and posters protesting against him. As far as Andrew was concerned, he was the coach, the big boss. He knew he'd have to be the top dog, or else he'd be a prisoner on two accounts, and a fool on at least one. He was a novice head coach they'd all try to make him prisoner, and yet he would have to be a magician to pull off this small miracle of appreciation.

"Andy, that was great!" Winthrop said to Andy as he came off the court, perspiring profusely.

"Thanks. I'm gonna take a quick shower. Have them shoot foul shots. I'll be back in ten minutes." Andy began to walk away laggardly.

"How'd you know you'd win?" Winthrop asked.

"Speed. Speed conquers all. He's everything but fast. If it was any one besides Williams, I would have lost."

The players were standing directly behind Winthrop and Bart by thirty feet or so. Williams was walking back to join his teammates with his head hung low, speechless. The players weren't riding him, but consoling him. They knew it was quite embarrassing to be ambushed by the suddenly aggressive young coach.

Andy looked over at them. Acting seriously, when he was quite obviously unable to go another one-on-one, said, "Next?" They were so surprised since he was apparently exhausted that they looked at each other, wide-eyed as could be, and Cory Jackson pretended to faint, falling into the arms of several players who caught him. Andy had to impress them, and he did. Andy then walked off to the showers.

Winthrop asked Bart, "What was the final score?"

Bart replied, "11–5."

Winthrop made a facial expression that was unbelievable, knowing that Andy had predicted the score so closely. He was only off by one point, and that point was in his own favor. "That was amazing," he said.

Bart replied, "If this guy's like this all the time, we're gonna see some serious shit."

"Come on. Let's get on with the practice," Winthrop replied as they both moved over to the players.

FOURTEEN

In the locker room, Andy stood in front of the mirror hanging above a sink. The water gushed from the faucet. He stared into the mirror at himself. Perspiration, combined with water, flowed rapidly down his face.

He could hear the thoughts in his head. *Oh, hang in there, Andy. Hang in there.*

He continued to look deeply at himself. Then he took a hot shower before returning to the battlefield upstairs, where the power struggle would take a vacation, but only a brief one.

CHAPTER

FIFTEEN

They walked down the stairs in the basketball arena holding hands. Andy lead Sheila down to the court area. There was hardly any crowd there as yet, just a few fans, as it was still quite early. Maybe about 200 people were in the stadium of the 9,000 capacity arena. Most of the people there were necessary to set up the game: radio announcers, sports reporters and other media people, security guards, and the coaches and players of the opposing team. Andy's team was probably just arriving themselves, and they were beginning to get suited up in the locker room.

"Andy, we've got good seats?" Sheila asked.

Andy turned back to look up at her. "Yeah, we've got real good seats. We're down in the front."

With a smile, Sheila replied, "Really, I've never been to a basketball game before."

"I know, you told me."

They continued walking through a sporadic crowd of people, down near the court. Andy led Sheila near the players bench.

"Andy, where are we sitting?" Sheila asked dumbfounded.

Andrew motioned with his hand to a particular seat, right behind the players bench. "Sheila, you're sitting here."

Nonplussed, Sheila asked, "And where are you sitting?"

"I'm not."

Sheila was now extremely curious. "What do you mean, 'You're not.' You have to sit somewhere!"

Just at that moment Winthrop approached Andrew and confidentially whispered in his ear away from Sheila. Andy shook his head affirmatively. A referee then came over to Andrew from the other side of the court, grabbed his arm, and said, "Coach Trella, my two associate referees are caught up in some kind of a traffic jam. They just called, so we'll be starting a half hour later than usual, which gives you about one hour from now."

Again, Andy shook his head in an affirmative manner. "That's fine. Thank you."

Sheila stood there in a monumental daze. She was utterly astounded as she was in the process of putting two and two together. She finally deduced that Andrew was the Western Chicago University's new head basketball coach, but she wasn't done accepting the knowledge. She had vaguely remembered reading or hearing something about some resignations, and the appointment of a young gentleman named Andy. But she never thought for a fraction of a second that this stranger she had only met less than forty-eight hours ago was indeed the current man in control of this university's basketball program. She stood frozen in disbelief. After the referee departed, Andy's eyes fell on hers and they regained each other's attention.

Sheila said, "So, you're the coach."

Andrew simply looked at her with a strong, handsome confidence and humorously said, "Well, I'm wearing his underwear."

"Why didn't you tell me?"

"I wasn't sure how to tell you! Sometimes sports turn a girl off. Listen, Sheila, take a seat. I can assure you I'll be back, but I'll be a bit busy tonight."

He leaned on one of the player's chairs and Sheila whispered in his ear, "Payback's a bitch, I'll get you later."

Andrew said, "I'll get you now," and kissed her on the lips. He stood up from his slouched position and buttoned his sport coat as he left her. Once he had gotten thirty feet or so away from her, he suddenly swiveled around toward her and yelled. "Hey, Sheila! Enjoy the game!"

She stood up from her chair and shouted, "You're gonna get a beating later tonight!"

Andrew fabricated an expression and replied. "Yeah? Well, I might be getting one in about an hour." He was referring to the ball game by either the other team or the student fans attending.

"Good luck!" she said.

Andrew raised his arm and crossed his two fingers, signaling acknowledgement. Then he turned away to join his disciples who were getting dressed in the locker room below.

Sheila sat down, still taken aback. She even started talking to herself, something she rarely ever did. *I can't believe this guy. He's the damn coach.* She sat there in amazed bewilderment.

SIXTEEN

Andy had his hands on his hips, pacing the sidelines while the game was taking place. He yelled at the referees, "Your ass! What do you think, his arm's a piece of chicken? What game are you watching?" He walked away abruptly, looking up at the ceiling, checking the scoreboard perched up in the rafters. His team was winning pretty handily, but you'd never know it by the way Andy was working the referees over. He raised his arms and gestured the appropriate signal for a Time Out.

The five starters hustled over to the bench area, sitting in their respective seats. The others cleared out and stood around in the customary enclosed circle to block out and pay strict attention. Andy knelt on the floor before them and started shelling out current instructions.

"All right. We're looking very good out there. Keep it up. We're not gonna do anything different than we're doing. No freeze. No delays. Just keep moving the ball. Don't worry about shooting, the shots will come. The most important thing is that we rebound. We need lots of rebounds on both sides of the glass." Then he stood up, backed up a step and said, "OK! On the floor. Let's go with the President's row."

Five players began to resume their positions on the court.

Their individual names were printed on the backs of their shirts, above their designated numbers. The five were: Washington, Jefferson, Kennedy, Jackson, and Johnson.

Andrew moseyed on over to the part of the bench where Sheila was seated. He said to her, "How are you doing?"

"Fine. This is exciting. The team is doing really good."

Andy asked, "Are you ready?"

Sheila, curious, asked, "Ready for what?"

"On the next time out. I want you to go in for Washington."

Sheila smiled, and Andy turned around and went back to work.

CHAPTER

SEVENTEEN

The players were all undressing, laughing and joking, showering and celebrating their way through the rest of the night. They were high fivin' it. Half were dressed in casuals, and half still in uniform. Andy entered the affable area. Both Winthrop and Bart were right behind him, standing like sidekick puppets. Andy began to address his team.

"Guys, hold it up a second. I just want to thank you all for winning tonight. This was my first game on a college level. Someone else will be here soon enough, so if you don't mind, I'd like to shake hands with each one of you individually." He proceeded on down the line, shaking hands with each and every one of them, as they stood in front of their own lockers. Winthrop and Bart were just taking in the stellar moment.

When Andrew approached Willie Jones, he noticed Willie didn't look too good at all. He looked both sickly and fatigued. "Willie, you okay? You don't look too good!"

Willie Jones appeared nauseous. I'm okay, Coach. Just feeling really tired. I might be coming down with something."

"Well, you get back to the dorm and get some shut eye."

"You got it, boss."

"Good." Andy continued to shake hands.

CHAPTER

EIGHTEEN

It was nearly half past ten when Andy and Sheila headed toward the parking lot. This was their first date, and it was quite a night for the both of them. Sheila saw a basketball game, her first ever, and she had been naturally overwhelmed by the surprise that her date was the head coach. For Andy, it was equally an eventful experience, especially since he had been on the victorious side of his first game.

At his vehicle, he was just about to insert the key to unlock the car door when a burly, short black man appeared on the opposite side of the car. The man said, "Excuse me, sir, but you won't be driving that car tonight."

"What do you mean? Who the hell are you?" Andy asked, maintaining a part curious, part nonplussed countenance.

"My name is Biggerman, sir. And you will no longer be driving that car while you're commanding this basketball squad at this university!" Biggerman threw out his arm and hand to show off the vehicle they now would be traveling in. It was a beautiful, brand new, black stretch limousine. Biggerman explained, "Compliments of Al Perkins."

Andrew and Sheila looked the long automobile over, both smiling. Biggerman said, "Of course, this is a short-term lease.

Once a new man is hired, this vehicle will be turned into a pumpkin in your regard, and he, then, will receive my services."

Andy replied, "Is that so?" Then he looked at Sheila and asked, "Sounds like a pretty good deal to me. What do you think?"

"I say we take it."

"We're not buying it, we're just riding in it," Andy commented, amused. He looked at Biggerman and said, "Ya know, Biggerman, once they get their hands on something, they don't let go."

"I know what you mean, sir!"

Sheila gave Andy the slightest of shoves.

"Madam, if you please!" Biggerman said as he opened the limousine door. Sheila entered, and Andrew followed her into the luxurious car.

Andy asked, "Where do you wanna go, Sheila?"

"How about the park?"

Andy leaned forward and said to the driver, "Biggerman?"

"Yes, sir."

"You look familiar to me. Have you ever been to New York?"

"No, sir. But I have family there."

"In the limo business?"

"As a matter of fact, yes. Why, sir?"

Andy changed his mind and just decided to quit the present conversation by saying, "No particular reason." He leaned back to rejoin Sheila, saying, "Biggerman, take us through the park."

"Yes, sir!"

Andrew and Sheila were relaxed, taking in the sights and lights on this special night. Downtown Chicago, Lake Michigan, Soldier Field all looked so enchanting as snow flurries softly began to curtain the night. They were sipping champagne, which was the perfect beverage for the night they had experienced.

"So, are you enjoying your prom?" Andy asked her.

Sheila replied, "I never went to my prom!"

Andrew drew the champagne glass to his lips, but before he drank, he asked, "How come?"

Sheila, deciding to become facetious and play a game with Andy's head, said, "I was pregnant!"

Andy immediately spit out a spray of the champagne as he was totally off guard and unprepared for that kind of remark. "What?" he said.

Laughing, she said, "Got you good that time!"

Andy just smiled as he blushed softly. She continued, "I had to get some payback for shocking the hell out of me tonight. I never thought for a single second that you were the new coach everyone's been talking about. That was a helluva surprise. You will never surprise me with anything as you did tonight." Sheila began to sip her glass of champagne.

Andy smiled, looked at her with a twinkle in his eye, and replied, "Oh, yeah? Wait till later!" Sheila instantly knew what he was referring to. She responded by spitting out some champagne that she had sipped in a toast to her own touché that backfired on her with Andrew's last remark.

Biggerman turned around and said, "Under your seat, I have an umbrella. Could you pass it to me? It's getting a bit wet up here!" He was politely and humorously informing them that he felt the spray twice within the past minute.

Sheila apologized, "Sorry, Biggerman."

"That's quite all right, ma'm."

Andy said, "Sorry, Biggerman."

"Thank you, sir."

Biggerman closed the window divider that separated him from them and any further activity. Andy and Sheila just snuggled and enjoyed the sights of this perfect evening.

CHAPTER

NINETEEN

Sheila was curled up in front of the fireplace, surrounded by a multitude of pillows that were set around the room like a constellation of stars. Andrew walked over and handed her a glass of wine. They were both fully clothed, and it would still be a couple of weeks before they would actually make love. They both wanted to and would have, yet they seemed to feel they could wait a bit longer. They were, of course, still in the primordial stages of their relationship. Sometimes when two people sleep together without knowing each other for a time, one or the other quickly loses interest.

Sheila and Andy were in agreement not to have too much too soon. Everything was great, happening so quickly, that rushing into sex so fast could possibly diminish their emotional development. The end result could thus jeopardize their relationship. They both seemed to sense that any premarital sexual activity should not be planned ahead of time, but should be in an environment where both participants knew the time was right. Making love with one another would then raise their common friendship to new heights where sex would not only be a backbone but an additional fringe benefit to the core of their love for each other. Besides, both of them seemed to think they had been traveling at the speed of light for the past couple of days.

"We shouldn't drink this much, Andy!" Sheila said.

Andrew knelt down next to her and said, "I know. This is way above average for me, but it's been a pretty special night.

"You can say that again."

Sheila smiled and Andy, for some strange reason, said, "Too bad it can't last longer."

Immediately, Sheila got aroused, trying to figure out what he really meant.

"What do you mean?"

"Well, even as we speak, the college is desperately working to get an experienced guy in here."

"Andy, would they still replace you, even if you kept winning?"

"First of all, there's no such thing as continuous winning, even Dean Smith of North Carolina. He had won over 800 games but he's also lost 250 times. But you wanna know something? Something happened to me tonight! I mean, I really had a good time out there. I enjoyed coaching that game! I didn't even hear the crowd at all. I mean, I knew they were there, yet in another way, I didn't even know they were there. If that makes any sense?"

"I follow that."

Suddenly, Andy had a change of heart as he thought about it and said, "Ah, I probably just got lucky tonight! They played really well."

Something went off in Sheila's soul, as if it a volcano erupted in her chest cavity. "Wait a minute! You did very well out there tonight. There's a hell of a lot of stuff going on out there, and you could have found a way to screw it up, and lose. Don't you think so?"

Andy's tongue slid over his front upper teeth smoothly, as he was digesting Sheila's remark. "I suppose you're right. I could have done worse. I could have done a lot worse."

Sheila interrupted, "Yes. You could have, but you didn't. You should be proud of yourself. What's the matter with you?"

Andy decided to raise the discussion to greater heights. "Let me ask you a question. Have you seen some of the signs and picketing going on around the campus in reference to this basketball team's new coach?"

"Yes, I can see exactly how that could demoralize someone. But, Andy, you cannot pay attention to that."

"Oh, yeah? And how do I do that? It's pretty hard every time I walk around a corner and see a poster board, and it says 'Dump Andy Trella. He Sucks'."

Sheila was giving him a good verbal fight, like a barracuda strung out on a fishing line. You have to ignore that. If you read every single sign and then think about it, it'll destroy you. You have to see it, read it, and then discard it. Don't ponder and evaluate it. That's ludicrous. That's suicide. Let me ask you a question. How come no one was screaming against you tonight?"

"That's easy. We were winning from the outset, throughout the entire game. If we were losing by one point, for one second, you would have heard a roar that would've cracked the sound barrier."

"You sure?"

"You bet."

Andy, you're getting all worked up and tense over this. Come here and lie on your stomach!"

"What for?"

"I want to see how tense you are. Then I'm going to relieve it for you."

Andrew turned over, stretched and sprawled out on the floor as she instructed him to do so.

Sheila sat close to him and began to engage in massaging his upper back and neck. She said, "Andy, I want you to tell me about the worst thing that ever happened to you."

"What?"

"You'll see."

"Let me think."

Andy closed his eyes, his face submerged into a pillow, searching for an event from his past. He was appreciating the dexterity of her fingers dancing on his back. It did not take him long to begin his story.

"Once when I was a little kid, we were playing football on the beach on a very hot summer day. There were a bunch of us, and we had all gotten so tired and hot, we all made a mad dash to jump into the water to cool off and refresh ourselves. I was about ten at the time, and when I dove in, there was this incredibly strong undertow, one that I never experienced before. It pulled me under, and was taking me out."

Andy turned over lying on his back wanting to look into Sheila's face before concluding his true story.

"I remember coming up for air for less than half a second, before another wave would climb over on top of my head and push me back down again and again. Within that half a second, I still had enough time to grab as much air as I possibly could, and then scream for help as loud as I could. But there seemed to be no one around me. Then suddenly out of nowhere I felt someone grab my arm firmly. I remember vividly and strangely, that we didn't struggle to swim back to safety. The moment, the very moment he clutched my arm, I was saved. I was hoisted out of the water completely. There were no waves. They vanished. It was like an evil hurricane that dropped dead as soon as he grabbed my arm, as if he parted the ocean. He brought me back to shore with such ease."

Sheila was extremely captivated by this story, and Andy was now telling it as if he was really back in time, reflecting and remembering it as it had happened.

"I was back on the beach blanket, and I saw many people on the shore line looking out at the ocean. There was commotion and screaming. I saw my mother screaming and my brothers were looking out at the lifeguards who were swimming around, holding their arms up in the air signaling they couldn't find anyone or know where to look. I remember seeing a terrified look on people's faces on the beach. Before he walked away from the beach blanket, the man said, Take care, my son,' and he left me. No one seemed to notice him when he walked away."

Sheila interrupted Andy once again. "Andy, this reminds me of the poem, "Footprints."

Andrew was not done yet, but he was surprised and taken aback when she mentioned the infamous poem.

He continued, "Sheila, when the man walked away, I watched him as he left, and I saw he left no footprints in the sand. Then I looked to the path where we both walked to reach the blanket from the water, and, unlike the poem, he didn't carry me to the blanket. I walked to it under my own strength. When I checked, I saw no footprints at all–mine or his. No one saw him bring me in."

Sheila was completely consumed and moved by his story, especially his last sentences. Instinctively, she put a hand over her mouth and said, "My God, it was Him."

Andy just looked into Sheila's face with true sincerity. He rose up to a sitting position on the floor and they embraced each other with meaningful conviction. Sheila even had a tear in her eye as she said, "He saved you for a reason. You were blessed. What did he look like?"

"Well, He was tall, thin, near his thirties. I guess. He had red, really short hair. He didn't have lots of hair and a beard, if that's what you're thinking." Sheila admitted she was. Andy continued the story. "About two or three minutes later…"

Sheila stopped him in his tracks. "You're not done yet? This story is not over?"

"No, it's not."

Sheila thought to herself, before he went on, that this guy Andy was really working on giving her a heart attack, constantly surprising her to the utmost. On the date at the game, earlier in the evening, and here again on the wrap-up of it. She also was thinking that she had been the foolish one to ask him to tell her a story. Before he'd finished it, she decided that she would never ask him to tell her one again.

Andrew continued, "Later, there was this huge crowd gathered around my blanket. Everyone, my brothers, my mother, were asking me, 'Who saved you?' I said that a man did, and I pointed in the direction that he went. My mother stood up, looked, and I guess she saw this man at a distance, walking by himself. I remember she left us with all these people crowded around our blanket. I assume she felt she had to go and thank the man responsible for saving my life. When she returned, she was completely quiet, like she was captivated by the meeting with this man. A week later, my mother was diagnosed with cancer and died a year later."

Andy was looking down at the floor. He couldn't keep his eyes on Sheila, for they were both emotionally affected. Andy's tears were flowing now. He couldn't help thinking of what had taken place between this great man and his mother one summer day in his childhood; that when they confronted each other, it was a simple thank you of appreciation. But apparently it was more than that. It was a swap. The man sent by God would not take her son. That would be too painful a life for her. Andy's mother's thank you was accepted, but Andy always thought that that man took his mother's life as part of the deal for saving his.

"Oh, Andy!" Sheila said as she wrapped her arms around him. Softly, she touched his face and cleared away the tears that were melting into his pores. While she was consoling him, she said, "Andy, I'm sorry about your mother, but I know she'd be proud of you. So you have to do one thing for me, I mean for you!"

Andy was content in just listening to her.

"No matter how many students and fans and players resist you–whether it's the athletic department, the media, or reporters that come down on you. Stand up to it! Fight it all. No matter who, or what, or how many. Stand. Stand tall!"

Andy looked at her as he was in the process of collecting

himself and understanding her revelation. He said to her, "You're something else you know that?"

"Yes. I do."

He jumped to his feet, walked over to the kitchen sink, ran some cold water, and splashed it on his face. Upon his return, he stopped by the parrot's cage and threw a sheet over it.

Sheila asked, "Why did you do that?"

"They shouldn't see this. They have a habit of talking about it then repeating it, and we can't have that."

Sheila smiled. She could tell Andrew was about to be seductive, and she was going to accept it. He turned off the lamp, got on the floor next to her, and kissed Sheila. The only light in the room was the one cast from the blazing fireplace.

In unison, both parrots started squawking, "You're an ass. You're an ass. You're an ass." Sheila and Andrew burst out laughing, interrupting their kiss. Andy suggested that Sheila get up off the floor and help him open the sofa into the convertible bed. They laid down and began kissing and hugging. They would do so for only fifteen or twenty minutes before passing out. They were both quite tired, and it was quite late. For them, it was quite a night.

CHAPTER
TWENTY

This time, they were not in the conference room. That particular room had been getting a great deal of use the past week. This time they were in Al Perkins' office, and there were only three of them: Al, Sam, and Andy. Andrew was standing, while the athletic director and his assistant were sitting. Al was seated behind his desk where a mountain of papers made it seem Al was in need of more file cabinets or more trash cans. Many of them were resumes of potential head coaching assistants. Al stated, "I think we're making headway, here. We're flying in three guys this weekend for interviews."

Andy quickly said, "Good."

Al asked, "How's it going for you?"

"Well, to put it in a nutshell, it's not easy. There's always rough spots on the court, off the court, especially off the court."

Al began making some notes with a pen. "I know what you mean. That's understandable. Hang in there. You're doing great! 1–0. Keep it up!"

Sam interjected, "You got lucky last night, hm?"

Andy immediately gave Sam a twisted stare. Then he turned to address Al. "Ya know, Al, I may be wearing my welcome out in the gym, but I didn't think I'd be wearing it out here. I'll see you later."

"Where are you going?" Al asked.

"I'm going to the chiropractor. I've got to get some of this tension and stress out of my back." Andy left the room.

Al said to Sam. "Sometimes you're such an asshole!"

Just then Andy reopened the door, took a step in and said, "He's right, you know. Al, thanks for the limo." Andy shut the door and left.

Al took the opportunity to scold Sam a bit. "Will you please relax and ease up on him? Don't you think he's brought down enough every time he spins around a corner or hallway, constantly seeing signs, posters, badgering him one after another after another? Did you ever think about that for one single solitary second? Put yourself in his shoes! Think you'd like it?"

Sam remained silent, finally understanding things from a different perspective.

Al continued, "Most people worry about their self-image every day of their lives. Well, he doesn't have to worry about it. Hundreds of students tell him about it every day, all day long." It was like a Godsend that Sam now understood. Sam felt one emotion, shame from guilt.

"You're right, Al. I'm sorry."

Al shouted, "Don't tell me tell him!" Sam got up to pursue Andy.

"Not now. The next time you run into him."

Sam closed the door after opening it and stayed in the room. The expression on his face counted him for an idiot.

TWENTY-ONE

All eleven of them were in the shower stalls with the overhead faucets running at full throttle. It was customary, as well as necessary, to shower after their daily intense practices. Only today's showers weren't of the ordinary nature. This shower was conducted right smack in the middle of a practice session. Andy was governing over it like a Gestapo general. All the players seemed to be upset. Their facial expressions revealed that this was a distasteful experience. Each and every player was in full uniform, jersey top and shorts, socks and the rather expensive limousines for the feet. This was the most upsetting fact of this strange penance or punishment that they were immersed in.

Andrew and his two assistants were standing at the entrance, on a foot high marble step that divided the shower stalls from the locker room. Winthrop was laughing being his jovial old self. Bart was smiling in amazement. The frowns on the player's faces conveyed that Andrew truly struck a vital nerve that made it such an unpleasant experience for them.

Sneakers to a black basketball player were worth their weight in gold, just as precious as a newborn infant is to a young mother. Nothing could be more painful than having their two hundred dollar sneakers, Nike's, Reebok's and other assorted high flying air pumps treated to complete submersion.

Each one of them was soaked from head to toe. Andy was yelling at them so loud that he was easily heard over the dozen or so shower heads currently in use. "You guys are not responding to me! You've decided to give me a hard time! Just because you won last night, doesn't mean you can do whatever you Goddamn please!" Andy began to walk into the shower stall, fully dressed with his suit on, minus the suit jacket he had taken off promptly and passed on to Bart before entering the six inch pond of a puddle that had grown in the stalls. Andy was now situated directly in the middle of the shower room. Like the nucleus of a molecule, he was the nucleus of this team. The water level, completely covering his ankles, submerged his dress shoes and the cuffs of his pants. The players seemed to forget about their own personal physical conditions, as well as their clothing, which could just as well have been in a washing machine with a little detergent added.

They all turned an about face so that the shower heads were hitting the back of their necks as they listened to Andy. He had six of them to the east wall and five on the other side, as he was now at center stage. If they were all statues, this would look like one of those exquisite water fountains exhibited in front of one of those elaborate Las Vegas hotels.

He said, "I swear to God, the brothers are gonna learn to be what a team really is. Not a single one of you knows what a team is really all about. One bad apple easily wrecks the whole Goddamn bunch. That's what we have here, only there's two, maybe three of you. And that's enough. That doesn't give us a chance. All it takes is every day, just one of you to screw things up. It could be a different guy every day, and you know what we have? Nothin'. Nothin' at all."

Andrew was pretty drenched from the mid-torso on down. The players were completely saturated. He decided not to let up yet, since he knew he had their attention.

He used the term again to make his point of attack clear. "I swear to God. If you guys don't learn this one frigging concept, I'll have you doing aerobics at practice instead of basketball. We won't play ball. I'm not kidding. You can dance to aerobic music and curse me out like you've been doing anyway."

He looked at each one of them singly, instructing them to shut the shower heads off. All of them stood silently, as the dripping from the shower splashed into the puddle below and the noise it gave off became less and less, until just quiet dripping remained. Andy began swishing along the water in preparation to step out of the shower room. Just before he was about to step out over the marble tiled step, he turned back to them. "This is what will happen to all of you, every time one guy steps out of line. One of the brothers curses me out, I wash all your mouths out with soap. When you win, you live like a team. When you lose, you die as a team, and when you struggle, you survive as a team. I hope the athletic department doesn't find a new Goddamn coach for three more weeks. I'll break your asses in, even if I have to house train every one of you. I look forward to a return engagement." Squeaking away out of the locker room, Andrew left them all.

The players looked around at one another, trying to figure out what the next guy was thinking. How were they going to react to this new young boss who was certainly resourceful, unconventional, and unusually motivated.

Jefferson broke the silence as they were all still soaked and dripping. "You'd better smarten up. This guy's not jiving. He's a motivated mother fucker. He's the type who's gonna take failure personally. And he's Italian from New York. Those New York Italians are the baddest. They don't forgive and they don't forget. They crawl up your skin so Goddamn fast you think you saw a ghost. I'd think twice before I'd get out of line."

The other ten of them just listened to Jefferson speak his words of wisdom. They all were white-eyed, letting the uncommon lecture by Jefferson penetrate and take meaning.

Jefferson ironically bent down to tie his shoelace while his sneaker was completely underwater. He continued. "While you are out dancing, singing, playing with the ladies, getting drunk, he's up at night planning this shit for us. You try to pull something. He's got something up his sleeve for it. I'll bet he has two dozen more stunts like this ready for us. Just waiting for us to screw up."

As Jefferson began to leave the shower area, he said, "I ain't fuckin' with this guy. I come to school to play ball, not this shit. Somebody screws up tomorrow, I'll be doin Goddamn aerobics." Jefferson disappeared and they looked at one another knowing Jefferson was insightful, meaning business.

Winthrop and Bart handed out towels, and lots of them, as the players filed out of the shower room. Each of the players seemed upset and preoccupied with the condition of his sneakers. While exiting, Washington said, "These are my new super pump specials shot to hell. All washed up."

Kennedy quipped, "Don't worry about it, so's your game."

TWENTY-TWO

It was 7:32 in the evening. The tarp of night had covered day. Andy was just leaving the athletic building and Sheila had come there to meet him. They were planning to get a little Chinese food for dinner. Andrew did not change his habit of picking up dinner on the road and bringing it home, even though he was no longer totally single. He had someone else to think about since he now shared dinner with not only his two pet parrots but Sheila also. For almost a week now, he'd have to think about another half of him to consult.

Sheila did not curb his way of getting his meals since they'd become an item. Andrew chose his meals as if he were still single. Sheila didn't care what they had to eat. She was just happy to be with him for approximately two hours each night during weekdays. They really couldn't spend much more time than that together during the week. Every day she would have papers to be corrected from her students, either tests or term papers, reports, and special assignments. At least once a week at night, she'd have to prepare a history lesson for the following day's classes. Sometimes she'd do a little extra research on a particular segment of a lesson. In this way, she would learn something additional, and enlighten the class with a little extra detail so that perhaps ten years from now, they might be able to recall something specific they had learned from her.

Andrew would spend the rest of his night on the phone, talking to an assortment of people. The subject matter naturally would be the college's basketball program. He'd draw plays on the chalkboard in his apartment. Twice a week, he'd take a ride to the university's dormitories and talk to a couple of the players for one reason or another. Pep talks basically and also to check up and personally see if any of them were playing basketball around the campus anywhere. A college varsity player of any sport was forbidden to play games in intramural sports, blacktop pick-up games, or with anyone else, for that matter. They were only allowed to play in the gymnasium under athletic department supervision. That was the price each player had to pay for accepting a scholarship to any major Division One school. One time or another, the players couldn't resist wanting to showcase their talent with the average folk. Of course, there were concessions the players received for accepting the scholarship. But the days of being shown how to pick out your new free car were over in college athletics.

Andy also wanted to see for himself who were the partiers. Who were the ones bird-dogging chicks at midnight on weekdays, and who were the ones drinking hard at the local college watering hole. He didn't partake in the practice of surveillance, that was not his job. Stakeout was not the name of the game, but making sure that their basketball play wasn't affected by it was. Just get an idea of who might be the wild ones.

Tonight, however, Andy and his new found girlfriend would not make it to the Chinese restaurant. They were walking down a steep hill in the grass on one side of the athletic building. They were holding hands in affection but also as a matter of caution. The hill was quite steep.

Suddenly, from around the corner of the building, five to six students started yelling at Andy. "You suck, man! You can't coach for shit. Give it up, asshole. Get a real job." They were cursing, badgering, and slandering him. Consequently, one of the kids noticed a good-sized rock laying on the ground after he had stepped on it and was now beneath his shoe. It was a perfectly good stone for throwing and striking someone right square in the head. That's exactly the course the rock followed, seconds after its discovery. Once it was thrown, it was targeted at Andy and raced through the air. Unfortunately, it had curved and struck Sheila on the top of her head, knocking her down.

Sheila instantly fell to the ground and remained there. Andy was alarmed. Moments later, he'd be furious. He screamed, "Sheila!" He hustled over to her aid as he was merely only a second or two away from her. "Sheila, you okay? Don't move. Just stay still, honey. Son's a bitches. I'll kill those bastards." The bastards had run off when they saw the damage they had done. Sheila laid there, dazed and hurt. Andy did not like the expression on her face at all. "Sheila, I want you to concentrate on breathing. Just take good breaths and rest." Sheila put her complete trust in him and concentrated on breathing. Andy could plainly see right off that she was definitely hurt, but she was more stunned than anything else. The stone did not strike her squarely. It had grazed the top of her head, cutting the skin underneath her hair, and the skidded off of her, continuing its flight elsewhere.

"Andy, am I hurt badly?" she asked.

Andy quickly looked around for help, but didn't see anyone anywhere who could assist. He looked down at her and placed his hand over the back of her head where some of her hair was soiled in blood. He felt the injured spot and witnessed the blood on his hand now. He said, "No, Sheila. It's bleeding a little bit, but it's not bad. Just relax another minute and I'll take you up to the infirmary."

Andy was lying to her. It was bleeding profusely. He felt she was hurt enough as it was, and he didn't need to make her worry needlessly. He grabbed a clean handkerchief from his pocket and placed it at the spot of the wound. He told her to put her hand on the spot and apply pressure to stop the bleeding. He had positioned her hand in such a way as to not get any blood on her hands and fingers. If she saw how it was bleeding, she could freak out on him, perhaps even faint.

She looked up at him and said, "Andy, I'm cold."

Andy instantly took off his coat, leaving him without anything but a white collared dress shirt that made him look coldly naked in the turbulent, windy night. Andy wrapped it over her upper torso, tucking in the sides close to her body. "That's better?" he asked.

"Yeah, thanks."

"Sheila, one more minute, and then we'll try standing up, okay?" Sheila just nodded her head, saving her strength. "Those mother bastards," Andy sputtered.

"Andy, my head hurts."

Andy bent over and kissed her on the cheek. He was gentle with her on the outside, but he was boiling over on the inside. "I know, honey. Come on, let's go see the doctor."

He gently and slowly assisted her to her feet. They began to walk down the rest of the steep, exceptionally cold hill. Sheila was bundled up, and she had Andy's arm tightly wrapped around her. She appeared dazed and weak. His arm was around her for a multitude of reasons: keeping her warm, keeping her path straight, and keeping her from falling down again. Andy looked so cold with nothing on but the dress shirt that now had a two-tone look to it. There was a stained red color that had arbitrarily been placed on his shirt. The man and woman who were becoming unusually great friends so fast continued plodding down the hill through the cold and dark night.

CHAPTER

TWENTY-THREE

Sheila was sitting in a chair with Andy crouched down in front of her. She had just taken seven stitches in her scalp. Andy looked in her eyes and said remorsefully, "I'm sorry."

"I know, but it's not your fault."

Andrew stood up sharply, took a couple of steps away from her and swiveled back toward her. As his eyes confronted hers, he said, "But it is."

Sheila was slightly stunned by Andrew's reaction. She had gotten hurt and didn't think Andy would confront her with any issue at all. She was wrong. "What?"

Andrew again made eye contact with her and seriously said, "Maybe you should stay away from me for a little while. Just until all this madness blows over."

Sheila returned fire with a strange, sharp look of her own. Her chin had tightened up, and her forehead constricted, revealing her feeling of disagreement vehemently.

Andy went on staking his claim. "It's too dangerous to be around me right now. Look what happened tonight."

Sheila bluntly said, "No way! Forget it! You'll have to think of another way to get rid of me …"

"Tough girl, huh!"

"You bet," she responded, "You'll have to kill me!"

Andy replied, "That ain't happening."

Andy lightened up on her drastically. He could see he was talking to a stone wall, or perhaps her thinking cap was a little discombobulated from the blow she had taken. He said, "I'd like to kill those sons a bitches, every last one of them." Sheila's eyes showed a deep seriousness. He bent down again, looked at her very closely, and said, "I love you, Sheila." He then kissed her ardently on the lips. She did not stop him.

After this special moment of affection, Andrew slowly stood up and called out, "Hey, Doc! Can we go now?"

Andrew heard a voice from clear across the room. "Sure, just come over here and sign this release form."

Andy said to Sheila, "You're gonna need someone to look after you, so you'll have to stay at my house tonight." Andy did not have a house. He had an apartment. By saying his 'house,' it gave Sheila a sense of the commitment he held for his personal possessions: she was now one of them. He walked away to sign the release form as the doctor had instructed him to do. Even though Sheila's head was throbbing, she managed a smile, and a tear of sweet contentment. It was a smile and a tear that no one saw.

CHAPTER

TWENTY-FOUR

Sheila sat in an armchair applying an ice towel to her head. She was simply resting herself. Andy was also holding the ice towel to her head, as he was in a crouched position. "How do you feel?" he asked.

"A little better, but my head is throbbing."

"Sheila, can you hold this for a few minutes by yourself? I just wanna draw something out on the board."

"Sure, how long will you be gone?"

He began to walk away from her and said, "About three hours."

Sheila smiled, acknowledging his attempt at humor. She pointed her finger in a manner for him to come back to her and give her a kiss, which he obliged. As Andrew left her on his way over to the blackboard, he said, "And don't take that ice pack off your head, or tomorrow you'll have a bump that'll make you look like the Elephant Man."

Andy was behind the fully portable blackboard on wheels that he kept in the living room for drawing plays when he got ideas on some strategy. Andrew was now completely shielded from Sheila as he was sitting on a chair, chalking out the blackboard.

Sheila said, "Can I go feed the parrots?"

"No. You feed 'em after midnight they multiply, that's how I got two of them."

Sheila laughed at his joke. "You're crazy, you know that? Hey, Andy, if I have a big bruise on my head tomorrow, I'm going to tear your body apart, limb by limb."

Andrew's head popped up above the blackboard. With a serious frown on his face, he said, "S&M?"

"No, pal. Strictly torture!"

They smiled at one another. Andy tucked his head back down underneath the top of the blackboard so that Sheila could not see him at all. Andy whispered to himself, "I wonder if she knows S&M is torture. I'll have to explain that to her one day." He sat on the edge of the sofa, beginning to draw out the play with the chalk.

Sheila started thumbing through a magazine she found on the table next to her, when all she could see was this huge, empty blackboard staring right back at her, since he was writing on it on the opposite side. There was silence in the room for a short time. Andy began to talk softly to himself, beginning to think the play through verbally while actually chalking it out.

"The guard brings the ball to the right side of the floor, kicks it into the postman, who sends it back out to the left Forward who fights off the screen and drives, the ball penetrates the lane and kisses it off the lip and scores."

Sheila listened to him, paying strictest attention to his word-for-word description, which had a sexual connotation attached to it. She impulsively got out of her chair and grabbed the top of the blackboard, pushing it down toward her in order to see his face and scold him. However, when she flipped her side down, the opposite bottom side flew up so quickly that it caught Andy solidly across his upper left forehead. There were two sounds that Sheila had heard: actually there were three. First, was the crack of a wooden blackboard hitting his head sharply. Then there was a yell that howled, "Ahhhhhh." Finally, and the last in the quick succession of out of the ordinary sounds, was the thud of Andy's body as it hit the floor. The bottom of the blackboard had struck him hard, flush across his head, and exactly where he had been wearing the bandage from the car accident. Andy screamed out, "Is this the beginning of your S&M campaign?"

Sheila did not say a word. She just threw her hand up over her mouth like all women do when they're sorry and surprised at something they've done. Her eyes were bulging as she saw him lying on the floor, apparently hurt.

Five minutes later, they were both in the bathroom together, looking in the mirror at themselves. Andy was looking at the bandage Sheila was applying to the side of his upper forehead with a fabricated, perturbed grin.

"I can't believe you hit me right where I got hit in the car accident."

"Our accident?" she asked.

Frustrated, he said, "No, Sheila, the car accident I had before our accident when we . . . accidentally met."

Sheila and Andy began to crack up laughing. They both became hysterical, laughing contagiously. It was so funny, what he said. When he started out, he was so frustrated and didn't know exactly what he was going to say when he finished his sentence. Just before he used the word accidentally for the third time, they both started to laugh, knowing he had no choice but to use that particular word. It was so hilarious to the both of them since they knew Andy was making a point so seriously, and it came out in such a humorous disaster that it contributed to their ridiculous conduct.

Sheila was absolutely uncontrollable. She really was trying to make him feel like a jerk because he deserved it. It was an accident to begin with that he had gotten whacked in the head by the blackboard. And he was trying to blame her. Meanwhile, not too long ago, in the very same evening, she had taken a fall that was meant for him, and had to have stitches in her head. It was justice that he'd find himself flat on the floor this night, and not as the result of some sexually comforting acts.

Sheila and Andy began to touch their bandages on their respective wounds. Their heads began to hurt from the laughter. Sheila said, "Calm down, Andy. You're not the only one who got hurt tonight. Put seven stitches in your head, and see how you feel."

"I know how it feels. I just had stitches taken out of my head. Now I probably have to have them put back in, thanks to you."

"I think maybe it's a good idea that we should stay away from each other for a while," Sheila said. "It might be too dangerous for us to be together."

"I agree, as a matter of survival," Andy quipped.

"Let me see that!" Sheila wanted to make sure his bandage was placed appropriately on his head.

While she was adjusting it, he said, "The walking wounded in formation."

"At least we're walking."

"Maybe not for long, the way we're going."

Just then, Andy's phone rang. He left the bathroom to answer it. Sheila remained, turning on the faucet and wiping down the sink. After she finished tidying up, she turned off the water and doused the light, leaving the bathroom to rejoin Andy in the living room.

When she saw him, he was hanging up the phone, staring at the floor in front of him.

Alarmed, Sheila asked, "Andy, what's the matter?"

He looked up at her and told her. He had a look on his face as if someone had just died. Someone did. It was John Connors' wife, Priscilla.

Sheila's countenance transformed from a look of surprise to instant dejection. Slowly, she walked over to Andy and nudged her way in, burying herself in his chest. Andy wrapped his arms around her, holding her close to him. Sheila remained silent.

Andy just stared at the wall in front of him and said, "This night's getting rougher and rougher." They stood there in silence, just holding on to one another.

CHAPTER

TWENTY-FIVE

It was not that cold today, about 44 degrees Fahrenheit. For some strange reason, there were no gusts in this land known as the Windy City. However, it was a bleak day, as a drizzly rain fell over the city. It was also completely overcast, which seemed to be the proper setting for the burial that was taking place in Windwood Cemetery.

One positive that Andy felt relieved about was he knew for sure, beyond a shadow of a doubt, that he wouldn't incur posters, sheets, or signs defaming his name in public that was so notorious within the boundaries of the college's campus.

The night before he dreamed that he was chained to the passenger seat of a vehicle that treated him like an electric chair. It was a drive that went clear across the states, the longest drive possible. From Portland, Oregon, it went diagonally to Miami, Florida. Every billboard along the way conveyed an acrimonious message, slandering his name, mind, body and soul. He even saw thousands of cows in the pastures on the journey. Instead of bells around their necks, they were small signs defaming the unpopular, neophyte coach. "Kill Coach Trella," "Andy Sucks," "Crucify Him." He was being stampeded mentally, which, thankfully, wouldn't be as painful or tragic as a physical stampede. Thank God it was only a dream, but in reality, it wasn't. The dream only symbolized life in the fast lane during these present days at Western Chicago University.

There was no picket. It was a gathering of a clan around the cemetery grounds. The casket just lay there, anchored in its final immovable resting place. The casket wasn't going to move anywhere, neither would the woman's corpse inside it. The entire gathering of people attending this dark day of final respects to Mrs. John A. Connors were in a naturally plaintive mood. For now it was time for the earth to be shoveled over the beautiful, shiny mahogany box. The people who were submitting their condolences took their respective turns tossing the customary flowers on top of the casket as it sat in its provided abyss. Soon, it would be time for the most depressing part of all, the final curtain, the dirt covering.

John Connors stood at the front of the grave and dropped the last set of a dozen red roses onto the expensive wooden force field that enclosed his wife. It wouldn't be the last time she'd receive flowers. John would be back on holidays, anniversaries, and both her birth and death dates. Then, he'd be alone, but he would never again have a dozen red roses for her.

Several folks couldn't help but break down and cry after witnessing John's final gesture of love to his wife, Priscilla. They were the ones who were naturally very close to John and Priscilla. Family and good, close friends were there. It was predominantly the women who had uncontrollably shed the tears. Big John turned away, paced a couple of steps back, and turned around once again to prepare to receive final handshakes and kisses from those who were in attendance this afternoon.

First came family and close friends. Then came the good old doctor, and finally, many university people, including Al, Sam, Dean Thompson, and the entire basketball team who were wearing suits. John Connors thought it was good to see them all dressed so well.

It was a shame to see that it took these circumstances to

witness that event. John's emotional state changed slightly, but it was upbeat when seeing the players. He shook their hands, touched their shoulders, and softly slapped their faces, as they each went by him. He was thinking that this was one of the rare times that they not only didn't smell badly, but many of them were shaved and wore cologne.

When it was Skin Head's turn to shake Connors' hand, John said to him, "What's that cologne?"

Skin Head bowed his head to let John see and smell that his head was cleanly shaved and had cologne applied to it. John broke into a momentary smile and pushed Skin Head along easily. Phil stood on crutches in front of John Connors with the cast on his leg and a single rose that was being crushed up against one of the crutches that he was holding with the same hand. He had to squash it, in order not to drop it.

John Connors took the rose from Phil and said, "You shouldn't have come. It's quite a struggle for you."

"It's okay, sir," he stated, hopping along out of the way. "Did you learn anything from the accident?" John asked.

"Yes, sir. I learned the hard way to try and control my emotions.

"Good. Take care of yourself, Philip."

"Thank you."

After Phil hopped out of there, it was now Andy's turn. Andy and John shook hands as Andy said, "I'm sorry, sir."

"Thank you. Andrew, how are you doing?"

Andy could never be insincere to Johnny C. He always had a tendency to open up. But since this was a funeral, Andy decided not to expose his hang-ups to his mentor.

"Yeah, everything's fine," Andy tried insincerely.

John looked at him carefully, detecting something definitely not right. Andy could not hide his feelings, not from John. John said, "Listen, if you're not too busy, though I'm sure you are these days, I'd like you to stop up at the house tomorrow night. I'd like to talk to you, if you don't mind."

Andy responded receptively since he had so much respect and admiration for John Connors. "Sure, what time?"

"How's 7:00?"

"That's fine. I'll be there."

"Good. I'll see you then."

Andy then walked to the left, following the others.

CHAPTER

TWENTY-SIX

Andrew found himself on the front porch of John Connors' home. The front door opened, exposing Mr. Connors who was wearing his suit slacks, shirt and tie, but no sports coat. Andrew was wearing dress slacks with a sweater pulled over a collared dress shirt. Both men looked very handsome. Both men were without female company. John, of course, from uncontrollable matters ordered by the Supreme One Himself, in taking his wife to her eternal resting place. Andrew's lack of female companionship was strictly by sensible choice. Andy said, "Hi, Coach."

"Andrew! Come on in!"

Both men were sitting down in a huge den or living room and Andy wasn't sure which. There was an abundance of space, plenty of chairs, a sofa and a fireplace. The television set was absent, but there was a stereo system in an incredibly beautiful rock wall on one side of the room. The opposite wall resembled a library, with many books tucked into uniform spots on the shelves. John was seated on the sofa. Andrew sat in one of those luxuriously comfortable arm chairs with a foot rest. He was, however, sitting on the edge leaning forward, not appreciating the comfort of the chair's foot rest feature.

Surprisingly, Andrew said, "You're coming back, right?"

John was thrown by Andy's sudden candidness. "No, I can't. Not for a while.

Andy was surprised. He had hoped John would return and the craziness on the campus grounds would surely vanish.

John continued, "Some say that would be the best thing for me, to bury myself in basketball. But I just can't think about that at all right now. It would be unfair to... "

Andy interrupted him and completed the sentence for him. "The university, the athletic department, the booster club, the players, and the student body."

John was being very perceptive, watching and listening to Andrew. He would learn a great deal about how Andy was handling this team by the way he spoke about it. John wanted to know what kind of shape he was leaving this team in.

He was going away for a week. He had to get away from the house for a time. All the house did was remind him of Priscilla, twenty-four hours a day. He couldn't think about basketball. It just wasn't important to him at this juncture. Besides, he didn't want to put himself through thirty or forty people each and every day offering their condolences on the passing of his loving wife. John had been the head man of the university's team for better than twenty years. He knew a lot of people, and more knew him. It would be two to three solid months of people approaching him on his recent misfortune.

John was also getting tired of it all. The work week's schedule was burdensome for a man of his age, not to mention the traveling. He really wanted to go up to the lake. He and Priscilla had purchased a small log cabin by Lake Erie on four acres of land. They did not use it much, so it wouldn't be so bad to go up there to do some fishing and reading. Their kids, all married now, had used it much more than they did, for boating and skiing during vacations and long weekends. When John returned from his sojourn, he'd probably put the place up for sale and maybe move into a condominium. Then, in all likelihood, he'd retire, and see much more of his kids and his grand-children.

In the meantime, John had wanted Andrew to open up, and that's precisely what he was doing. Andy got up out of the chair, walked around the room, and spoke.

"It's just there's so much involved besides doing the actual coaching. And that's enough in itself. There's just so much going on, I don't know how anyone does it …"

John stopped him saying, "You're doing it."

"I'm having a pretty tough time of it!"

"Yes, but you're doing well. Besides, you were thrown into this from what I understand. It's only temporary."

"Yeah, but that doesn't dismiss the difficulty of the task at hand."

"Andrew, sit down and listen to me!" Andy followed his instruction obediently.

"First, ignore all that's happening around you."

"That's a tall order. Do you know what's going on?"

"Yes, I read the papers. I know all hell's breaking loose on the campus grounds. It was even on the news a couple of days ago."

Andy jumped up. "On television? That's just great! Quite a reputation I'm getting. I feel like the second coming of Bin Laden. Soon they'll be printing up tee-shirts with my face on it, with a circle around it and a bar running through it on the campus.."

This was the signal for John to get up off the sofa and approach Andrew. John had a smile on his face as he was amused by Andrew's recent tirade. John told Andy to sit down and relax, that he'd be back in a minute with a beverage. John returned to the room after fetching a half a glass of wine and handing it to him. Andy was holding his forehead with his hand.

"Something else happened I didn't count on just now."

"What's that?"

"I'm falling in love with this girl!"

"Well, I think we should talk about that for a moment if you don't mind."

"No, it's okay."

"It's quite obvious a lot is happening around you these days."

Andrew looked at John solemnly and said, "That's an understatement!"

John asked Andrew a question that would let him know if the team was in good hands or not. "Andrew, is this girl by any chance keeping your mind off your job?" Do you find yourself thinking about whether you should call her or not, and what you're going to say to her?"

"Oh no. This relationship fortunately is not like that at all. I couldn't afford to be thinking if I'm doing and saying the right things. That would drain me. She's really helped me. In fact, I think I'm getting my fortitude from her."

"Good, you have to keep your mind on the team right now."

"That's no problem, it's the side shows that get me down."

"And that's what they are, side shows," John said, showing concern. "The main event is that you have tunnel vision right now. Stay focused. I'm going to be gone in a couple of days. On my return, I'll be putting this place up for sale. I can't live here anymore, it's impossible. If you need some help with anything, some advice, or you're having trouble with a particular individual, feel free to call."

"I'll do that, Coach."

They got up in unison from their respective chairs and walked out of the room.

Andy said, "Well, who knows. They'll probably have me replaced by the time you return."

"Probably."

"Coach, I can assure you I'll do the best I can until they do.

As they shook hands, John said, "Atta boy."

They exchanged good night's and Andrew left.

TWENTY-SEVEN

Andy and Sheila had just come out of an ice cream parlor on a side street near Lake Michigan Avenue. It was odd that they'd have ice cream in the middle of winter, especially at night. Naturally, it would be much colder when night time held its watch while the sun took its turn getting some shut-eye. The wind that escaped Lake Michigan would hit the avenue, manufacturing the bitter wind that Chicago was known for. But every so often, they would be inclined to have a craving for the sweet dessert of ice cream, even if it had been bankrupt from their diet for a period of time. Just as soup is served in Ecuador, so too would ice cream in the frozen land of Alaska.

They walked arm in arm down the side street, leaving the bitter cold of Michigan Avenue at their backs. Sheila said, "That hit the spot."

"Good, I'm glad you enjoyed it. Now, for some hot chocolate."

"Cocoa. Your place or mine?"

He hesitated, made a face like he couldn't decide either way, then said, "Yours."

"Okay."

While they were walking diagonally across the street, a

commotion appeared before them involving four people. It seemed to be in the primordial stage. Three teenagers were harassing a younger, small boy and his bicycle. The boy was like a baby crab, only caring about fleeing the fisherman's net. The teenagers weren't about to let the boy escape their web of fear so easily. The boy was backed up against a stairwell when one of them wrestled the bicycle away and tossed it aside. Another one came closer to their prisoner and placed a strong hand around the boy's thin, quivering neck and began to squeeze. The boy could not scream, but he was crying and quite petrified of the three bullies. The odds were not in his favor. It was one vs. a team. He was small; they were bigger. However, very soon it would be an even fight, even if the boy's side was handicapped with a female and himself.

The other two culprits were watching their friend, laughing, as he began to seriously hurt the boy.

"Leave him alone!" the sudden voice demanded. It was Andy. He and Sheila appeared before them, out of nowhere. The one applying the force against the boy's neck went flying off of him as Andy grabbed his arm and upper side, flinging him around and off the boy like a spinning helicopter. He had spun two, maybe three times around before he fell into some side street garbage cans. When the other two charged him, Andy turned around one time so quickly, that when he kicked his first target, it was by complete surprise and sent him reeling backward into and over several shrubs. His chest was surely hurting, as Andy was fortunate to hit him squarely before he tumbled into the grass. Andy then let loose with a straight-forward thrust of a punch that stifled his opponent's attack immediately. He had not broken his nose, but damaged it enough to cause it to bleed. By now, the original, bigger guy had gotten up off the pavement and swung himself in a position where he could actually tackle Andy within two seconds.

One thing about Andy, he was quick. He was fast on the

basketball court as he had proven earlier when playing against Jarvis Williams in front of the entire team.

He was just as fast, maybe even faster on the streets of New York where he grew up. Now, he was that way in front of Sheila. If there was one thing he had learned from his father, it was to always be quick. His father had schooled him, revealing that you never had to be big and strong, but many times in life you would have to be quick. If he could master that trick, he could alter disaster and kick tragedy out through the gates of hell.

Andy stepped aside and grabbed the aggressor's fist with his hand and whipped it back behind his back, stretching his arm out in a position that would leave you to think he was asking for him to say "uncle." Then he coiled his other arm tightly around the guy's neck. He would never be able to escape this forceful entrapment unless he had outside help, which was now on the way.

As Andy held his captive's head against the brick side of the stoop, he said, "You like choking? It's fun, isn't it?" One of the culprits began to reconstruct a charge to Andrew's blind side in hopes of a rescue. As he did, he was impeded by the bicycle that came flying suddenly out in front of him. It had an invisible rider on it, for Sheila had wheeled it hard, directly in front of his running knees. He never saw it until it was too late. He tumbled, doing a complete somersault over the falling bike. Sheila had struck her target, and he was abruptly tackled by the two-wheeled missile. Sheila's maneuver had bailed Andy out of imminent trouble and left her assailant out in the cold, preventing any further attack.

Andy finally let go of the one who was now coughing and choking quite convincingly. The one who was bleeding from the nose on to his leather jacket pulled a chain out from his pocket. He stood about ten feet away from Andrew and was thinking about moving toward him. Andy took his coat off in such a debonair fashion that this changed the thug teenager's mind.

Andy said, "If you don't back off, I'm going to break a bone!"

The teenager looked at both his friends who were on the sidewalk. They were not getting up. "Take your friends and get the hell out of here!" he yelled. "Now!"

The young guy placed the chain back into his pocket and instantly began to help his friends as they scampered away from the scene.

Sheila looked at Andy with honest amazement as he went to help the boy who was trembling severely. He was sitting upright against the side of the brick staircase, crying. When he had seen what Andrew was doing to the thugs, he was more afraid. Andy was consoling the boy. He wrapped his arms around the boy and picked him up slowly, saying, "No one's gonna hurt you!"

Sheila was about six steps away from them and said to herself with a look of befuddlement, *He's a Samaritan, too. Where did he learn that?* She walked over to them and rubbed her fingers through the little boy's hair. "You okay?"

The boy shook his head affirmatively and wiped the tears from his flushed, red cheeks. Andy walked over to the bicycle, propped it up, and strode it over to the boy. The boy was still trembling as he could not rid himself of his fear. He could hardly say thank you, but he was able to receive the bicycle from Andy. Sheila asked the boy, referring to the bike, "Is it okay?"

The boy looked at the bicycle and said, "Yes, I think so."

"Is it okay if we walk you home?" Sheila asked. The boy's eyes revealed that she had just said the magic words that opened his heart with a key.

"Yes, could you, please?"

"Sure," Sheila smiled.

As Andrew picked up his coat from the cold sidewalk, Sheila asked, "You okay?"

"Yeah, just aggravated." He looked down the street to see what the three victims were doing. They were hobbling along their way without looking back at the party that had intercepted and foiled their dangerous fun.

The boy started to walk his bicycle along. Sheila was next to him with one arm around the boy's shoulder. Andy was on the opposite side of the bike. Sheila kept looking at Andy as they walked with a stare that wouldn't quit. Andy was dusting himself off and kept turning to take a gander at the three departing stooges.

"What?" Andy said.

Sheila could not help herself. "Where did you learn that?"

"Joe Chen's School of Fighting and Self-Defense."

"Oh," she said.

"Queens Boulevard, Forest Hills," he continued.

"You really could have hurt one of them, or you could have gotten hurt badly yourself."

"Violence knows no wisdom, Sheila," he said simply.

"Oh, that's great!"

"Look! You grew up in Milwaukee; I grew up in New York. This is Chicago. Quakers don't live here. And what about him?" meaning the boy. "Did you see how much pressure that kid was applying to his neck?"

"Shhh," Sheila said. Trying to quiet Andy down, she realized she'd opened a can of worms, and it was definitely the wrong time.

Andy went on, "That idiot was feeling power and getting off on it. How much longer do you think he could have withstood it?" Andy stopped himself, then softly said, "If he didn't let up, that could have been fatal."

Suddenly, one of the three young terrorists yelled out from a distance to Andy, "Hey, Mister!" Andy turned around quickly and saw one of them pull his pockets inside out in the front of his pants. He held them upward with each hand and yelled out, "Do me a favor and kiss the rabbit between the ears."

Andy yelled out over the avenue, "Yeah. Come back here." He faked a charge for a few steps. The culprits turned away and began running in the opposite direction. The derelict party needed to verbalize in order to feel they had gotten the last lick.

Sheila decided to continue to ask since the boy showed that

he had now collected himself. "How come... Why did you learn to fight?"

"You saw what happened tonight, and how many stitches did you get the other night?"

"Seven."

"Yeah, well triple it, and that's how many I have in my arm."

"Really." Her mouth gaped.

"Yeah. I once got stabbed at the Feast of St. Gennaro in New York." That final announcement by Andy of his little story was true and stifled Sheila from any other questions. The three of them walked on down the street in silence as snow flurries began to tumble down on them.

CHAPTER

TWENTY-EIGHT

The double doors opened wide with a thunderous blast, and the players ran through the hallway jubilantly. They were celebrating an obviously close, nail-biting victory. Andrew came through next, and behind him were a crowd of people. Al, Sam, Winthrop, Bart and Phil, who was hobbling on his bad hoof on crutches with great difficulty. There were many others behind them. Because Andy was at the front of the pack, he had a microphone thrust in his face. The microphone was attached to the arm of a female reporter. She was urgently trying to get a live interview to be broadcast to the television network where she was employed. Everyone was walking at a rather brisk pace. They were on their way to the traditional press conference that took place after each and every game. Whether the university's team won or lost, it didn't matter, a press conference unfolded immediately following a competition's conclusion, give or take twenty minutes. Everyone was walking unusually faster than normal. That was because they knew the home team had escaped by stealing a last second win by one single point.

The reporter asked Andy, "Coach Trella, this is your third victory in as many tries. How do you feel?"

"It feels great!"

She fired away again. "How do you explain your outstanding success, especially since the general student body seems to have labeled you as an amateur coach?"

"Whether you win or lose, there's always a multitude of reasons why."

"I'm sure, but there's got to be some particular reason why this team that seems to be just mediocre only seems to win under your coaching."

He suddenly stopped walking when he came up to the locker room door and said, "I don't know!" He pushed the door in and was gone. The female reporter was left in the hallway holding her microphone with no one to interview. That was okay. The night was still young, and she'd get a second chance. But Andy would finish that interview just as he left this one, walking out on her. Only the next time he'd have much more hate in his consciousness. Others followed Andy in, but many were forced to accompany the reporter, not being allowed to advance. This was the pre-press conference. The real McCoy would follow soon enough.

TWENTY-NINE

They were gathered inside the huge tent that was constructed for the purpose of interviewing players and coaches. The customary press conference was about to take place. There were many reporters and people with press passes that permitted them to be present and ask questions of the appropriate people.

The tent was made of beautiful white satin and stood as a permanent fixture within the Rosemont Horizon. There were school logos and pictures of Eagles pinned to the wall, representing Western Chicago University's sports teams behind the dais. At the dais were five or six chairs, a microphone at each position. There were several security guards posted who were on the lookout for anyone not having a press pass pinned to their lapel. They would be escorted out of the special area as if they were rubbish. The three security guards walked a total of seven people out before the press conference commenced. Fortunately, Sheila was given a press pass by Andrew much earlier. She was not there to ask questions and stood way in the back of the tent to witness and listen to the press conference.

Finally, Andy came out with two of his playing performers, along with Al Perkins. People clapped for them as they entered the well-kept, shiny tent. There were about one hundred people present, some sitting, some standing. Most of them were making notes on pads, holding microphones, and a few were taking pictures with their cameras.

After the fellows representing the team sat down at the dais, a male reporter stood up and said, "Mr. Trella, what was the biggest reason the Eagles won tonight?"

Andrew leaned forward into his assigned microphone and said, "Well, I think it was that we scored one more point than our opponent did." Andy smiled as the crowd roared with laughter. Sheila smiled and clapped in the back.

Another reporter yelled out, "Coach Trella, how do you explain all this winning taking place since you've been placed in the head coaching role?"

"When you win, you win for many reasons. The players have to understand their roles. They have to play within themselves. You have to execute, communicate, and with Washington rebounding like he is, Jefferson scoring, and Bennett handling the ball virtually error-free, (I think he had only two turnovers), it makes it easier."

Another reporter jumped up asking, "Mr. Perkins, can you give us any of your insight as to why the team's doing so well?"

"Well, the nature of this sport or any sports game is that your team can play great, and you can still lose; and yet, on any given night, you can play poorly and still be fortunate in winning the game. However, Andy Trella has been doing a super job for us despite some popular opinion, and the team is playing well under his direction."

Still another reporter stood and asked, "Mr. Perkins, is the athletic department still looking for a permanent replacement?"

"Yes, that was the arrangement. Andy knows his sudden promotion was only a temporary solution. Like I said, he's done a great job for us, but we're still campaigning to bring in a big name guy, probably from the Ivy League."

The same reporter asked, "Can you speculate as to who the candidate might be?"

Al stated simply, "No, I'm sorry, but I can't at this time."

Another reporter yelled out, "Coach Trella, how do you feel about being relegated back to being an assistant, especially after being virtually perfect so far?"

Andy answered, "Well, if a new head coach weren't coming in here, I can assure that it's very unlikely a perfect record would continue. Besides, a lot of people who have voiced their concerns against my appointment would surely take a much more active and detailed one once we've lost."

The woman reporter who had originally addressed Andrew in the hallway stood up and said, "Coach Trella, we understand that you recently have a girlfriend."

Andy's face immediately focused strict attention on her, as did Sheila, who was still standing in the back of the tent. The subject matter she was bringing up was not considered a proper topic for a press conference, having nothing to do with basketball.

"How come you're going out with a married woman?"

Sheila's knees buckled out from under her. Her face yielded a sign that led you to believe her heart had just been pulled from her body like a drain from a full sink of water.

Andrew was astounded and followed by saying, "What?" He paused and continued, "Wait a minute. This is a post-game basketball conference. That's all we're discussing here. Nothing else. That's personal and none of your business." He stood up at the dais and yelled out forcefully at everyone, "Besides, that's a complete falsehood." He was scolding her and others who might be against him. "You people are unbelievable. No matter what good happens around you, there's always someone trying to find the dirt on you, even if it's not there. I'm out of here." Andrew immediately began to march off the dais.

Sheila stood quietly in the back of the tent, listening to his every word. She said quietly, whispering to herself, "Good for you, Andy." Then she scampered out of there like a squirrel. She knew the next time she saw Andrew, he'd be irate at her and that she'd have some explaining to do.

CHAPTER

THIRTY

Andy Trella was fuming this morning. The rain that turned into a light sleet made the early morning start as though he had gotten up on the wrong side of the bed. But it was the conviction for a traffic summons at a hearing ten minutes earlier that escalated his mental position from dreary to extensively aggravated.

He had received the violation nine months previously and had postponed it twice. Once, because of a work-related road trip, the other due to vacation time. The hearing office also postponed his court date twice. The reasons were unknown, although he did speculate as to why. He figured that the officer who rendered the summons was unable to attend for some cockamamie reason, or perhaps the assigned judge was taking a three-week fishing trip. For that, he believed, it was grounds for immediate dismissal of the charge.

The violation was not that serious; it was not speeding or a DWI or anything of a hit-and-run nature. He had been traveling westbound on Interstate 41 and was getting off at exit 23. The traffic was inhumanely bumper to bumper, as it always was around 5:00 p.m. on any given weekday in any major city where the workforce was in the millions.

The weather was very bad that January day, extremely

windy, cold, and snowy. Andrew decided since he was only 100 feet away from the designated off ramp to pull out of the right lane onto the shoulder. He could not justify sitting at a standstill when he didn't need to be. He was getting off the interstate altogether. But what he did was cross over those special white lines a tad too soon. Those ever so sacred white lines. What purpose did these lines serve? This was a major expressway with hundreds of automobiles just sitting still like franks on a grill on the Fourth of July.

The white lines simply prevented maneuvers by the drivers to get off at their particular exits earlier than they otherwise should. Andy thought the basic idea behind city ordinances with respect to driving regulations was to keep traffic moving as swiftly as possible without jeopardizing safety by one iota. These lines only added fuel to the fire by not only preventing bottlenecks, but actually contributing to their survival. These very special white lines were dusted ever so slightly with snowflakes from the storm that was only two hours old. So the infamous white lines had company that transformed their specific featured directive into one continuous patch of white blocks that had range, density and length as far as the eye could see. It was quite a marriage: white lines formed by man, white snowflakes formed by nature. The result was an obstructed traffic directive, which inclined State Trooper Sal Basilia to once again commence issuing his assigned quota of summonses to the town's people. The quota was three a day: one for breakfast, one after lunch, and one before dinner. Needless to say, two of the three meals were held at Dunkin' Donuts; the other was usually a freebie at a regularly patronized delicatessen.

He was behind on his quota for this week, with his pregnant wife, Judy, in her ninth and final month on his mind. Today he was aggravated, and he sure as hell wasn't going to let Mr. Andy Trella escape so easily. Whether it was justified or not, snowstorm, windstorm, rainstorm, come hell or high water, Sal Basilia was in a bad mood and was taking it out on the driving public. It was a good thing he didn't have to shoot any of the culprits he administered tickets to. He had already written up a six-pack and was working onward to double digits with three hours left on his noon to eight shift. By the end of this day, he would record a whopping grand total of nine traffic summonses served, which would leapfrog him from a despairing deficit to putting him one over his assigned quota for the month with two weeks to go. The officer who'd compiled the most summons served each month from his precinct wouldn't get an award, trophy, or medal for exceeding his quota. It was just natural orders handed down from his captain. Meet the quota or you'd be walking a beat in Beirut. Or they'd transfer your ass to Kalamazoo if they could. However, the captain of the precinct did manage to display a head shot of the officer of the month in the Leisure Room for the highest total of summons served each month.

Thus, Officer Sal Basilia was back on course. After all, he had a third party coming to live at his house any day now. He didn't need any extra heat or concern from the people on the inside on quota. A word that didn't grow on you. A word that he'd learn and grow to hate.

Andrew was still upset walking back to his car thinking about the conviction. He didn't mind losing, but when the officer misrepresented the truth, that bugged him, and it bugged him big time. He even lost his cool and bellowed out in the miniature-sized courtroom, "That's not true!" He was severely challenging Officer Sal Basilia's testimony.

The judge always asks both parties, the police officer and the defendant, to raise their right hands and swear to tell the truth. For that reason, he, the judge unequivocally believes whatever is said by either party. The case cannot be decided by the factor that both parties disagree on one specific point or incident. It is not the judge's job to decipher and shred away until he exposes the true liar. To a judge, who is telling the truth is simply not important. He broadcasts his verdict based on the material he is spoon-fed and quite lucidly decides. The judge, without thinking twice about it, never doubts that he's listening to true testimony. Swearing to tell the truth, the whole truth, and nothing but the truth, is never in question.

Andrew's outburst condemning the officer's misrepresentations doesn't exist in a court of law. There were some thirty other law breakers in the court in regard to traffic offenses. All were sitting in the courtroom directly behind Andy and Officer Sal. It would be very bad for the whole judicial system if Andy proclaimed crazily, harping on the officer's disregard for telling the actual truth in front of all the onlookers as his main defense. If the judge took that and instantly decided in Andrew's favor by throwing the case out in Officer Basilia's face, it would surely have showed everyone in the court that all we have to do is jump up and down, scream a little, violently proclaim the officer is falsifying his report, and they'll let you off, scot free.

Unfortunately, it didn't work that way. The judge would never dismiss a case because he centered his decision on false testimony by a figure who represents upholding the law. The judge would never condemn a police officer, even if he knew for sure the officer was misrepresenting. Ironically, he'd ignore it. No, the courts, judges, and police were all one and the like. They'd back each other up, and only for profit.

The issue that the officer misrepresented was the snow. Officer Basilia claimed that there were snow flurries, that the storm had just started only a half hour earlier, and that there was no accumulation whatsoever at the time of the violation. Andy was beyond a shadow of a doubt sure about the accumulation. The city received seven inches that night, and drifts to the side of the road were well over a foot high. It really didn't matter that much. Andy had only one previous conviction fifteen months ago for an illegal left turn that registered only two points on his driver's license. The improper passing would add three more points, totaling five, and the original ticket would be off his license in just three months time. It wasn't like he drove for a career in order to make a living. If he had been a courier for a major transportation company like UPS, drivers had to be very leery about acquiring summonses. They immediately had to report it to their supervisor, record it on their evaluation file, and worry about not obtaining additional violations that would surely lead to suspension, demotion, or even termination.

Still, Andy remained very upset, not for the check he wrote to the cashier clerk for seventy dollars, plus an additional seventeen dollar surcharge. It didn't sit well that the police were in cahoots with the judges, yet they still had to misrepresent on top of that in order to swindle beefing up the state's supplementary revenue.

As he drove back to the university, Andy decided to stay away from Interstate 41 and took side streets and back roads in order to arrive at the university in time for the 3:00 practice session. He was thinking to himself that he wasn't going to take out his frustrations on the players as a result of his current mood. He knew he gave them enough grief as it was.

THIRTY-ONE

The ballplayers were playing a five-on-five half-court offensive and defensive assigned drill. Andrew was at the other end of the court, standing at the foul line. He was immersed in conversation with Bart, Winthrop, Sam, Philip, and Al. A scrimmage was taking place on the east end of the arena, and a huddle was being conducted on the west end of the court. Andy was demonstrating a specific strategy by gesturing with his arms and hands and was facing the players on the opposite side of the gymnasium. His counterparts were facing him, with the backs to the action that was taking place behind them. The event that had just occurred was a development of devastation.

Andrew, in the midst of his discussion, suddenly stopped speaking. His face flushed with the element of pure trauma. The others stared at Andy, wondering what possibly could have alarmed him. Perhaps it was a huge, horrifying monster that had appeared in the middle of the gym. It was a monster, but of a different kind. As they all swiveled around to discover what Andrew had witnessed, Andy bolted right through the five listeners. He almost knocked both Al Perkins and Winthrop off their feet.

Andrew picked up speed as he dashed in his full suit and

dress shoes, even though he had such a short distance to cover. He could see the team motioning with their arms to come quickly. They were all yelling, asking, pleading, begging for help. No matter how quickly Andy and the rest of them had covered the glossily polished parquet floor, Willie Jones was in big trouble.

All Andy could see was one of his players lying on his back, sprawled out like a helpless, little, injured bird. He was not so little, and he was more than injured. One of the teammates was screaming, "Oh, man, he's not breathing."

Andy finally reached his fallen player. Willie had taken one too many whacks of cocaine, and his heart was malfunctioning. It was a major cardiac seizure. Al yelled for Sam to call an ambulance. Sam did what Andy had done. He sprinted out at full tilt, exiting the frenzied gymnasium.

Willie's life depended on it. His eyes were wide open, and it was obvious he was in big, big trouble. He was begging for help without saying so. Andrew's colleagues gathered around him. He was kneeling before Willie, and he noticed right off the bat that Willie's breathing was impaired, as his eyes suddenly closed.

Quickly, Andy pinched Willie's nose with two fingers and started to administer CPR. The stench Andy immediately picked up was distasteful. The sudoriferous scent, along with the odor of some substance, was more than revolting. The seriousness of the event and the adrenalin that pumped through Andy's brain and body discarded the unimportant effect. Andrew really wanted to save poor Willie Jones. Even though Willie wasn't one of Andy's favorite players, in a certain sense they were all one and the same. He felt a common bond as their current leader, a duty of obligation to each one of them. This apparently sudden development went way beyond being an instructor and mentor of his present-day disciples. As Andy exhaled oxygen into the mouth of the unconscious body time and time again, a thought popped into his mind. It was a selfish thought, but Andrew kept it in perspective. Nothing would be as important as saving Willie's Jones' life for Willie's sake. But if he failed, he would always be known as the head coach of the university's basketball team who had a player drop dead right on the court during practice. The fear stayed in his mind as he continued relentless CPR. His troubling thoughts persisted. Would Andy Trella be held responsible that he could have done something to prevent such a tragedy? In fact, if Willie did perish, even though he expected to be replaced by a more experienced and superior coach, they could simply let Andy go. Forget about being relegated back to his original coaching position. They may simply decide to terminate him.

Suddenly, Andrew got shoved aside by Al Perkins. He tumbled off to the side, falling on the court just two or three feet away from the body in distress. Al Perkins yelled out, "Look out! Let me try something!" Al squatted down on top of Willie Jones and began a series of punches to Willie's chest. Al repeated the act a half a dozen times. The players, standing in a huddle, could not believe the punishment Willie was receiving. Al was dishing them out like a broken machine. Willie was actually dead already, and he was being beaten like a rag doll. To the players, it was a horrible, ghastly sight to witness and understand.

Andy loosened his tie. His bloodshot eyes filled with tears as he saw all the players crying, while Al Perkins continued mounting an incredible barrage of punches into Willie's abdomen. None of them could have been sadder as they watched the horribly frightful sight continue.

Finally, Al stopped hammering away both from fatigue and the evidence that he was fighting a losing battle. Willie's respiratory system did not respond. Al checked his pulse, put his ear to Willie Jones' chest, and checked Willie's mouth, which was half open. There was nothing. Al sat upright and stayed there motionless for seconds that seemed like minutes. Finally, Al said, quite depressed, "He's not there, he's gone."

Al looked up at the others, and it was clear they were at a

loss for words. They were all quite red-eyed, with tears streaming from their eyes. The uncontrollable crying had started. Dark days would now fall on Western Chicago University. For the time being, they all stood around, not knowing what to do. They were desperate, down, and lost. Sam re-entered the complex quickly, but he was forced to stop short and just stand still. He did not have to yell out that an ambulance was on the way. It would be the undertaker they would need now.

CHAPTER

THIRTY-TWO

Andrew sat on the sofa in his apartment. His feet were up on the coffee table, littered with several bottles of beer, watching the television. Winthrop and Bart were both standing up on either side of him. Phil Conig, without his crutches, was sitting on the sofa next to Andrew, resting his injured leg. They were watching the news reports about themselves. The reporter was standing in front of the church as the Western Chicago University basketball players acted as pallbearers, carrying their beloved friend and teammate's coffin down the front steps of the church and into a waiting hearse. There was a shot of Andrew during the report wearing sunglasses to hide his eyes, making the sign of the cross.

The reporter began his editorial analysis during the somber procession, which aired in every home in the Chicago area that was tuned into that station. He said, "Tragedy and dark days continue to fall over Western Chicago's University in downtown Chicago. This is the latest and saddest of developments, as nineteen-year-old Willie Jones shockingly dropped dead while playing ball during a daily practice session at the university's basketball team facility. Autopsy reports have been completed but have not been disclosed to the public, leaving only speculation as to the cause of death. Was this a self-inflicted tragedy as a possible result of substance abuse, or was this one of those rare but seemingly growing unrecognizable heart ailments in young, tall athletes. This has been the second funeral in five days at the university, as long-time coach John Connors recently resigned just prior to his wife's passing. The university's basketball team has been losing coaches left and right recently for various reasons, and rumor has it that there is about to be yet another major coaching change soon. Again, the inside track has it that well-known Ivy Leaguer Nolan Castwell will be coming to the midwest, replacing the young neophyte, Andrew Trella, whose tenure as head coach has been a mere nine days. Strangely enough, in the last three years, five college athletes have died suddenly while playing basketball for their respective universities. In all five cases, the head coach of the university was terminated, irrelevant to whether the cause of death was a result of a physical problem or a self-induced one. So, I think it's fairly safe to say that the University of Western Chicago may very well have seen the last of its new coach, Andy Trella. For WICN Television, this is Carl MacElroy."

Andrew had the remote in his hand and disconnected any further transmission as soon as the reporter concluded his report. He then began a tirade. "I can't believe this shit! I'm gonna get fired now! I didn't even want to do this in the first place! I was just doing a favor! Now I get kicked in the ass for it! Was 3–0 and I'm not even going back to my old job! Just kick me out!" Andy looked at Phil and said, "I might as well just leave the country!"

This was Phil's signal to reciprocate and scold Andy. "What's the matter with you? You're talking like you assassinated the ass. Forget about that shit. The department is down coaches. They're going to place you back where you were. And it's not your responsibility for what happened. You did all you could to save him. He was a heavy coke addict."

This sounded an alarm in Andy's head and he asked Philip, "You know it was substance abuse, not a heart problem?"

"Of course, it was."

"How do you know that?"

Winthrop and Bart watched Andy and Phil as if their conversation were a ping pong match. Their eyes went back and forth, fluctuating as each one of them took their verbal swing at bat.

Phil stated, "Because I have been known to party with him myself on an occasion or two."

"Willie was into coke?" Andy asked.

"Big time!"

Andy's next remark came with a touch of relief to it. "That's a little bit of a relief."

Winthrop interrupted, "Why's that?"

Andrew explained, "Because if it was a heart problem and the university knew about it or didn't and should have through physicals and testing, they'd be responsible and the family could sue for millions. But if it's drugs, then the choice was made by the individual. The family can't sue for a dime. Regretfully for his family's financial sake, the individual pays the price."

Phil attached the exclamation point by saying, "Not to mention losing his life!" Andy looked at Philip and made a smirk that he agreed.

Bart blurted out, "What do you care whether the school gets sued or not. It's not your money."

"Hey, I just wanna save my assistant coaching job. If this was a heart problem, the school would have to pay a million dollars. They'd want to take it out on somebody clean house and fire the medical staff and all coaches. If it's drug-related like Phil says, I can at least make a stink and negotiate to stay on. If not, I'll be flipping hamburgers at Burger King." Andrew picked up a glass and took a drink.

Phil said to him, "Andy, have you heard from Sheila yet?"

Andy instinctively said, "No. I'll deal with that later." Then he walked out of the room away from them.

PART TWO

CHAPTER

THIRTY-THREE

There were about a dozen or so people sitting in the conference room. The pressure appeared to be lifted from Dean Thompson and Al Perkins. The mood of the athletic department was lighter, almost comforting, for the first time in two weeks. However, this state of mind was innocently presumed and astonishingly erroneous. Everyone in the room thought the near future would be bright. A new era, a new beginning, for the end of this season and the start of a new one next year. They were wrong. The pressure that seemed to be lifted from them hadn't even started. The mayhem had yet to deliver its full, massive attack. The chaos and confusion previously on campus was not over by a long shot.

Sitting in a chair directly opposite Al Perkins was Nolan Castwell. He was just about six feet tall, sixty-five years of age, with gray hair kept very short like a little boy's crew cut. Everyone was cordial and cooperative. Andy sat quietly, hoping that he'd get along with and like Mr. Castwell. He felt he probably would because he'd certainly try to. He'd be submissive, cooperative, and never attempt to dominate a man of such age and experience. This attitude wouldn't last.

There was one serious problem with Mr. Nolan Castwell. He

conducted himself like his haircut looked–a fully-decorated colonel. This was to Al and the dean's liking. They wanted someone who'd have a tight-fisted grip on the athletes, especially after the terrible tragedy that had just occurred. If any of the players had a habit with respect to substance abuse, alcohol or even late hours, Nolan would know and he'd do something about it.

Dean Thompson's goal was to lift the university's athletic program, bringing it to new heights. When they selected Nolan Castwell, they were operating in a cautious mode, instead of pursuing a master motivator of young athletes. Due to Willie Jones' tragic death, the philosophy had come to be one of protective vigilance, foregoing their previous commitment of having the promising athletic program become persistent over-achievers.

Al stood up, announcing, "Gentlemen, I'll have you all know two important things. One is that the coroner's report on Willie Jones revealed he had serious levels of cocaine in his blood system that caused cardiac arrest. There will be no lawsuit brought against the University of Western Chicago." There was a round of applause in the room. Andy did not join in.

"The second piece of good news is that Nolan Castwell will be the new head coach at Western Chicago for the remainder of this basketball season." Again, there was applause punctuating the announcement. "Nolan, would you like to say anything?"

Nolan Castwell stood up as a matter of respect for his immediate audience and said, "Not particularly, except that I'd like to thank Al and Dean Thompson for offering me the position. I can assure you all, you will have no further problems with the Western Chicago Eagle Team regarding discipline and/or foul play."

Andy's eyes rolled as this remark clearly pointed a finger at him as being the one responsible, thus fueling his emotional conclusion of taking it personally.

If Nolan Castwell could see the future, he would have realized that he had just put his foot in his mouth and would be astounded by the developments that would occur in just one week's time. Strange and peculiar occurrences had been unfolding the past two weeks, and they would continue for another two weeks. It was as if the devil and God decided together to put a 30-day curse on this university. If it wasn't a curse, it surely was a jinx.

"I look forward to meeting the players," Nolan continued, "our first practice, and naturally our first game together. Thank you all." The complete table applauded once again, including Andrew. But his accolade was from possible peer pressure, not from voluntary approval or respect.

Dean Thompson took his turn, standing up and proclaiming, "Well, I'm sure things are in good hands here. If you don't mind, I've got to get back to some regular business. Good day, everyone. And good luck, Nolan."

"Thank you, sir."

After Dean Thompson left the room, Nolan suddenly announced a decision he had made and had totally forgotten to mention previously. "Oh, by the way, I've decided to keep Mr. Andrew Trella on as my assistant coach, along with the young man with the broken leg."

Andy looked at Nolan in a way that might lead one to believe that if he had a knife in his hand this current scene could be a reenactment of Brutus and Caesar. Nolan Castwell made it sound like he was doing Andy a big, special favor.

Nolan was sure of himself and was going to do things his way, and he was smart enough not to draw enemies from the start, except for one. He thought it would be a gesture of good faith to permit the present assistant coaches to stay on. Even Winthrop and Bart could finish out the season, but they would just be employed as water and towel boys at this point.

Some people's intentions are good, but then they go out of their way to put their point across in a half-hearted manner. This only jeopardizes and discounts their good intentions, making things worse. This was Nolan Castwell's way. Nolan would have done better if he hadn't said anything at all with respect to Andrew's status. As long as he didn't personally fire Andy, naturally he would have stayed on as his assistant.

Andrew knew he was not going to be in favor of his new boss. When he came out of this quick, formal meeting, he was depressed. He wanted things to be the way they were, and he wanted to like his new boss. He could tell Nolan was an egotistical, power-hungry admiral who'd satisfy only one appetite–his own. He knew Nolan was going to release all assistant coaches at the end of the season and hire a completely new staff for next year. The only reason he didn't let anyone go now was his unfamiliarity with the squad itself. He would gain valuable information, assessing the talent of the team and the positions they played. Nolan would live and die by the answers he would gain from his assistants for the first couple of days or so. But by season's end, tournament or not, Nolan would clean house and gather in his own hand-picked garrison of noblemen.

Thinking to himself, Andy couldn't believe that Al Perkins and Dean Thompson put their heads together and this is what they came up with–a fully-charged leader who was more like a general preparing to command an army rather than of a simple college coach. The university's team needed a teacher. Even though it wasn't an academic class, the basketball coach was a teacher. They went out and hired Robocop, instead. Then Andy thought about what had happened when he was at the helm of Western Chicago. His tenure was just shy of ten days, and he had a death on his resumé.

CHAPTER

THIRTY-FOUR

Nolan Castwell stood aloof right smack in the middle of the basketball court. He was wearing a gorgeous navy blue satin sweatsuit, and hanging from his neck was a beautiful solid gold whistle. It had an "N" inscribed on one side and the figure 200 chiseled on the other. It was given to him by Princeton University after he had won his two hundredth game. Nolan got great use from the whistle. It was a present he loved to wield.

Today he was hardly coming up for air. He whistled it loud and clear all throughout the practice. His cheeks were starting to acquire a common redness from the constant inhaling and exhaling that the whistle required in order to function. The constant puffing that he accumulated thus far would have put him through three-quarters of a pack of cigarettes. Judging from his current attitude, he was surely going to exceed the two-pack-a-day habit. When he exhaled into the whistle, it generated sharp shrills, signifying the drills to commence.

Thus, they ran, and they ran, and they ran. Nolan made the entire team do suicide drills, one after another. They'd run to the foul line and back to the base line, then on to half court and back to the original baseline. Then to the other foul line, past half court, and on back to the baseline: then baseline to baseline.

They did it over and over. No breaks. No rest to speak of and if there was a rest, it was only a minute's worth.

Andy stood on the base line underneath the hoop near the players, where they completed the last leg of each exercise. Needless to say, his eyes were once again rolling. He couldn't believe that Nolan was conducting the practice like the players were in boot camp. Each time the players approached the baseline, he'd hear comments from the exhausted participants:

"He's lost his mind."
"The man thinks he's the track team, Coach."
"I came here to college to play ball. I woke up in the morning as a Marine in Cambodia."

They were now on a momentary break. Each of them was resting in various slouched positions along the baseline under the basket near Andrew. They were all perspiring so profusely that the next thing to come through their pores might be blood. The suicide drills were extraneous, burdensome, and lengthy. Surprisingly, no matter how fatigued they were, they were still be able to offer their comments. "We've already had one man drop dead on this court, what's he want ten more?"

Andrew was having a tough time in controlling his thoughts. He specifically didn't want to show his feelings against Nolan to the players who were gasping for air and or water. However, when he heard the last comment by one of the dissenters, "What's he want, ten more to drop dead?" Andy summoned the impetus to approach Mr. Nolan Castwell. The players all showed the whites of their eyes when Andrew began his stroll. Each one of them knew that there'd be a confrontation, and they were definitely not going to miss it.

As Andy confronted Nolan, he said, "Excuse me, sir, but how much more running do you want them to do? They've been doing this for twenty-five minutes straight."

"I'll be the judge of what's enough and what's not," Nolan stated in a controlled manner.

"With all due respect, sir, they are so exhausted right now that they won't even be able to pick up a basketball."

"That's the problem with this team. These boys haven't had a real good workout. That's why they have the energy to go out at night, gallivant around, chase women, drink and do drugs."

"Are you kidding? They'll be so tired, they won't even be able to get up for class in the morning."

Nolan walked away from Andrew, signaling that their discussion had come to a quick conclusion.

"They're a basketball team, not a combat unit," Andy protested.

Nolan didn't turn around or respond in any manner to acknowledge Andy's remark. It was as if he was on auto-pilot and Andy wasn't even there. Nolan was reacting as if he had no mind of his own but had been programmed by a high-tech computer.

Andrew just shook his head in disbelief at Nolan Castwell's antics and way of running the practice.

"Set 'em up for passing drills!" Nolan bellowed out to Andy without even turning his head.

THIRTY-FIVE

Andrew entered the locker room that was adjacent to where the Eagle players had their lockers. These players' lockers were set apart from many of the students who used them as part of their gym classes. This gave the players some degree of privacy and also a feeling of prestige, having exclusive double sets of lockers for themselves. So, Andy could actually be in the locker room and none of the players could see or hear him.

Cautiously, he stopped walking and remained still in order to hear the comments without giving himself away.

"This is total fuckin' bullshit! We don't have to put up with this fuckin' asshole."

"Oh, yeah? What can we do?"

"We can be fuck-ups. We can have attitudes–be late for practice. Not show at all. We can protest!"

Oh, no, not that! Andy thought. He'd had his fill of protest and revolt for at least a thousand days. Andrew stayed in the back part of the locker room, content to listen to the complaining dissenters.

"Are you kidding? Man, we can't pull that shit. They'll pull our scholarships out from under us."

"Then what's we gonna do?"

"We got to do something."

"Like what?"

"We can't do shit except live with this is how things are gonna be."

Kennedy just kept saying the same thing. "It's bullshit, man. It's total, bullshit. We don't need this crap from that old geezer."

"Fellas, I'm thinking about quitting," Turner said seriously.

They all paid strict attention to Eric Turner's words since several of them had actually had the very same thought, never giving it credence. They were more than willing to give Eric their ears. Andy was not about to scramble on out yet; he felt compelled to finish this stakeout.

"I'm serious. I'm a senior. There's only three weeks left in the season, and I'm not going pro."

"Don't do it, Eric, hang," Jefferson offered.

"Screw it. What the hell for? I'm going back to the streets: Chicago, New York, Philadelphia. Makes no difference. Same shit. Hassles on the street are easier than this bullshit. It's over here for me. Maybe not for you, but it sure is over for me. Why prolong the agony? I'm writing my letter of resignation tonight. Tomorrow I'm out!"

They all remained quiet, letting the silent moment hang on.

Andy lowered his head dejectedly, quietly turned away, and exited the locker room with his eyes focused on each footstep he took. He thought to himself that by just talking about their problems they were, in fact, doing something. He also knew he was powerless for a solution. Something was surely meddling in his heart and head, but he couldn't quite put his finger on it. When he was able admit it to himself, it would be clear. But the time was not now. Once he realized it, it would be soon.

CHAPTER

THIRTY-SIX

The score of the game was shown high above the scoreboard that hung like a chandelier from the top of the center roof. Home Team: 54–Visitors: 81. The Western Chicago Eagles were on the short end of the stick. The student fans were doing what they did best when in unison–booing in a big way. The Eagles had lost by 27 points. The Eagle players ran off the court quicker than they had run all night during the contest. Their destination was out of the arena, so they were as quick as possible to get away from the extremely vocal partisans chanting their disapproval. They were not going to escape so easily, for Mr. Nolan Castwell would let them have it in five minutes time, and he'd tirade for a full twenty minutes.

It was Nolan's first game, and it was a loss. It was a disgrace for the home team Eagles to give such a poor showing. The university's fans were not used to their team winning each time out, but they were certainly not used to this lack of effort by home team itself. They hadn't lost by this kind of deficit in over two months. They had lost one game by 22 points when John Connors was coaching, but that loss was on the road against a superior Illinois college team. Tonight's loss was especially degrading, since playing at home was supposed to be such a sizable advantage. If it was any consolation, they did lose to a superior club. Dayton was having a great year and was ranked in the top 25 of the country.

Nolan marched off the polished floor, shaking hands with the opposing coach. He ignored the waves of boos. He kept in mind that he was just getting to know his club and that the Dayton team was on a roll. Nolan's countenance did not show he was taking this to heart. He'd show that in the confines of the Western Chicago locker room.

Even Andy knew that if he was still in the forefront, in all likelihood, this would have been his first loss. But it did bother him that they had played so badly. It was obvious to him that they were missing an integral component. They did not seem as energized as they were only a week ago. And he knew that Nolan was the reason for it. Nolan Castwell, the supposedly expert motivator, had an imposter side to him that conquered the opposite factor.

Andy did not want the team back by any stretch of the imagination; at least he didn't think he did. He didn't need all the bullshit in his life. He was just trying to figure out what the team needed that it now lacked. He was taking notice of the current situation and categorizing it. Plenty of questions. Plenty of answers. No solutions.

THIRTY-SEVEN

Six on one side, five on the other were sitting on the benches set up in front of their lockers. They were divided into thirds when it came to categorizing their current state of dress. Fully dressed. Undressed with a towel wrapped around the waist after showering. The other third were still in their uniforms. They were all being reamed out.

Nolan Castwell was delivering a fully-charged emphatic lecture that would have sunk a Navy submarine and maybe a battleship, as well. The sermon he was serving up was not one you'd likely hear on Sunday morning in church. The vulgarity in his vocabulary arsenal was considerable. He was irate, progressing to livid.

"You looked like shit, played like shit, which means that's what you might be! Never in all my years have I coached a team with no heart, no energy, and no motivation. That was a despicable display of basketball. More than half of you were playing soccer out there, kicking the ball all over the Goddamn place. The fucking girls' team could have given them a better game."

The team members were all looking down at their feet. Not one of the brothers were capable of looking Nolan in the eye.

They were upset and dejected. Andy noticed, or instinctively felt, that collectively, they didn't seem to care.

Maybe their spirits had been broken. Perhaps too much had happened to them over the past month. Andy thought he couldn't blame them for falling apart like a tree's leaves withering away when winter comes to call. Facing the facts, the resignations in the formerly stable coaching staff were mind-boggling. There were protests and pickets all over the campus practically around the clock. There was an unfortunate tragic death. On top of that, even more head coach swapping. How could you blame the players for not responding to each and every command. The Western Chicago Eagles lacked one thing above anything else–balance and stability. Whether the goal sought was the erection of a tangible commodity, as in a house, or an intangible, as the spirit and chemistry within a team concept, a foundation would be required. The Western Chicago Eagles were clearly lacking that prerequisite.

Nolan wasn't succeeding in putting the team in proper perspective at all.

The charisma and chemistry that the team had once had was now separated like vinegar and oil. The Eagles were headed in one and only one direction, and that compass pointed directly south. Mind, body, and spirit. They were falling faster than the temperature when the sun went down. And this was only the beginning of the Nolan Castwell era. With anything in life, it's such a slow tedious struggle battling to get to the top. Yet, when heading in the opposite direction, one can get there sliding down skid row in a Miami minute.

With Nolan Castwell on the scene, it would be a monumental climb just to get to the break-even point. Financial analysts were not the only ones who needed to surpass the break-even point. Everyone who was ever born, lived, and died had the need to move on by the break-even point. Western Chicago University's athletic program and the balance sheet were no exception.

For Al, Dean Thompson, and the top echelon, it was not such

a big deal to lose this particular game. Before the season started, they'd pencil in an 'L' in the column next to Dayton. Besides, most people of integrity and intellect figure that sometimes you have to take two steps back before you can plot a course forward. Only the University of Western Chicago couldn't afford to take any steps backward at this juncture. This wasn't the board game Monopoly, where in going backward you'd go directly to jail and then re-roll the dice. However, in an ironic way, current events at Western Chicago had a great deal to do with money. The university was attempting to make their way into the monopoly game with the television networks. In the meantime, the school would be sifting through all the rubble to get to the gold.

They knew Nolan needed some time. Time to learn the team and time to get his message across. He was undoubtedly accomplishing the latter but wasn't a needle in a haystack close to the former. Judging from Nolan's experience and track record, it wouldn't be long before they'd be on the upswing. There was an hourglass involved here. Not on Nolan but on negotiations with the cable network and board of Western Chicago. But the fact remained inside Andy's head as he stood behind Nolan as he persisted in verbally degrading the players. Nolan was not just taking a few paces backward to build up some steam in his attempt to railroad this bunch on the right set of tracks. He was certainly railroading it all right. He was railroading them off the tracks completely. It would be a runaway train going in the wrong direction before long. Andy pondered. He deduced that he, Coach Castwell, and the players were all in big trouble now, and chances were it would get much worse before it got better.

Nolan finally concluded his speech by saying, "Well, gentlemen, and I use the term loosely, you'd better get some rest tonight, cause tomorrow, we're gonna run."

The teammates each flashed an expression as if they were drowning, gasping for air. They didn't mind being scolded to the maximum degree. That just rolled off their backs at this point.

But the last thing they wanted to hear was what they would have to endure the following day.

Nolan turned an about-face and left the pessimistic atmosphere of the locker room. Andy stood leaning up against the door, holding it open so Nolan could pass through. If the door was closed, Nolan would probably have passed through it just as easily as if it was open. Andy raised his head, focusing on the teammates who looked at him as if pleading for salvation. He didn't want to confront their eyes. He was embarrassed to be part of this situation. He had never looked at any of them in this kind of way before. He observed that every single one of them was looking at him. Andy didn't know what to think, didn't know what to do or say. Each of them knew the answer to this problem but Andy did not.

Jefferson stood up, and as he approached Andrew, said, "We're all going to the Groggery Pub. Can you meet us there?"

Andy looked away from Jefferson and glanced at the others who were hanging on for his response. "Sure. I'll be there."

The players started to move about, preparing to leave the locker room. As Jefferson moved away from him, Andy said, "I don't have any answers for you."

Jefferson turned back and snapped, "Like hell you don't!"

Andy's eyes ballooned, trying to figure out what he meant. Andy watched them gathering their belongings. The expression on his face was ambivalent. You couldn't decipher whether he was in favor or against. But he'd find out soon enough at the Groggery Pub.

CHAPTER

THIRTY-EIGHT

The tall, black players walked into the tavern one by one. The bartender's expression exhibited the look in a western saloon when the villain gunfighters strode in. Andrew appeared in the midst of them and caught the bartender's fear. He edged his way forward into the bartender's view and said, "Don't worry, basketball team." The bartender instantly showed relief and let out a sigh.

Andy led them to a corner of the pub, keeping them secluded and private from the other patrons. They all scuttled around, pushing several tables together before they sat. Only one young couple had to get up from a nearby table and move away from the large group.

"Will you need menus?" a waitress said on approaching them.

"No, thanks," Andy replied. "Just bring us three pitchers of what's on tap."

"Three? What're we gonna do with three?" Washington interrupted. "That won't even fill up a cavity."

"Okay, make it four pitchers," Andy said to the waitress.

Washington said, "Four pitchers! What are we gonna do with four pitchers! That won't…"

Andy stopped him. "Chris, if it's cavities you got to fill, go to the dentist. We're not here to guzzle."

The waitress, having waited patiently, was instructed by Andy to bring the pitchers. They all sat down at the huge table they had arranged.

Andrew did not know exactly how to start this discussion, since he didn't know its course or direction. He knew everyone was unhappy. So he decided he'd try to break the mood and alter their frame of minds by saying, "Hey, you guys. I heard this great joke today."

"Listen to this," Travis Bennett said. "We didn't come here to tell jokes."

"Hey, Travis, I'll be the first one to admit the real joke. It's what's happening to this team. But I want to tell you this joke," Andy said. The teammates sat with their arms folded, waited for their beer, and let him go on with his joke before the serious shit was to come.

"So, there was this Jewish guy who was so horny cause he hadn't gotten laid in so long, just like Jefferson here." They began to smile slightly, realizing Andy was goofing on Jefferson, even though it wasn't the truth. Andy continued, "Anyway, he was so horny, he took a thousand dollars out of the bank, went into the city, and hired a hooker. But what he also did was he decided to videotape it. Since he was spending so much money, he wanted to be able to watch it over and over to get his money's worth. So, days and weeks went by and he continued watching the video every night. But the thing was, he got hooked on watching the tape in reverse. He watched it over and over backward. Why do you think he got caught up in watching this one part over and over in reverse?

None of them could come up with the answer, and a couple of them asked, "What?"

"He loved the part when she paid him back the thousand dollars."

They all laughed out loud. They were expecting him to say

something about the sex, and it all had to do with money. They laughed and had a good roar. Except for Turner. He just kept looking at Andy.

Andy noticed Eric Turner wasn't laughing. He let his smile fade, looked serious, and faced Eric. "What's on your mind, Eric?"

Boldly, Eric said, "Mutiny. Mutiny on the Western Chicago bounty." The smiles on everyone's faces were wiped clean. Turner went on, "If it rains tomorrow, this asshole will make us do our runnin' outside. Man, I'm not running in no torrential rain. I may be black, but I'm no fool. So tomorrow, I'm quitting. I'll join up with the track team. They do less runnin' than we do."

Andy just listened to him then said, "That's good. Anybody else packing it in?"

Kennedy raised his hand and Andy asked, "And what are you going to do?"

"I'm going back to what I was doing before; it's back to the streets for me."

Andy bellowed out, "Okay, enough with the bullshit! Nolan's been pulling his crap and now you're doing the same. The streets will be there the rest of your lives."

Washington, taking his turn, griped, "This is total bullshit! What's going on around here? It's fuckin' ridiculous. An hour of running every single day and only forty five minutes of ball time."

Andy interrupted, "Washington, I agree with you. You saw me complain to him yesterday. I disagree with his tactics, and he admitted to me you won't have to do it much longer. In one week's time the running will all be over with."

Skin Head said, "That's the best Goddamn, news I've heard yet. I'll drink to that."

The waitress had just arrived at the table with their thirst-quenchers. The beers were poured in the glasses, and they threw the slugs down their throats in unison. Coming up for air, Washington said, "Andy, we want you back in charge."

Dumfounded, Andy answered, "No. Forget it. It's not about what you want. It's what the athletic department wants. It's what Al Perkins and Dean Thompson want, and they don't want me. I don't want it anyway. Once was enough. Don't you remember what this campus was like when they put me there?"

"That's bullshit," Washington sputtered. "The same principles that apply to us, apply to you. So you had some adversity just like we do now. You're just as frustrated as we are. At least before, we were all on the same page. We stepped out of line, you corrected us. This guy corrects us before we've even made a mistake. We've had three different coaches this month, and if we keep losing, we'll get another."

"No, you won't. Castwell's contract is guaranteed for the rest of the season. He's staying, boys. You better get it through your skulls."

"Well," Johnson asked, "what if we lay down on this guy? What if we throw every game he coaches?"

"You can't do that."

"Why the hell not?"

"I'm going to tell you why. Besides it being unethical and wrong, if someone found out it was true, it would be suspension and revocation of your scholarships. Plus, no other college program would pick you up. You couldn't even transfer out. Besides, even if you're not playing well, Nolan will take you out of the game and put someone else in. You know as well as I do, there are pro scouts at every game. If you're a starting ball player, you play to stay there. If you're a sub, you play to crack the starting line-up. That never changes. You may be able to throw one game and get away with it, but it's unrealistic to think you can throw a string of games together. There's just too many intangibles that come into play with that scenario."

"Look, man," Washington pleaded, "We want you back. We

don't like this guy. We don't want to like him. Isn't there something we can do to get you back in charge?"

"Sorry, guys. I'd like to help you out, but I can't. You've got to make it through this one on your own." He got up from the table and began to leave.

Washington stood up and said, "Get ready for a long losing streak, Coach."

Andy turned to look at them and said, "If it's meant to be, it's meant to be."

Washington countered, "No matter what you say or what you know or what you believe, you have to be just as frustrated as we are, maybe even more. You think about it!"

Andy stared at Washington for a long silent moment, then looked at the others who were sitting there in silence. Then he left the bar. On his way to his car, he stopped, stood and pondered, thinking to himself, *You're right, Washington. The same principles that apply to you apply to me.*

Andy strolled over to his vehicle as a light drizzle fell from the sky. If there was such a thing as invisible handcuffs, Andy felt he was wearing them.

THIRTY-NINE

The game was out of hand by now, and it wasn't even half-time yet. Nolan Castwell had his arms folded like Chief Hunting Bull, with an expressionless face that didn't reveal a thing. You couldn't tell if his team was losing by thirty or winning by twenty. Unfortunately, it wasn't the latter.

The crowd was wildly belligerent. You'd think it was the Roman Coliseum when the task masters would order a contest. The competition in those days was man vs. animal, slave vs. lion, and they'd give the sword to the beast if they could.

Thank God there was no Las Vegas in Roman times. How would the kingpins assess their handicap in such a contest? A competition where one only became the winner by draining the blood of its victim like a vampire in the fog of a London night.

There was no half-time, either. Imagine if there were, by current day standards, the sports announcer during intermission of a New York Jets and Miami Dolphin football game:

"And here are some updates: Vikings 27–Rams 14: Cowboys 21–Cardinals 12: Packers 20–Falcons 10. Over in Italy, at the Roman Coliseum, the Roman Legion Lions 7–Human Slaves nothing. And to the highlights: Watch here in the first quarter.

Here's how the Roman Lions scored half of their points on this apparent take down; watch as the aggressor severs the arm from his opponent. Last word here is that they are now tied at nine apiece, as the one-armed, bloody slave has forged a remarkable late rally comeback, forcing the contest into overtime."

The losing team couldn't wait any longer for it to be over. A rare state of mind for any black athlete who loved his basketball. The score was now Wisconsin 62–Western Chicago Eagles 38. In fact, Andy didn't know what to do or what to think. He just sat there, embarrassed at this team's representation; but then again, so were about eight thousand other people in this sports edifice.

It started at seven minutes and five seconds left in the ball game. Suddenly, there was no more booing. The decibel level fell like an anvil. The boo's had evaporated so swiftly that it could have been pulled through a wind tunnel vacuumed and sent into outer space.

The chant began ever so gradually. Andy's head rose slowly, like an awakening, as if a ghost had appeared right before his eyes. He looked deeply into the audience. Straight ahead. Twelve o'clock. Upper mezzanine level. The ball players who were currently not playing but keeping the bench warm also gave this strange event their strictest attention. This was an unprecedented occurrence, and they left the game's happenings immediately behind, like dust in the wind. The crowd began, and never stopped as it gained momentum like a colossal tidal wave.

"We want Andy! We want Andy! We Want Andy! We want Andy! We want Andy!"

Andy was astounded. Sheila, who was sitting four rows behind him in back of the home team's bench was surprised and mesmerized. It was totally unexpected. This was only the fourth time she had ever been in this building to attend a basketball game, and both times she witnessed incredible developments. Instantly, she felt there was going to be a series of more unbelievable events to unfold before this season was eventually over.

She couldn't have been more right. Sheila glanced down at the floor, but all she could see was the back of Andy's head. She could tell that his attention was held captive by the bellowing crowd.

The fans in the bleachers were now much more than observers. They began to stand. The chant was building with magnificent strength at a riveting pace. The score was: Wisconsin 92–Eagles 67, but it didn't matter. It was purely academic. All anyone heard was a large crowd revving up and sounding off. "We want Andy! We want Andy! We want Andy! We want Andy!" A deaf man could probably have heard it from afar. It might have fueled an earthquake and caused the Rosemont Horizon to come tumbling down. It made the Chicago Bulls vs. the Boston Celtics, who were playing five miles away across town, seem like Romper Room, especially since the Michael man and the Bird man were both retired.

The referees allowed the game to continue, hoping that their choice to permit the action on the court would override the roar of the chants. But their strategy to drown out the ever-persistent crowd was dubious. They couldn't have been so wrong, just as the match-up of the two teams were so decidedly wrong.

The calls for Andy's resurgence were totally out of control by now. Everyone in the sports facility was on their feet, continuing their harmonious signal, like a chorus line singing their hearts out with vivacious commitment. They were calling the three words, asking for reinstatement by process of impeachment.

Nolan Castwell did not want to call a timeout, even though it seemed to be necessary, especially since there was such lack-luster performances by the Eagles. The players were probably playing at half-speed. A timeout at this point would be devastating. It would only give the crowd an opportunity to build its chants even stronger, if possible. On a scale of one to ten, the audience's enthusiasm was, minimum, nine point five. And why not? The game was devastating. How much more dreadful could things be for Coach Nolan Castwell from his point of view? They really couldn't have been much worse. He refrained from giving the signal for a timeout.

Andy could not take it anymore. He bounded to his feet like a springboard. He made that impulsive decision as if he weren't relegated back to being an assistant under Chief Hunting Bull, Nolan Castwell. Andy turned to his left and began walking down the sidelines, juxtapositional to the inbounds play of the court. It was quite obvious to everyone that he was leaving the arena—unauthorized.

Would his action be deemed a resignation? Maybe. Would it call for a discharge? No way! Could it mean promotion? Unlikely! Nolan did not call Andrew back. He had much bigger problems on his hands.

At least now, Nolan felt that Andrew joined him in the dog house. Castwell could only see abandonment and desertion. Absent Without Leave. Missing In Action. Military policy court marshal and then shot or hung as in the olden days. The noose was ready. They'd use the net from the basketball hoop on either the west or east side, whichever was closer. Only it would be Nolan's neck, not Andrew's. If Castwell reprimanded Andy at this moment, he would provoke close to eight thousand people. Castwell wouldn't be fired, he'd be mobbed and beaten to a pulp.

Nolan decided not to stop Andy. Why incite anything further? It would only lend itself to his own personal banishment or perhaps even self-sacrifice. With the intention of self-preservation, Nolan chose not to impede Andrew's walk-off. He even acted like he didn't notice Andy leaving the arena.

Meanwhile, Sheila did the opposite. When she saw Andy rise and then leave, she rose up from her box seat and ran down the stairs as fast as she could. When she reached the court's floor, she turned left and followed the trail Andrew had taken as if she were Lord Baltimore, the great Indian tracker. He was in view, approximately ninety feet ahead of her. Andy was surely headed for the double doors with the illuminated exit sign from the playing area. His head was down, and he walked without looking to his left or right. He was undoubtedly avoiding eye contact at all costs. He pushed the door open, went through the portal, and disappeared. Sheila was right behind him and had to use caution to avoid the swinging double doors. A timeout was called, but it was by the game officials, not either coach. Sheila continued following Andy. The double doors were getting a workout tonight. At least something was, since the players in uniform sure as hell weren't. As if they were in a dungeon's chamber, Andy and Sheila could still hear the muted chant: "We want Andy! We want Andy! We want Andy!" Although the doors muffled the sound somewhat, they still heard it.

In the corridor, Sheila tried catching up with Andy. The two of them seemed to have a certain knack for meeting that way. After all, that's how they had originally met. Sheila called out to him, "Stop, Andy!"

Andy turned around immediately and saw her. He hadn't expected to. She was, understandably, the furthest thing from his mind. She confronted him. "Where are you going?"

He walked back toward her. He was very angry and confused. The confusion came because these were the very same people who were protesting and screaming for his head two weeks ago. These were the people who voiced their opinions with signs and posters and demonstrations and rebellion bordering on riots, deprecating his existence. Now, they were chanting for his immediate reinstatement. He was thoroughly confused.

When he reached Sheila, he said, "I don't know where to go. I think I've seen and heard it all now. Tragic death, accidents, protests for and against. My head is spinning so fast I couldn't even tell you what day it is. Where would you go, Sheila?"

Quickly she responded, "Right back in there where you belong."

"Are you kidding? Can you hear that?" He opened one of the double doors slightly to increase the decibel level of the enthused student body calling his name. Needlessly, they listened to what they had both heard before. Andy continued, "What planet are you on? This sort of thing doesn't happen to me every day. How can I go back in there? How the hell can he continue to coach in that environment with me sitting in his face?"

Andy let the door go and walked back to Sheila. He turned around to her and said, "This team, with everything that's happened to it, needs only one thing. It needs me. And I don't have the authority to make that happen." Andy finally said it. He let the craw out of his gut that had been subconsciously gnawing away at his insides. Deep down, he longed to get back at the controls and fly this plane, even if he was away from it for just a short time. He gave Sheila a dead serious look as he finished his last syllable.

Sheila just returned the favor and said no more. She stood in silence and realized he was right as she watched him turn and walk away.

Andy took his sports coat off as he walked down the hallway. He was in a tirade. "I don't understand this. I didn't want this. I don't know what's going on anymore. I can't follow this."

Sheila stood still and watched him in his frustration. A tear surfaced as she truly felt sorry for him.

CHAPTER

FORTY

He was bearded today. Andrew's beard was about fifty-two hours old, and it made him look quite handsome and rugged. Another twenty-four and the aging beard would make him look scrappy and scrubby. By this time tomorrow he'd be fully clean-shaven. Andy was sitting on one of the campus' park benches by himself because he wanted to be alone. He was depressed. He often resorted to outdoor public park benches when he was disconsolate.

Whenever Andy got that way, which was rare, he'd think back to what really got him gloomy. Today he was reminiscing about his grandmother who had passed away less than a year earlier. He used to call her Nana. She lived in St. Petersburg, Florida, and died at the age of 85. St. Petersburg is an unwritten designated city where elderly folks go to live out the rest of their lives. It is one of the retirees' summits of cities in the United States. If you could afford to retire, this is where almost twenty percent of the elderly go.

Andrew had been in St. Petersburg to visit with her three weeks before she had passed on. He was there for Thanksgiving. At this point in her life, 15 years shy of the century mark, she could hardly take care of herself, especially since she lived alone.

Andy decided it would be nice for her if he flew down south to spend a special Thanksgiving feast with her eldest grandson. He'd flown into Tampa International Airport about 12 miles north of St. Pete, two days before Thanksgiving. The first thing he did after their initial great big kiss and hug was to take her car over to Pizza Hut and share some pizza with her. It wasn't real pizza like the north had, with soft glowing white melted mozzarella cheese, but to Nana it was a real delight. Even though the pizza place was on Fourth Street and First Avenue around the corner from her home, she never went there unless her grandson was with her. He'd purchased one medium-sized extra crispy pie with sausage and pepperoni. Nana did not need much to satisfy her appetite at this ripe old age. She'd have her one small slice, and he'd have the other five. One thing for sure, when eating pizza with his grandmother, they never had to be fearful or embarrassed over taking the last slice. It always worked out perfectly. She required very little, and he needed a lot. After eating dinner and talking, they relaxed in the comfort of her home, watched a movie on television together, and talked some more. Nana cherished her comforts as well as her privacy.

She had had a bad marriage, which catapulted her appreciation of privacy, security, and comfort. Her marriage produced one child, a daughter, whom she had named Shirley, Andrew's mother. Nana's name was Lillian, and her husband, Warren, was a merchant marine always on ships and always away from home. Warren wasn't a typical sailing partier, nor did he chase women. He just had his own way about him and didn't feel comfortable sharing the responsibility of marriage to the fullest. They were married for almost thirty years but lived together for only six. Neither one filed for divorce, since both knew they'd never marry again. At least Shirley was the one and only beautiful and positive thing that their marriage had produced.

Shirley was born after a most difficult pregnancy. Four out of five doctors said that Lillian could not have children. The pregnancy was a helluva one that nearly killed her. But come hell or high water, Lillian was going to have a baby. It was a one-shot deal. If she miscarried, she knew in her heart and soul that she'd never get pregnant again. So. Lillian fooled them all by having her one and only child. She would be very happy as Shirley married a lawyer and had three sons of her own, one of whom was Andrew. The other sons were Raymond and Joseph, both married now, and living and working in New York.

Lillian now had three grandsons to love and cherish. They were her family, her only family. Sadly, Andrew's mother Shirley had died of cancer at the age of 35. It was Hodgkin's Disease, which not much later became one of the few cancers that was totally curable.

Now it was Lillian's turn for cancer. Her's was lung cancer, which came from smoking two packs a day for nearly an unbelievable 47 years. After Shirley had died, she wasn't going to stop. Lillian's two best friends were Benson & Hedges 100 and a cup of coffee. She always seemed to have their company, separately, simultaneously and together. Lillian didn't give a damn. Any fears she'd had were wiped clean when the Mighty One decided to take her only proud treasure away from her.

Lillian was near the end herself. She really had trouble breathing. She was literally out of breath by a short walk from the bedroom to the bathroom. Her body was wearing away. She had lost so much weight and was down to about 77 pounds. She could hardly eat, not because she wasn't hungry, but because she just didn't have the energy.

Dr. Light, who ironically was black, promised her she would never have any pain. That's all Lillian cared about these days. However, she hated the idea of taking medicine. She was always doped up, which she found to be pretty wild for a woman who never needed as much as an aspirin her whole life. Even in the end, she would not exceed her dosage of codeine and her assortment of pills. She took her prescribed dosages to the tee.

Once Yvonne, the woman who lived downstairs and who looked after and cared for Lillian, poured her codeine about a quarter of an inch too high in the plastic measuring shot glass. When Lillian saw this, she made Yvonne pour all of it back into the bottle and then re-pour to the proper amount. She knew if she took more medication than she was allowed, she could easily overdose, which would be considered suicide. That did not sit well with Lillian. So she only took her prescribed allotment and not a drop more. She wanted to go naturally, in God's way. She had already lived fifty years longer than her only daughter. She was not going to commit suicide now. She wanted to go quietly, peacefully, at God's calling.

One thing that amazed Andrew about his grandmother was that she was still as sharp as a whip. With her body quickly eroding away, Lillian was very quick mentally. She read newspapers and magazines from cover to cover and watched the news on Channel 13 twice a day. She knew everything going on in the world, even though she was confined to this one-bedroom condominium. This made Andy feel as if he knew nothing of what was happening in the world. She knew all the current events, the tragedies, the political issues, stock market swings, Hollywood gossip, and even who was gay and who was not.

Three weeks after he left his grandmother following Thanksgiving, he received a telephone call from his stepmother in New York. His father had remarried after Andy's mom died, and he and his new wife had an additional three kids. His stepmother's name was Terri.

"Andy, I received a call from Florida this morning. Your nana passed away."

Andrew was stunned and started to weep when he heard the news. He thought that no matter how much you know, something like this is bound to happen. You're never quite prepared for it when it does. He knew it was going to happen but still couldn't believe it when it did. No one ever does. Terri told Andy that she loved him. She felt it was the only thing she could say to ease his pain. She truly felt sorry for his loss. She also told him to be careful driving home from the university that day.

Andy would leave work early, call his brothers, and make flight arrangements back to St. Petersburg.

Sitting on the park bench, wearing his overcoat on this brisk day, Andy was remembering that he'd had to fly to St. Petersburg, think about the funeral, settle the estate, and secure the condominium. Andy knew Nana gave many keys out to other senior citizens so they could come in and check on her. Andy was concerned about so many people having keys. He knew Nana had acquired a great deal of jewelry for the better part of sixty years. She also had a couple of furs. With several sets of keys out, it would be rather easy for one person to pilfer the apartment before he or his brothers could get down there. The only valuables left in the condominium after his brothers took the jewelry and furs back to New York were three color television sets and a microwave. The rest was Nana's clothes and several pairs of shoes that Andy didn't have the foggiest notion of what to do with. But he really didn't worry about that. That was a trivial detail to deal with later.

Andy recalled that when he went to see Yvonne, she told him about his grandmother's final days. Yvonne lived in apartment number 8B and came upstairs every day to wash, feed and food shop for Lillian. The first thing Yvonne did when Andy came down to see her was grab, hug, and kiss him on the cheek. He felt this was pretty strange from a woman he never met before. Then she said, "Your grandma made me promise her to give her three grandson's a great big hug and kiss for her when I saw them." Yvonne told Andrew that she was the one who had found his grandmother when she died. Yvonne was an elderly woman herself, with hair that was a snowy beautiful white.

"I came into your grandmother's apartment around 9:15 in the morning, as I do every day. I remember not hearing a sound at all; usually, I hear coughing. She coughed a lot, especially in the mornings. So first, I figured she was probably sound asleep. When I walked into her bedroom, I found her lying across the bed, perpendicular to it. Her arms were hanging over one side of the bed, and her feet were over the other. Apparently, she had been trying to get out of bed."

Andy had tears surface instantly.

Yvonne continued. "Her feet were black, her body was cold, and her eyes were open, which I immediately closed." Andrew could not fight back the tears as they continued streaming down his cheeks.

"Last week she couldn't even talk on the phone or to anyone else. She'd whisper gingerly, only to me. She saved her energy in case she had any requests. Three days earlier I came in, and Lillian was lying on the sofa in the den with the television on. She lay there motionless. I thought she was dead."

Andy said, "She was sleeping."

"No."

Andy waited impatiently for what Yvonne could possibly say if she wasn't dead and wasn't sleeping, either.

"She was in a coma!" Andy's eyebrows pressed into his forehead as he listened and tried to understand. "I saw Lillian's fingers move slightly. I began to wake her, but she wasn't responding. Suddenly, she woke with a fright and swung violently at me with a magazine. 'Why did you wake me? I was going. He was taking me. I was talking to my mother and sitting with my daughter,' she moaned."

Andy was appalled. "She was mad at you."

"She was furious. About a week ago, I came in and Lillian was on the floor, trying to get up."

"She fell down?" Andy asked.

"Yes, she was trying to get up but couldn't. She had a glass framed picture of your mother. The glass had broken and cut her hand when she fell. Not bad, but it did cut her. She was carrying a photo of Shirley around the apartment and telling us that she was soon going to be with her daughter."

Yvonne then told Andy that his grandmother was praying to God for Him to please make her die. By now the tears were uninterrupted, a steady flowing stream falling from his eyes.

Yvonne apologized to Andy for making him weep so much and offered to stop telling him about his nana's last days. It was amazing to Yvonne that the tears kept coming.

When Andy left St. Petersburg, the condominium was naturally empty of any human inhabitants. This made him feel sad and lonely. The airport connection limousine service came to pick him up and take him to the airport for the trip back to Chicago. When he called the limo service to set the time for his pick-up, the dispatching clerk told him they'd pick him up five hours before his flight departure. This infuriated Andrew right off. He knew that Tampa Airport was only twenty minutes away. He argued with the clerk over the phone, "What am I going to do in the airport for four and a half hours before my flight leaves?"

She responded, "I'm sorry sir, but it's the holiday season. The airlines want all travelers to check in two and a half hours before departure. We also have many people to pick up. Andy was still ticked off at this. He wanted the extra time to tidy up the condo, making it presentable, as well as take care of any other final details. Andrew tried to make a point when he replied, "Well, let me ask you a question. If I were leaving next Saturday, when would you have to pick me up... like twenty minutes from now?"

The dispatcher chuckled as she said, "No, sir. I'm sorry for the inconvenience. We'll be picking you up at approximately 2:30 p.m."

"Okay fine," he replied and hung up the phone.

When Andy entered the coach van, he was feeling quite sad. It was the first time he had left St. Petersburg that his grandmother wasn't there to kiss him good-bye. As he moved down the aisle, he noticed two couples, senior citizens no less, already seated inside. They were on their way to Las Vegas for the holidays. Andrew worked his way to the back row of the van and sat down. He was reserved, lonely, and remorseful, and he wanted to be that way. A final tribute to his grandmother, showing his love for her. The van pulled out from the curb of the Winston Park condominium complex. The last thing he wanted was a steady flow of conversation. He wanted a quiet trip to the airport. Andy was going to be denied. The two couples were yapping away. They were talking about the Tampa Derby Downs, the dog races that were so popular in the Sunshine State.

One woman was nauseating to Andy as she started telling her story. "It was so wild to see one of the dogs while running the race, suddenly stop on the dime and start to scratch his privates. He must have had a flea attack. Another dog decided to take a short cut to the finish line and took off right through the inner grass circle. When he got to the middle of the area, he stopped running and began rolling around playfully in the grass."

Andrew just looked at her inquisitively. It annoyed and embarrassed him that these people were talking about something so insipid and that he had to listen to it. He was morbidly thinking that if he had a gun he'd shoot them all, right there and then. As they all sat there dead in the van, he'd say something like, "So, you're all going to Las Vegas for the Christmas season. That's great. Gonna gamble? Have a good time. Too bad you're all going as corpses. How do you like that!" Then he got mad at himself thinking of the word 'corpse', as that was the exact condition of his grandmother. He just sat quietly for the rest of the ride to Tampa. He paid attention to every word they said, not because he wanted to, he had no other choice.

The plane ride back to Chicago was even more nauseating than the twenty-minute taxi ride to the airport. It wasn't caused by turbulence, but Andy was unfortunate to be sitting right next to an extremely voluminous woman. Since this was a night flight, the passengers were given dinner. Every time she used her fork, she did so like her food was prey. Her elbow crossed over her arm rest by six inches, digging into his ribs every single time she forked her food. She was indulging into her food, thus digging into his ribs. Andy thought she should have been an archaeologist. He was very uncomfortable and exasperated that this woman couldn't manage to devour her dinner without trespassing into his zone. He wished that she had been seated on the other side of his airplane window seat. He was thankful that he wasn't shorter or that she was taller, for the preservation of his skull. He thought, *Can you believe this lady, shoveling her food like coal into her mouth, like a black hole?*

The woman asked the stewardess if she could have a second full dinner, and the stewardess obliged her. Andrew wished she was a furnace and would just blow up. Then he realized she had already done that. He was thinking that if the pilot had to drop a bomb, he could use her. She'd probably kill forty or fifty people. Then, the US of A could clone her as a military weapon, worse than chemical warfare. How would anyone like to see a screaming four-hundred-pound human falling ten thousand feet out of the sky on top of their ass.

Just before dinner was served, she dropped her newspaper on the floor under the seat directly in front of her. Andy thought that was pretty interesting. He was personally going to witness first-hand whether she was going to attempt to pick it up or not. He was thinking if it were he, he'd kick it farther under the seat so it would eliminate the chance of her struggling to resurrect it. However, he knew she was going to go for it, and she did. Andy figured there was a better than fifty percent chance she'd trap her shoulder against the bottom of the seat in front of her.

He was amazed at the battle she gave to get that body in position to pick up a single newspaper from the floor. If she got pinned in, they'd probably have to put a huge sun roof in the plane so that they could use a high-powered crane to pull her up from her position. She was a perfect illustration of being stuck between a rock and a hard place. Finally, she was capable of sweeping up her newspaper and getting back into her original position. Andrew thought he could easily complete the five minute mile, before she concluded her ordeal.

Andy suddenly awoke from his drifting memories of the last

time he'd been to Florida. Still sitting on that park bench, he wiped a tear from his face. As his focus returned, he saw a woman walking with purpose toward him. She was maybe ninety yards or a football field away from him. Even at such a distance, he could tell who it was. It was Sheila. It seemed as though she was marching, heading straight in his direction. It was time they dealt with something. They were about to have it out, and he was in no mood. Andy knew a sermon was about to be served up while she torpedoed toward him. He knew she'd be the shipper and he'd be the recipient. They would need no account number. But the charges could turn out to be very expensive.

CHAPTER

FORTY-ONE

Andy still had his butt parked on the wooden bench. He'd been there for so long he couldn't tell where his butt started and where it ended. Both the bench and his ass were hard and cold, making them partners. He had just passed some gas, which kept his seat warm momentarily. The good thing about it was there were no ill aroma side effects. The infamous wind of the windy city blew it away like dust off a cleanly wiped counter.

Sheila was now standing right before him. They were both wearing winter coats. Andy's was gray and left unbuttoned, while Sheila's red down jacket was zippered up to her neck. Andy kept his hands in his coat pockets. He was looking down at the dirt in front of the bench, smoothing the pebbles about, turning them over and repositioning them with the hard surface of his shoe. Perhaps by nightfall, he'd have constructed a small pyramid.

Now that Sheila was within speaking distance, she said, "Feeling sorry for yourself?"

"No."

"Then what?"

"Just upset, depressed. It's all coming apart, the team. You, me."

"Why is it coming apart Andy? Tell me why? Don't tell me you're letting that basketball team come between us. If things aren't going good, then quit if you can't take it. If you love basketball, and I know you do, just because your team is not doing so well, don't let that affect your relationships. That's immature and shallow. What are you going to do when you're married one day? If your team loses, you'll come home and fight with your wife; and every time you win, you're gonna break out the wine and make passionate love. That's pretty goddamn shallow!"

Andrew eyes were deadly fixed on hers as he asked, "So when do I find out that you have kids? Next month?"

He knew that was the wrong thing to say, because all it did was hurt her. It bothered Andy greatly that she never told him she had been previously married. It had a lasting effect only because of the manner in which he learned that she was, which embarrassed the hell out of him.

"No, Andy, I don't have any kids. I was married for two years, and it's over now. He lives in Michigan. We don't speak, write, or see each other at all."

"When was the last time you saw him?"

She collected her thoughts for a minute and said, "Over a year ago." She felt her answer would be impressive to him.

"Sheila, how come you're not divorced yet? You've just said there's no children involved?"

"Take a guess."

"Money?"

"You've got it. We had a house, cars, boat and a horse."

"A horse? What kind of a horse?"

Sheila looked at Andy with a weird dumbfounded expression, wondering why he'd interrupt her for some unimportant detail that didn't concern them. She continued on, "Look Andy, I drive a beat-up Volkswagen. I have a measly one-room studio apartment. I have nothing in a savings account. What if I'd have gotten into a car accident like your friend Phil? I wouldn't be able to teach, and I wouldn't be able to keep what little I have right now. Why shouldn't I fight for what's rightfully mine? I should just give it all up? The lawyers are fighting this battle out, not me, and I could get anywhere from twenty to seventy thousand dollars. I'm not being greedy. I'm just refusing to be a stupid fool, like you are now."

Now it was Andy's turn. "Sheila, it's not all you. It's mostly all team-related. The Eagles are in turmoil right now. We lost a player in a dreadful disheartening manner, and we gained a coach who's an idiot."

Sheila countered," Life is not a bowl of cherries. Sometimes all you have is the friggin' pits."

Andy replied, "In case you don't know it, it's been a helluva of a crazy month."

Sheila wanted to end this discussion and, opting for a different conversation, said, "Okay, Andy. If you wanna see me, just call me!" She turned around and began to walk away.

Andy got up from the park bench, reached out, grabbed her arm, and spun her around. Sheila made a sound that revealed she was moved and wanted to be taken by him. He looked at her face intently for a few brief seconds then lunged his mouth toward hers. They kissed each other passionately then slowly fell to the frozen ground. They were lying on the grass kissing, and Andy started to unzip her red coat.

"Andy, what are you doing?" Sheila asked.

"I thought maybe we'd switch coats, yours looks warmer than mine," he answered humorously.

Sheila's teeth were pure white as she smiled at his joke. Andy spoke in between all the kisses, "Actually, I should rip all your clothes off and leave you out here as punishment."

"Please do!" Sheila answered. They continued on kissing each other in the uninhabited park. They were on the same page once again. They were turned on to each other, not only because of their attraction for each other but because they genuinely liked and loved each other. What made this special on this afternoon was this was the first time they were making up. Making up was fun to do.

Andy said as he took a break from kissing her, "Maybe we should get on the bench."

"I got a better idea," Sheila responded.

"What?"

"We could go inside on a bed somewhere. Have you ever thought of that?"

"No," Andy said, "but I still think we should do something else first."

Sheila asked curiously, "What?"

"I still think we should switch coats."

They smiled and laughed with each other as they got up off the cold ground. They started walking at a brisk pace holding hands.

"You like red, hmm?" Sheila asked.

"Yeah, on a girl," Andy answered. "Red nails, red lips, red toes, and big boobs!" They both laughed really hard as they walked off the park grounds holding hands, content that they were back on course.

CHAPTER

FORTY-TWO

About 500 students were outside the university's athletic building. It was raining hard, but they were still there anyway. Once again, they were doing what they do best when gathered all together. They were immersed in lobbying, picketing, and revolting before the Athletic Department's top caliber decision-makers.

Andy drove his vehicle onto the university grounds with Sheila in the passenger seat. As he pulled the car into a parking spot, both of them paused to witness and try to figure out what was happening. From around the bend, it seemed like there were 50, maybe 100 people. But now they'd both agreed that there were a helluva lot more people than that. The amazing thing about it was the steady rain didn't seem to bother these people. No one was running for cover. They were there for a purpose, for these were the loyal ones who supported their college's basketball program as if it were a Sunday school. Their obvious standoff meant something, but neither Andy nor Sheila were sure just what.

"What the hell is going on!" Andy asked.

Sheila answered even though he was not expecting an

answer, "I don't know. Why is everyone standing in the rain like that?"

Andy responded, "I don't know." Andy had the car parked, and they both sat there with the engine still running. Fortunately, no one was able to detect them, especially with the rain and foggy windows. They both sat trying to decipher what was going on.

Then they saw the signs, the posters, the white cardboard contact sheets, and there were many of them, wide, long, and tall. Each writing, each illustration, offered an opinion directed at the university Athletic Department on what should be done in order to regain success.

"Fire Nolan"

"Castrate Castwell"

"Say Goodbye to Nolan Castwell"

"Castwell Should Be Cast Off and Wished Well"

Andy said, "Well, I'll say this, at least they're consistent."

There were many posters degrading the new Nolan Castwell. There were also other posters. Not only did the student body lobbyists render their opinion of whom to get rid of, they also stipulated and voiced their alternative solution of who they wanted to have as their head coach.

It was the same guy they were calling for to be reinstated at the last basketball contest just two nights ago. They wanted Andy Trella.

"Andy T for President"

"We Want Andy"

"Andy T is 3–0, Nolan C is 0–3 — Make the Switch Before it's Too Late."

"Don't Do it for us, Do it for the Money"

"A Mutiny Always Takes Place at Sea. This One's on land!"

It certainly was a mutiny that was now taking place on the campus of Western Chicago. It seemed to be a common denominator of late.

"Come on, let's get out of here," Andy said. "I know another gym we can go to."

Upstairs in an office window, Dean Thompson was looking out through the venetian blinds. In the room with him were Al Perkins, Sam Hastings, a secretary, and several other key executive officers of the university board of directors.

Dean Thompson said, "Look at them. Can you believe it? It's teeming out, and they're out there standing in it as if they were in a museum. In fact, the crowd's getting bigger." Still looking out the blinds, he looked to his left and saw a crowd of 40 more students march toward the athletic building, as if it was a fort in hostile territory. They were in full rain gear and had plenty more posters. "Al, come look at this," the dean said.

Al obeyed and saw what the dean had witnessed first. Then Al looked down below and saw ten garbage pails set on fire one by one. They were in the form of a huge octagon, with the pails placed in strategic positions on the perimeters of the desired shape they'd chosen. Al looked at the dean and said, "It's only 1:00 in the afternoon; wait until 3:00. There'll be 1,200 students out there."

"Are you kidding?"

"No, I'm not."

"Will it get violent like the last time?"

"No it won't. They learned a lesson last time. This is worse though,"

"What do you mean?"

"Well, last time was like a riot. It reached its climax, a few people got roughed up, it was over and everyone went home. This started yesterday. It's calm, controlled, but they don't leave."

"What do you mean, they don't leave? Everyone disperses when it gets late."

"No, Mel. It's a 24-hour a day demonstration. It's an around-the-clock vigil. It's a membership club. It's not growing, it's multiplying, and it's not going away. They're setting up tents."

Dean Thompson, flabbergasted by these developments. said, "When will this nightmare go away?"

From his seated position, Sam answered, "Probably not until school's closed!"

The dean reiterated, "Probably!" as he went to take another look out through the venetian blind-covered window. Then he said, "I wonder if they know something that we don't.

It was now Al's turn, who said, "Maybe so."

Sam asked, "What do you mean, Al?"

"I'm saying that maybe we had a great thing and didn't realize it."

"You can't mean Andy Trella as head coach?"

"Yes. That's exactly what I mean."

"But, that's ridiculous, Al. You saw he can't handle it."

The dean said, "I saw that he could handle it."

Al picked up where Dean Thompson left off. "If he wins, that's the only criteria."

Sam said, "We just contracted Nolan for $50,000."

"And that's $50,000 we threw away," Dean Thompson grumbled.

"Well, let him finish out the season for us," Sam offered.

That's what I'm afraid he's doing. He's finishing our season before we intended it to be finished. Al, what would you do?" Dean Thompson asked.

"I don't know. I can't call this one. It's a really, really big decision."

"That's what we get paid for."

"You talking about firing Castwell and reinstating the kid?"

"Yep! And let me make it more monumental for you. WGNB is just about ready to offer a contract to the university to televise the full 30-game schedule next year for $3.2 million. But we must get a bid to this year's tournament first. The network will not pick up the coverage if the basketball program isn't elevated to one of the rising one's in the country. Plain and simple. We get in the tournament, the university gets the full $3.2 mil. We don't, it's nothing. So, I ask you again. Would you keep Nolan Castwell? Can he turn it around right away?"

Al gave Dean Thompson a dead serious look and said, "No way! I don't think he can turn it around right away. In fact, I don't think he will turn it around at all."

The dean said, "Good. Decisions made. Castwell's out. Al, you'll have to dismiss him right away. I don't want him near the ball players for another hour."

Sam and the rest of the executives shook their heads in disbelief. They had just paid 50,000 bananas for this guy to answer their prayers, and all he did was debilitate and jeopardize their chance to lift the athletic program to the elite status that they had hoped for.

Sam said, "I can't believe this."

"I can't believe it either, Al said, "But we gotta do what we gotta do."

The dean said, "Exactly. Al, after you dismiss Nolan, tell that young Trella kid he's back in the saddle. And don't tell him anything about the television deal with the three big ones."

"You got it, Mel."

One of the executives very firmly asked Mel, "Mel, can this kid carry us through?"

"I don't know gentlemen, but I'm playing a hunch." Al said,

"What hunch is that?"

"Gentlemen, sometimes good things come in small packages."

Mel left the room, and the remaining participants were left looking at each other.

Al was speechless for several seconds, then said, "It is what it is."

CHAPTER

FORTY-THREE

The door slammed shut with a thunderous blast, and General Nolan Castwell came out of the room. He was fuming, to say the least. His face was flushed red. He was talking out loud as if he had a listener, and he did not. People in the hallways could hear every syllable he pronounced. It was as if he was speaking at a convention. Everyone stopped their normal course of business to pay attention to the quite loud speaker. The decibel level of his voice automatically shifted everyone's attention like a magnet.

"Never in the history of my entire life, professional or social, have I ever been subjected to such cruel and unusual punishment. For them to think for one conscious moment of the day that that young punk can out-coach me and run a college squad better than I can is absolutely absurd and ludicrous. Here I am hung out to dry without so much as a court-martial."

Castwell continued his tirade in public, even though the content of his speech should have been private. He was beyond embarrassment since he had just reached the apex of it only a minute ago. He marched around the corner of the hall like a thoroughbred on the loose. Actually, he was on the loose. Al had just done that to him.

Inside the room that Nolan Castwell had recently left, Al said to Sam, "Well, that went well." He smiled while Sam laughed.

Sam said, "What do we care, it's not our money."

"Precisely," said Al.

CHAPTER

FORTY-FOUR

Andy walked around the track that surrounded both the free weight equipment area and the hydraulic weight lifting machines at Lincoln's Health Spa. Tonight he had a guest, his girlfriend, Sheila. They had planned to use the gymnasium at the university, the weights, and the track, but with all the fuss and commotion, Andy decided to high tail it out of there and head off to the local private health club. Besides, he was spending way too much time at the university. Normally, Andrew went to Lincoln's Health Club once a week to attempt to get some exercise. It would also give him time to be alone and think. Some people would think it foolish for him to go to a health club when he could easily use the facilities at the university for free. So, once a week, he'd press and pull some weights for an hour and a half, twenty minutes on the track, a half hour of swimming, and then back and forth in the Jacuzzi and steam room before the final, long, hot shower. Another benefit of not being at the university facilities was that he'd be guaranteed not to be interrupted by students and players who'd recognize him and want to chat for several minutes.

Andy and Sheila were on a brisk walk around the running track. They were also doing some light chatting. Andy asked

Sheila if she was going to join the aerobic class that was due to start in ten minutes. The class ran for twenty minutes or so, and she was delighted to get a chance to bop and weave to the music. But before the class commenced, as they rounded one of the turns on the track they spotted Philip, Winthrop, and Bart entering the establishment as if they were cops issuing a search warrant.

"Look who's here," Andy said to Sheila.

"What are they doing here?"

"While you're finding out, I'll go catch one more set of aerobics, okay?"

"Sure, go ahead." They kissed and she departed.

When he reached the three of them, he asked, "What's up, guys? Wanna go for a swim? I'm gonna jump in right now."

Philip countered, "No, you're not."

"What do you mean?"

"Al Perkins wants to see you right away. He's still in his office."

Andy looked at his watch and said, "It's a quarter to ten. I've put enough overtime in to last the next two seasons."

Phil reiterated, "Andy, he wouldn't have sent us to find you if it wasn't important. He wants to talk to you right away."

"Why can't it wait? If I'm going to get fired, it can wait until tomorrow."

"Because the team is in turmoil right now, and it's not gonna change overnight."

"Yeah, it's true the team is in shambles right now. Al can thank himself and Nolan for that."

"I thought when the going gets tough, the tough get going."

"Yes, that was last week. But you know what, Phil? I'm not the head coach this week; somebody else is, and it's his problem. So tell Al to look for Nolan."

"He doesn't have to look for him. He just sent him packing."

"Get the hell out of here. You got more stories than the monkey, you know that, Phil?"

Phil took a step closer to Andrew, looked at him real hard, eye-to-eye, and said, "Do I? That's what you first thought when I called you about Coach and Bob Saunders. I wasn't lying then, and I'm not lying now."

Andy just stared at Phil for a few seconds, waiting for the prank to be over. But it wasn't a joke. Andrew looked to his left at Winthrop and to his right at Bart. Their facial expressions indicated that Phil definitely wasn't telling a fib. Andrew's face changed dramatically when he fully realized that Philip was speaking the truth.

"You gotta be kidding me! I don't believe you."

"Why don't you come see for yourself?" Phil turned and walked away from Andrew, while Andy just remained looking at Winthrop and Bart. Then he turned from them and walked away. After seven steps or so, he stopped walking, stood still, and looked down at his sneakers with his hands on his hips. Obviously, having better sense and second thoughts, he changed his mind and turned back, half-yelling to Winthrop and Bart as Phil was already outside.

"Hey! Tell Phil I said I'll take a quick shower. I'll be in Al's office in half an hour."

Winthrop and Bart smiled as if, somehow, some way, they knew Andrew would quickly change his mind.

FORTY-FIVE

Andrew found himself walking alone in a dark corridor, headed for Al Perkins' office. It was now twenty minutes past ten in the evening. The hallways were deserted and amazingly peaceful, unlike the way they were when the students were protesting the athletic department's decisions over the past three weeks. Andy left Sheila at the end of the corridor. She was sitting on a large window sill waiting for Andy's meeting to be over.

When Andy reached the designated door, he placed his hand on the door knob and turned back to look at Sheila for a moment. She was occupied with looking out the huge window and didn't notice that he was observing her. He turned the knob, heard the click, and sent the door ajar, then entered the office. What his eyes saw was a shocking surprise. In the room were Al Perkins. Sam Hastings, Winthrop, Bart, and Phil. The unexpected surprise was that the entire basketball team was present.

Immediately, Andy said, "Fella's, this can't be a surprise party, cause it's not my birthday. What's going on here?"

Al said, "Yes, it is, and we've got a surprise present for you."

"Oh, yeah? What's that?"

"Well, Andy, you're back in the saddle."

Andy was totally nonplussed as he wasn't quite sure what he

had heard. Then he looked around the room and saw big, wide smiles from each and every one of them. Andrew was unequivocally stunned. Finally he asked, "Where's Nolan?"

Jefferson came forward and announced to Andy, "He's history, man. Mr. Perkins gave him his pink slip tonight."

"This is really unbelievable, you know that?"

Al said, "You may not have much experience or the track record behind you as a head man, but these guys play for you, and they win under you. We've got eight losses, and that's too many to get into the tournament. But a slight winning streak and a win against Carolina will give us a great chance to receive a bid by the selection committee. Andrew, I want you to do me one favor–rev these guys up and beat Carolina."

Andy took a step forward toward Al, looked at him, and said, "I only have one question. Why are you guys in uniform?"

Washington stepped up and said, "Coach, we're ready to go to work through the entire night. We need to practice. We haven't played much lately."

Andy looked around the room at all of them and said, "Okay, let's do it. Let's play some basketball."

The door to Al's office opened with a thunderous blast. Andy came out first.

Sheila looked up the corridor from a distance and focused on what she saw. Behind Andy, she saw Winthrop, Bart, Phil, and the entire team filing out of Al's office like toy soldiers. They were all walking next to and behind Andrew, filling up the entire width of the hallway. The march had begun. They were all soldiers with an obvious quest on their minds, not to be denied. Sheila noticed they all seemed to be walking with a quick confident air about them. They appeared as a small army of marines on a mission from God, and they sure as hell were.

Sheila started a slow, hesitant walk toward the aggressive committee that was headed for the gymnasium.

Upon reaching her boyfriend, Sheila asked him, "Andy, what's going on?"

"We've got work to do?"

"What about Nolan?"

"What about him?"

"They fired him?"

"Absolutely. To put it in Nolan's words, it wasn't an honorable discharge."

Sheila smiled, lifted her head, and kissed him on the cheek. "Can I watch for a little while?"

"Sure, but you'll be all alone."

"That's okay. Good luck, Andy."

"Thanks."

They approached the double doors leading to the basketball arena. Winthrop and Bart each opened one of the sets of huge double doors entering the gymnasium. What Andy saw captivated his emotions and his soul. There were perhaps 1,000 students sitting in the stands, clapping their hands, giving him a standing ovation. They were sticking around for the all-night practice about to take place.

Sheila was more overtaken than Andy, who was also quite surprised, as the players started to run onto the basketball court.

Sheila said, "I'm not gonna last two months going out with you. I'm definitely gonna have a heart attack. I'll probably have gray hair by next week."

Andy said as he started to take his sweater off, "You know, Sheila, in two weeks, it's Christmas. I think a double set of pacemakers is in order for us."

He started to walk on the court to join his players as the audience continued clapping.

"Go get 'em, Andy," Sheila said.

He smiled and said, "I guess you're not gonna be alone. Here we go." He walked away from her toward the court, rolling up his sleeves.

FORTY-SIX

Andy was now suspended at this opportunity for success. It was as if head coaching had been converted from a previously hated jail house warden into the throne of a king. For the very first time, all obstacles had been removed, except for the one that is natural–the opposition. Many challenges that impeded his task were overcome with the decision leading to his reinstatement. Andy did not have to fight any longer against his players for the struggle of power and respect. He had it. He did not have to ignore the student body who were constantly rebelling against his previous appointment. The booster club and athletic department were done guiding and controlling him. They threw away the reins; the harness was shed. Somehow, he had now gained a fully charged endorsement.

If a head coach and his players were to excel against the big boy schools, they would need all the encouragement and support that the university could muster. The players would need encouragement from the student body to assist in fortifying their belief in themselves that they could accomplish something special in such a turbulent season. The University of Western Chicago had that kind of enthusiasm and inspiration necessary for their young, incredibly energetic new leader. The basketball team and the university were a single large force to be reckoned with in an attempt to snatch victory from the other, supposedly superior schools.

On the practice court, something unique was taking form. The usually eccentric black players were no longer jiving, laughing, joking and carrying on through the practice. They had lost a special friend and teammate in Willie Jones, and Andy never let them forget it. He used that as an additional component to fuel the fire within their hearts in order to produce dedication and commitment to become better than they ever were before, singularly and collectively. The impetus of his own conviction with being given a second chance, based upon his own personal merit, consummated the fortification of his and the team's common goal.

If Andrew had told them all to take a long walk off a short pier, they'd make it a short walk off a short pier. He was the power button. They were the amplifier, operating like a relentless machine on all gears, with all cylinders on full throttle. They jumped and leaped, and passed, and shot, and ran like the wind until 2:00 in the morning. Thank God the next day was Saturday. No classes. Sleep in.

In front of the whole squad, Jefferson told Andy, "Hey, Andy, you want us to do aerobics? We'll do aerobics. You want us to jump rope? We'll jump rope. You call the shots, bro. Not one of us is getting out of line with you ever again. It's time for this group to accomplish something before it's too late."

Andy took his words to heart and showed them by his facial expression that it meant a great deal to him. The astonishing degree of encouragement and cooperation, especially from the team itself, led Andrew to say, "Guys, one thing I want you to know. I'm gonna give you my best." That's all they needed to hear from him, and that's all he needed to hear from them.

Andy was totally inspired, enthused and focused, more than ever before. When they made him head honcho the first time, he had no subjects to command, just confrontations from every angle. Now he was the MAN, and he had a platoon of men behind him. And the team had an army of university students behind them. The magic carpet ride was about to begin as the force was now with them all.

Andy perched on a tall ladder leaning against the backboard of the ten-foot-high basketball hoop. He reached up and pointed to markings on the backboard that he wanted the players to touch in order to get the most of their jumping ability. He waved a 24-inch ruler, pointing it at the players as he instructed them. Standing three feet above the rim, he said, "Travis, my grandmother is dead in her coffin, six feet under. Even today she can still jump higher than you. Now come on, jump, goddamn it."

Travis Bennett ran and jumped extremely well, and the rest of the team followed suit. They were all dunking the basketball like they were munchkin donuts in a cup of coffee.

CHAPTER

FORTY-SEVEN

In Andy's personal life, other things were developing as a result of his return to the helm. Biggerman was back as his personal limousine driver. Firms had contacted him and asked him to endorse their products for advertising, from sneakers to automobiles, from McDonald's hamburgers to life insurance companies, from credit cards to breakfast cereals. Even Fedex, with its marketing and advertising headquarters based in Chicago, contacted him to do a single commercial displaying the overnight priority letter when it absolutely, positively has to be there. The McDonald's hamburger commercial was a joint venture with none other than Chicago's Mr. Michael Jordan, featured throughout the Chicago area.

Several local television networks were asking to corral his time and services for brief interviews. He was on the cover of three magazines in the month of December. He signed autographs on the campus grounds for little kids. He found himself at several charity drives, endorsing their existence and boosting the revenues for cancer funds.

At home in his apartment, he drew plays on his portable blackboard. He worked diligently at his desk, outlining strategies. He viewed game films of opponents to uncover and dissect weaknesses, identify their strengths, and whittle out game plans until two or three in the morning.

Sheila would surprise him with a plate of spaghetti as he worked at his desk. Naturally, she'd have to get a kiss in return for the dinner she had prepared.

One day while Andy and Sheila strolled on the campus grounds, new cement was being poured next to the grass near a university building. Andy noticed three kids putting their hand prints into the wet cement as he and Sheila walked by them. Andy stopped and signaled to Sheila, whispering that these were the very same culprits who had thrown the stone that struck Sheila in the head several weeks earlier. They retraced their steps, pushed the kids into the newly wet cement by kicking their buttocks, then pushed them all head first into the unformed concrete. The three punks rolled over, wondering what had happened. All three were covered with wet cement.

Though these were busy and good times for Andy Trella, he was still able to find the time to purchase a dozen red roses and greet Sheila at her door with a big smile when he picked her up for a date. Sheila's response was the same smile, and she rushed at him, charging like a pro football defensive end, eliciting a hug from him.

The city of Chicago was now alerted to the second upcoming hot basketball team. Jordan's Bulls were the top flavor of the town after six championships. But these days in December, charging toward the New Year, brought a second hot commodity. It was Andy Trella and his Western Chicago Eagles who were soaring, soaking up the city's interest, captivating their hearts and their souls.

CHAPTER

FORTY-EIGHT

Bobby O'Brien sat behind his desk in his office looking very much like the president of a Fortune 500 conglomerate. At Carolina University, he was treated not like the president of a company but as if he owned it. He was highly respected. His ego was in another stratosphere.

On the far wall were plaques of recognition, and in a display cabinet were various trophies, awards, and pictures distinguishing him as an accomplished current-day legend. He even had several photos of himself with popular celebrities of both the sports and entertainment field.

Across from his desk were four chairs, currently occupied by his four assistants. They all appeared intelligent and sophisticated. Two of them were well into their forties, and the other two were in their early thirties. The four men were all wearing their usual executive-type suits. Bobby O'Brien wore his usual slacks, white collared shirt with the two top buttons left open, and a cardigan sweater that was buttoned halfway up his shirt. He wore what he liked, and they wore what he insisted on.

He began addressing them. "Have any of you been aware of what's going on over at Western Chicago University?"

One of the assistants replied, "Yes, sir, Coach O'Brien.

They've been switching head coaches like musical chairs, which is extremely rare at this point in the season."

"Yes, I heard about what originally happened. I know Connors took a leave of absence, and his wife passed away. His first assistant took the head job at Idaho. So what have they done about it? Can any of you brief me as to what's going on over there?"

The same assistant who had originally spoken, continued, "Yes, sir. They supposedly have this young kid who is one of those guys with beginner's luck. Anyway, he took the Eagle team for ten days and put three victories in his pocket. Then they brought in Nolan Castwell of Princeton University to finish up the season for them in case Connors wanted to come back next year. Well, Nolan did much more harm than good, and they lost three straight under him, which seriously dampened their chances of making the tournament. So the athletic department turned around and decided to release Nolan and give the team back to the kid."

Bobby O'Brien's eyes lit up, showing that he was actually very surprised at this last piece of information. "Are you kidding me? They actually went through with that?"

"Yes, sir."

Watch the opposite happen. The kid probably won't win another game the rest of the season."

One of the other assistants finally spoke up, "They say he's crafty and spirited."

Bobby O'Brien said, "How old is he? Twenty-seven, twenty-eight?"

"Hey, Paul, every year, we hear about this. Same old story, same time of year. Some new upcoming hot shot coach with a very limited, mediocre team leads them to a great season. All of a sudden, he's the new genius of the game, and every year they get annihilated. You guys have been running this tune at me every year at this time."

"Yes, sir, but that's usually a guy who's been coaching as a head man for three, four, five years. This kid got nothing behind him. No track record at all."

Bobby O'Brien said, "Not to worry. We'll blow them out by 40 points.

When are we playing them, Saturday or Sunday?"

"We have Illinois on Thursday night and then Western Chicago on Sunday night."

Bobby O'Brien threw his body back into the luxurious reclining office chair and said, "I'm worried about the Illinois game. I may let one of you coach the Western Chicago game."

They all laughed as they knew he was jesting, implying that he may not even be needed for a victory versus Western Chicago.

Bobby O'Brien yawned and said, "How about some lunch, guys. Tell Sylvia to call the delicatessen. I'll take my usual."

FORTY-NINE

Winthrop, Bart, and Phil were sitting on the sofa and chairs in Andy's living room, their feet up on the coffee table. There were two cardboard pizza boxes lying on the table. One box was empty; the other had just one slice left that no one seemed to want. Andy was occupied with feeding his pet parrots. He spoke as he finished handing the last cracker to Spartacus and Moses.

"Okay, guys, time to go over defensive schemes. We have the basic two-three zone, the box, and one if that guy Rayford has a typical hot game. I like the one-three-one, also."

"Why don't you go straight up, man to man, against them?" Phil asked.

"Actually, I'd like to. We're playing best in man-to-man, but you cannot play that against Carolina."

"Do you think you'd like to employ full court presses or half-court traps?"

"I'm not sure." Then, a light bulb suddenly lit inside Andy's head. "Wait a minute. Why is it everyone institutes traps and presses when they're losing by eight, ten, when it's late in the game? Maybe we could shake this thing up a little. Play the beginning of the game like that. Foil their rhythm. Shake their feathers a little. They won't expect it. Change the entire tempo of the game. Play it in a frenzy from the start. If we can get the upper hand early, we can go to multiple defensive zones, preventing them from adjusting.

"That's not bad, Andy," Phil said. "I like it. Play the game in reverse. Instead of just feeling each other out the first eight minutes or so, a fast pace first half, and a slow down in the second half."

"Sounds good!" Bart said.

"Sounds real good," Winthrop echoed, "Providing we get the lead."

Phil said, "It could work."

Andy approached them. "It just might work. All right, guys, we're gonna have to split this scene. The White Tornado will be here in fifteen minutes."

Winthrop and Bart's eyebrows were raised in curiosity. Winthrop asked, "The White Tornado? What's that?"

"The cleaning lady," Phil answered. "She's unbelievable. You heard of Robocop. Well, this is Robomaid. She comes in with the face of a mad bull, messes the whole place up worse than it is now for an hour, and then cleans it all up in fifteen minutes. Looks like a wicked witch, works like a wizard."

Winthrop looked around the room. "I gotta see this lady."

"At your own risk, pal," Andy warned. "You better put a helmet and shoulder pads on, and I'd wear a cup, too."

"She hits below the belt?" Bart asked.

"Something fierce," Phil answered. "You'll feel like you're sparring with a cyclone, and she looks like a Cyclops."

Andy laughed. "A Cyclops has one eye. She's uglier than that."

Bart threw a friendly punch and connected with Winthrop's shoulder. "Oh, she's perfect for you."

They were laughing hysterically when both the doorbell and the phone rang out at the same moment. Winthrop answered the door, and there she was, the White Tornado, with a grimace on her face as if she wanted to choke a gorilla with her bare hands.

Winthrop was laughing, an uncontrollable laugh that would actually hurt most of his body, since thirty-five percent of it was stomach.

Bart and Phil were laughing, too, but not to the extent Winthrop was. Winthrop's state of laughter broke new ground when she looked him over and said, "Outta my way, Fatso, before I harpoon you with this mop."

Winthrop fell down in a chair as the three of them continued laughing in a contagious roar. They thought it was so funny that she was wider than he was, and she had called Winny, Fatso. Besides that, he wasn't embarrassed being called obese, when in other situations, he probably would have wanted to strangle the culprit who called him fat.

Having picked up the phone during this eventful moment, Andy wasn't laughing or smiling at all. In fact, a very new and different event was developing. It was Sheila on the other end, crying and upset. Andy's smile turned sour.

None of the others had noticed Andy at all, for they were mesmerized in the gales of laughter. All Andy said into the phone's mouthpiece was, "Are you home?" When he heard the response he said, "I'll be right there." He slammed the receiver down hard into the holding position.

He grabbed a coat and his car keys, using one fist for each, and in a flowing motion, hustled through the living room for the front door. Philip noticed Andy's alarmed state and shouted out, "Andy, what's the matter?"

"I don't know," Andy rushed on, "I think Sheila's hurt. I gotta go." He disappeared through the door a moment later.

After he left, Phil said, "Jesus Christ, I wonder what the hell happened now? I hope to God it wasn't a car accident." The three visitors stayed in Andy's apartment as the White Tornado vanished into another room.

Phil hobbled to the door on his crutches, opened it, and yelled out, "Don't drive too fast. Believe me when I tell ya." Then he looked down at the cast on his leg, reminding him of his own disregard for personal safety as a result of emotional preoccupation while driving. He was just passing the advice along to Andrew, since he knew that his friend's state of mind was somewhat equivalent to his at the time of his misfortune. The first prerequisite was met. Andy's emotional state of mind was quite impaired. But the second condition was not, Philip was not with him. Thus, he'd probably be safe. Andy could not hear Phil's remarks as he was already in his car and had started the engine.

When Phil closed the door and reentered the apartment, he looked at Winthrop and Bart, dumbfounded. "Come on, let's get out of here." Suddenly they heard pots and pans banging and sounding like they were falling all over the place. The three of them looked at one another without commenting. They'd leave that to the parrots.

Spartacus said, "Look out! White Tornado."

Moses said, "On the loose."

The two parrots scrambled about their cage, looking for cover as if it were a Chinese Fire Drill.

CHAPTER

FIFTY

Andy's Chevy Camaro was airborne. All four tires were a full six inches above the pavement on this quiet Gildersleeve highway. The incline of the road, combined with the inertia that the automobile manifested, forced the vehicle to have the trajectory of a missile in flight. Andy did not take note of the rolling hill in the road up ahead but realized its presence at a moment too late, leaving him no choice but to ride out the seven foot jump. The Chevy zipped into the air, doing close to 40 miles per hour, knifing through the stratosphere as if Evel Kneivel were bronco busting the metal machine.

He was fearful, as the hang time lasted nearly half that of a football kicker's 4.8 kick-off. Since Sheila's well-being had inhabited one hundred fifty percent of his concentration, he was not thinking that Officer Sal Basilia could possibly be on the other end of the road, plotting to nail him once again. But that was okay, he wasn't. He was in the waiting room of Mercy Hospital, biting his nails, chiseling them away as if he were a squirrel who thought he was transformed into a sculptor. His wife, Julie, had just given birth to a new, 10 lb. 4 oz. baby.

Fortunately, Andy was able to steer the car perfectly straight as the tires reacquainted themselves with the familiar road. His frame of mind readjusted as he realized he was in too much of a hurry. He wasn't sure if it was life or death. However, she was seriously alarmed, and he didn't know why. When it came to Sheila, no matter what, when she was in distress, it was like life or death to him. With that thought, the speedometer pushed forward once more over the speed limit. If possible, he would have broken the sound barrier if he could get to her in one piece any sooner. His hands were at the ten o'clock–two o'clock position on the wheel that he held tightly in preparation for a possibly dangerous situation. Once the tires made the commitment to reconnect with the earth, it would be a kiss that wouldn't happen again. The next kiss would be his upon Sheila the minute he saw her. But for the present, Andy was a pilot in a cockpit, looking only to reach Sheila.

Even as the vehicle was pulled down with the force of indefatigable gravity a minute ago, Andy whispered to himself. "What's the matter with me? Slow down, asshole! What's the big deal? So what if you get there thirty seconds later." He then slowed the vehicle down, but a minute later he was back up to 55. Sometimes, some things just don't matter when you care for something, or in this case, someone else, more than yourself. That was Andy and how he felt about Sheila.

With the episode of the car having shot above the pavement over, Andy could concentrate his thoughts on Sheila. What could possibly be wrong with her? He just prayed she wasn't hurt. He had seen her that way once before, and once was enough. It didn't matter if it was his fault or not. He just couldn't have her hurt by anyone for any reason. Case closed. If she wasn't hurt, then he deduced that something had happened to someone else she knew. He said to himself, "Please, not death. There's been enough of that lately." The one thing he knew was that he could comfort her, and he just couldn't wait till he could. He had four and one-half miles to travel. He'd be there in three minutes.

CHAPTER

FIFTY-ONE

Andy sprinted over the grass of the house where Sheila was renting her studio apartment. A thin branch from a nearby oak tree nearly poked him in the eye as he ran past. He noticed the front door was wide open, which caused many wild thoughts to fill his mind. He raced the rest of the way at full tilt until he found himself in the front foyer.

Andrew fixed his eyes on Sheila, who was sitting on a sofa in the unusually large foyer, her eyes tearfully bloodshot.

"Sheila, what happened?

She got up from her sitting position and approached him. "My sister and her husband were in a really bad car accident in Green Bay. They're in the hospital, and both are in critical condition. They might not make it, Andy." Sheila was crying, tears rolling down her cheeks, causing emotional pain for Andy. Her tear-filled face took on a different form from what Andy had seen before. It did not bother him to the point where he was turned off to her. It did bother him tremendously that she was so emotionally troubled and shaken.

He grabbed her, pulled her close to him, and gave her a strong hug. "They'll make it, honey," he said forcefully. "They're both in the hospital, right?"

Sheila backed off from the embrace, wiped her nose with a crumpled up tissue, and responded, "Yes."

"Are you going home?"

"Yes, tonight. I just booked a flight."

"What time?"

"9:00."

"Come on, I'll help you pack." He grabbed her hand and started up the stairs to her apartment. His take-charge attitude managed to comfort her to a small degree. Andy led the way, and Sheila was a half step behind him.

"Andy, can you drive me to the airport?"

"Of course, I'll drive you to the airport. Do you think I'd let you hitch-hike?" Sheila smiled slightly. He continued, "I'd drive you back to Green Bay if I could, but I can't really leave these parts these days, if you know what I mean."

Understanding his point Sheila said, "I know. It's like you're a doctor on call twenty-five hours a day."

"You can say that again but don't. How long will you be?"

"Five days, through Sunday."

Andy thought that was four days too long as they reached the top of the staircase and entered her apartment, forgetting to shut the door behind them.

CHAPTER

FIFTY-TWO

They were at the departure gate. The airline had just called for boarding for the seat she had been assigned. This particular wing of O'Hare International Airport was unusually and unexpectedly quiet. Sheila kissed Andy and parted from him.

"Wait a minute, Sheila," Andy said. "I have something for you. Give me your hand." He grasped her hand and pulled it toward him gently as Sheila looked at him curiously. Then he wrapped a quaint gold bracelet around her wrist. This was the last thing in the world she expected. It was such a sweet gift due to the element of surprise. It probably wasn't the most opportune moment for him to offer his first gift to her, but in another way it was. He knew for sure that it would make her flight back home a lot less burdensome.

"Is this why we stopped at your place first?" Sheila asked.

"Something like that."

On the return flight, she'd have a lot of answers to her questions regarding the condition of her relatives. However, on the flight there, all she would do was think and worry and wonder about her family. By giving her the bracelet, he knew it would give her some brief moments of happiness, replacing some of her worry.

"Since you'll be gone so long, I just wanted you to have something from me. I haven't had a girlfriend in quite some time, and I want you to know that I care about you. I'm gonna miss you while you're gone."

Sheila was consummately swept up, as it was such a perfect goodbye for such a temporary absence. She moved closer to him and looked him in the eyes, then kissed him passionately and said, "The next time you blink, I'll be back."

"I wish that was true."

"Well, I'll be back soon enough." As she walked away from him she called out, "Thanks for the bracelet, Andy."

"You're welcome," then in a determined way, he added, "Hey! Don't forget you're going home, and you're bringing good luck to your family, alright?"

Sheila shook her head affirmatively, manufacturing a positive outlook. "I'll call you tomorrow night."

"Have a good flight."

She strolled through the boarding gate, turned around, and waved goodbye. Andy watched her, thinking she looked like a little girl going off to her first day of school with noticeable apprehension.

Sheila disappeared into the gateway's tunnel, and Andy missed her already. She wasn't gone for five seconds, and he wouldn't see that lovely face for at least five days. That didn't appeal to him at all. He dreaded it. But then again, he knew he was going to be quite busy.

CHAPTER

FIFTY-THREE

It was 4:00 in the morning. It was quite dark and utterly quiet in the apartment. Even the layers of air seemed still, dead to existence whatsoever. Andy tossed and turned as he couldn't sleep. He threw the blankets off him like an Olympic javelin performer and sat up on the edge of his bed abruptly, as though beamed into that position. He felt that he was frozen in time. It was like he had been photographed and was really contained in the picture. Possibly it was insecurity. Maybe it was that he was thinking of Sheila and wondered what she had found out about her family. Whatever their conditions were, it was sure that Sheila knew by now, but he did not. This was insecurity in its worst form, being up and alone during the dead of night not knowing.

He knew why he couldn't sleep. It was a combination of reasons; Sheila was one. The second concern was the very big contest against Carolina on Sunday night. It was still four days away. One thing he was certain of was that it would be quite a contrast of the sounds, or lack of them, in his apartment as compared to the roaring crowd's noise on Sunday night.

Andy knew he had more work to do in preparing the Eagle team for Carolina. It was so strange, but it was an absolutely valid contention. This particular basketball game was not a championship game, nor was it one to determine first place position. It was a simple single game on the schedule. But it was distinctly, uniquely important for Western Chicago University. To upset a Carolina university team would be great for the psyche and ego of all Western Chicago leaders and its student body. A victory would almost guarantee an at-large bid to the post season National Collegiate Tournament, which would bring in additional revenue to the university. This, in turn, would probably be the true overriding factor for WBNB cable company network to consummate a deal to broadcast the complete thirty-game season back into the Chicago area next year for a handsome price of $3.2 million, payable to Western Chicago University.

Western Chicago was nineteen and eight. Carolina University was 27–3, tied for the third best record in the entire nation. A good game, a sound performance, might secure the Eagles team a berth in the upcoming March Madness tournament. A win would clinch that berth. The selection committee would offer bids of invitation to the universities to enter the extravagant single elimination tournament. The committee selects 64 schools out of a possible 396 Division One universities across the United States. The University of Western Chicago had never been to one. They just wanted to get there one time. They knew they could never win the whole goddamn thing, but they just wanted to get there. A win versus Carolina should clinch that, and, of course, would bring in revenue to boot. It would also do something else for the financial interests of the university, but Andrew knew nothing about that at this point. It was basically simple mathematics. If you bested one of the best, you were deserving of an opportunity to represent your university by competing in the classic basketball extravaganza in Division One college basketball's March Madness.

The CBS television network signed a billion dollar deal to broadcast every single tournament game, back to each university's home town. Naturally, certain games would be televised nationwide during prime time hours. But the $1 billion CBS paid was for a full seven-year term.

These tournament games only took place three weeks out of the full 52 weeks in a fiscal year. One billion dollars for 21 weeks of televised coverage over a seven-year span. It wasn't an understatement by a long shot that there were exorbitant amounts of cash thrown around the lights of college basketball and football programs. A win by Western Chicago on Sunday would practically force the selection committee, obliging them to offer a bid to the college.

Andy was thinking that there was so much left to do. One: finalize a complete game plan of attack versus the opponent. Two: motivate and prepare the squad emotionally. Such a fine line to attempt to conquer. The Eagles needed to be confident but not overconfident, loose but not wound, and yet not be intimidated. For a moment, his mind switched to wonder if Sheila would be back in time for Sunday night. Then, just as fast, his mind switched back to Bobby O'Brien. Andy knew that to beat Carolina, the players would need to do more than to outplay them. He would have to out-coach the great Bobby O'Brien.

O'Brien was the best coach in college athletics. Four national titles to his name. He was a legend in his own time. He had compiled the best win-loss percentage of all college coaches in the entire country. Bobby O'Brien was closing in on the century mark of wins for the fourth time against only 92 losses in his entire college coaching career. He was selected to the basketball's Hall of Fame in Springfield, Massachusetts.

As great a coach as he was, he was quite a controversial figure. He projected intimidation to a forbearing degree. Habitually, he resorted to intimidation tactics, which could have altered the referees from calling a fair game. It may have been unusual, but Bobby O'Brien's Carolina teams always had less fouls committed against them than their opponents. It had been four years since his team had committed deliberately more illegal fouls than the opponent, and that time his squad of players only committed two more than the other team. Not that Bobby O'Brien's teams didn't foul, for they were excellently coached and disciplined from that behavior. They would get away with a half a dozen or so non-calls per game. They weren't a dirty team that played flagrantly. They simply got away with illegal pushes and shoves more than any other team.

Bobby O'Brien would erupt like a volcano when a decision went against his team, and he would let the referees know about his displeasure. By displaying this tactic, he was sure that the referees would not call many of them, even if they did occur. For they would get an earful from Coach O'Brien, intimidating everyone who came into contact with him.

He also had four assistant coaches he had groomed, and all had specific areas to cover. They were good at it. All of them from Ivy League schools, just as Andy was. When they'd enter the arena on Sunday night, they'd look like four attorneys, all working on one insurance negligence case worth millions of dollars. The boss man they'd report to was the judge himself, Bobby O'Brien.

It was a devastating fact for Andy to acknowledge that Bobby O'Brien had eons of experience more than he. He had more knowledgeable assistants, better players, and the referees in his pocket. Realistically, it was as if Bobby O'Brien was the godfather of rural society on the college basketball level.

There were two things Andy felt really good about at the moment, and he'd come up with more over the next three days. First, this was a home game, which was a big consideration for Western Chicago, and second, when the game started, the score would be even at zero to zero. Unless, of course, Bobby O'Brien could figure out a way to manipulate the referees to alter that scenario.

Andy suddenly had a flashback and pictured in his mind the time he broke his wrist playing basketball in high school. He had fallen to the floor so hard that his wrist snapped, pointing his hand in an unnatural direction. Andy was now nine years past that suffering event, but he sat in bed holding and rubbing the wrist that had been fractured so many years ago. He got up to get a drink of water, then went over to the parrots' cage with cheese and crackers. It would be a good way to let the rest of the night pass.

CHAPTER
FIFTY-FOUR

Andrew was perched over the stove in his kitchen. It was 6:35 a.m., and daylight was gradually seeing its way through the kitchen window curtains. He was cooking some breakfast. Since he'd barely slept a wink, he thought the least he could do was start his day on a full stomach. Andy had eggs frying sunny side up in the pan.

He also had the clock radio on, and the song currently playing was a love song by the group Heart. The repetition of words throughout the song had succeeded in completely captivating his attention. He was mesmerized to the point of being lost within it. The song's lyrics kept needling him each time they were sung. "What About Love?" was a hit single by the group from their first best-selling album, along with their fame and fortune.

Andrew's eggs were almost black. He was so wrapped up in the song, permitting the essence of its meaning to reflect into his own personal love life. He was so hypnotized by the song that it only reminded him of Sheila, causing him to forget totally that he was cooking. The look on his face was as if he were in a trance. He was not worried about losing Sheila at all. She was just as much involved with him as he was with her. He managed to realize, and for the very first time, that he was definitely head over heels about her. He knew he loved her. The relationship had taken off like a rocket. But because she was gone on a short sojourn, it made him aware of not only his desire for her, but his truly unblemished need for her.

He finally looked down at his breakfast-to-be and saw that his eggs were post mortem. They were more than fried, they were barbecued. Once he had taken note and comprehended what he had done, he said aloud to himself, "Jesus, I'm really in love with Sheila." He then went over to the refrigerator and pulled out a bottle of barbecue sauce. He sat down at the kitchen table and poured a flood of sauce over his eggs.

Look what love does to you, he thought to himself as he ate. *It certainly makes you crazy. Look at me. Barbecue sauce over a half-dozen eggs. I wonder if I should mix some tuna fish in and probably a stomach pump for a chaser.* He tasted the concoction and thought it wasn't as bad as it appeared. Then he again thought to himself, *Andy, you've got a job to do and a pretty tough one at that. Stay focused. Be in love, but don't go bonkers. The Eagle team will accomplish that trick for you.* Then he threw out of the rest of the eggs, having only eaten one of them.

CHAPTER

FIFTY-FIVE

Andy walked up the driveway to his apartment carrying a briefcase. He seemed exhausted by the sluggish way he carried himself. Explosively, he became charged up as a rivet of enthusiasm bolted from his spine to his toes and back up toward his head as he heard the telephone ringing inside his apartment. He guessed that it was Sheila calling him from Wisconsin. He opened the door in a second, flung his briefcase onto the sofa so quickly that it would have frightened the dog, had he had one, and raced toward the phone.

Once he picked up the receiver he was relieved, as Sheila had called to check in with him, as promised.

"Sheila, hi. How are you?"

"I'm okay."

"How's your sister and her husband.?"

"It wasn't as critical as I was led to believe. They're going to be okay, just like you said."

"I'm so relieved. I thought it could be fatal. Well, it's a good thing you went home. I guess you brought good luck with you."

"I know."

"So, what's their condition?"

"My sister, Sandy, had to get ten stitches in her arm and also fractured two of her ribs. Her husband, Paul, broke his collarbone and also has a concussion."

"How did it happen?"

"Some idiot lost control of his car and jumped the divider. The police officer said the driver was DWI."

"Thank God they'll be alright. They just need time to get better."

"I know. Andy?"

"What?"

"I miss you."

This made him so happy. He was on cloud ten. It was the first time she had said it.

She continued, "I love my bracelet, also. It's great."

"Great things for a great person."

"Andy, you always say the right thing."

"Thanks."

"How are you doing? Anything crazy happening since I left? I know it's quite ordinary for bizarre stuff to occur in your line of work."

"Believe it or not, nothing out of the ordinary has happened since you've been gone. It's been a great pleasure. So, do me a favor and stay in Green Bay."

"Ha! Hal Ha! Very funny, wise-guy. Maybe I'll do just that."

Andy decided to get serious after his attempt at humor. He said, "Are you kidding? I'm going through withdrawal here. Cold turkey, girl."

"Really?"

"Yes."

"Me, too."

Sheila felt very content and more than appreciative for the way he was admitting his feelings about her. In the past she resorted to skating away from men that came on strong, at the primordial stages of a relationship. But with Andy, it wasn't that way. There were several clandestine occurrences that made her believe she should trust her feelings and him, as well. For one, the way they met. When each one of them seemed to take turns in being preoccupied with themselves and ignoring the other person. There was the very unusual first date, where he never informed her that he was the coach who had just been promoted on a temporary basis and ended up receiving so much publicity around the campus, as well as the city of Chicago. Just as they say, things usually happen in three's. What really became the clincher that knocked her off her feet was when she was literally knocked off her feet when the rock was thrown at him, striking her instead.

She had seen how upset he was, how much he consoled her, took care of her, how livid he was at the culprits. She adored how poised he was with her during the small crisis and how gentle he was with her during it. His anger at the guilty participants only manifested how much he cared about her well being. Aside from that, they really were best friends, maintaining an honest interest and appreciation of each other, along with their charismatic sexual desire for one another.

Andy said, "I just have one question for you. What day and time are you coming back?"

"I'm flying back into O'Hare on Delta Flight 4206 on Sunday, arriving at 5:45 p.m.

Andrew was alarmed. "Oh, no! I can't pick you up at that time!"

"Why not?"

"The Carolina game starts at 6:00."

"Oh, Andy, I heard it's supposed to snow on Sunday. I can't have one of my girlfriends pick me up. It's an hour's ride back to the university. If it snows, I can't tie one of my girlfriends up for three hours on the road in a snowstorm."

"Yeah, that's true. Listen Sheila, take a cab right to the Horizon. I'll pay for the fare."

"You don't have to do that."

"Wait a minute, just because we might be considered an item

here doesn't mean I can't reimburse you. If there wasn't a game, I'd be picking you up, right?"

"Right."

"Now it might cost you fifty bucks. I'm paying for it, and you come straight to the Horizon, okay?"

"Okay, Andy."

Sheila resigned herself to listening to him. She liked when he took charge. It was one of those instances where the woman liked very much when the man took charge.

"Okay, honey. I'll see you Sunday night."

"Andy?"

"What?"

"I love you."

"I love you too."

"I'll see you Sunday."

"Hey, Sheila, bring a little of that good luck back with you Sunday night. I think I'm gonna need it!"

"You got it. Goodnight, Andy."

"Good night, Sheila."

Andy hung up the phone and felt exuberant. He was astonished that he wasn't nearly as tired as he had been twenty minutes ago. Sheila's phone call brought life into the remainder of his night. His battery was fully recharged, and now he wouldn't be able to sleep for a while. Then he thought how all he did was speak to her. Imagine his mood if she was there with him. Electrocution, followed by nuclear explosion. But the reality was she wasn't there. She was in much colder Green Bay, Wisconsin, and the snow season was approaching the midwest in full force. But what he did have was a concrete day and time that she would be back.

After throwing some crackers to his pet parrots, Andy sat down on the sofa with a pen and pad and started to scratch out game plan strategies for the Carolina game. He needed solid strategy and plenty of backup plans in case any of his elective strategies were thwarted by Bobby O'Brien. Tomorrow after practice was concluded, Andy would hold one additional 45-minute strategy lecture. He'd brief the entire team on plans, tactics, and basic strategy against Carolina. He'd even open up the discussion for opinions from the team itself, figuring they might give him two or three ideas that would assist in their mutual goal of victory. Andy knew he needed everything possible to pull off this single small miracle. He wanted to cover all the bases, even if there were a thousand of them. He did not want to make the mistake of omitting one of them.

CHAPTER

FIFTY-SIX

One of the ball players had just hit a basket to end the daily hour-long scrimmage that was played to conclude each practice session. Andy walked onto the court with Phil, Bart, and Winthrop. Winthrop and Bart handed out water bottles and towels. Andy said, "Okay, guys. Good strong practice. I like what I'm seeing very much. It's great to see you all working so hard. Why don't you hit the water fountain and come back and take a seat. We're going to have a little chat about Carolina."

About half of them stayed there with water bottles being passed around like an old Indian peace pipe. The other half took off for the water fountain.

The coaches and some of the players were standing about the foul line. Andy used the brief time to instruct Jarvis Williams on some defensive strategy that he was getting burnt on time and time again. He informed Jarvis on the proper way to front a man, lanes to let him run into, and what lanes not to permit him to enter. Andy moved about the top of the key area, positioning Bart and Winthrop as pawns, representing fictitious players and continuing on to developing a scheme that was giving Williams so much trouble.

Winthrop looked more like a buoy, stipulating the boundary lines of shallow water in the channel of a bay.

Upon the return of the other players, Andy said, "Okay, gentlemen. We have a lot to talk about."

Everyone began walking toward the sidelines and into the stands about five rows up from the floor. They sat in the bleacher seats, leaving at least two or three empty seats between all the players. The three assistants also sat down in a formation just as the players had.

Andy stood alone and elaborated. "Guys, we have a claw to clean. This school has only played Carolina two times. Lost by 46 and 34. This year, once again, they're one of the top five in the nation." He bellowed out, "Do not let those bastards scare you!" Immediately, he calmed down just as quickly as he had gotten charged up. "Jefferson, stand up. Are you a senior?"

"Yes, sir."

"Washington, stand up. Are you a senior?"

"Yes, sir."

"Bennett!" Andrew did not have to tell him to stand, he naturally did. They were beginning to catch on to his flow. "Are you a senior?"

"Yes, sir, Coach."

"Skin Head and Skin Brain. Are you guys seniors?"

Uniformly they recited, "Yes, sir."

"We have five seniors and four juniors on this team. They have two juniors and one senior, and the rest are freshmen and sophomores. Yet, everyone says they're the more experienced club. They may have the more experienced and better coach, but he can't play in the game. It's you guys against his guys and that's all there is. Don't be intimidated by them. If a guy pushes you, push him back. If a guy punches you, punch the mother back. Don't worry about Bobby O'Brien and all the bullshit he brings with him. If you guys are taking care of his boys on the court, I won't let you down. You all know he brings his bag of tricks and works the game over like a magician. I've been preparing for all his shit, just like the few episodes I had with you. Now, they have two really good players: Rayford, the scorer, and Nathan the rebounder. Skin Head and Washington, when a shot goes up, I don't want both of you to go for the rebound."

"Say, what?"

"I want you to take turns. One of you goes for the ball, the other goes after Nathan. Screen him away from the ball. This will confuse and frustrate him. He won't know what to do. Don't foul him, just stand face to face with him. We're gonna play this game in reverse. Full court pressure from the start. A box and one zone to stop Rayford in the first half. In the second half, we'll abandon both the press and the box and one and go with multiple changing zones on every defensive set. This way, they can't make adjustments to our adjustments. Tomorrow night, Carolina's not going to play basketball, they're going to be guessing on how to play basketball. I'm not worried about rebounding, scoring, passing. I know you all will do a great job. Just remember one thing. Play smart by using each other. You only have to be better than them for forty minutes, not thirty, not fifty, not three days. Just outplay them for forty minutes.

"It's Saturday night. Who's going out tonight? Tell me the truth, guys. It's no big deal. My skin's white, but I'm still one of the brothers, you all know that."

Kennedy raised his hand and said, "I was taking my girl dancing tonight."

"Why don't you go see a movie with her and make it an early night, Kennedy? It's not like you play only three minutes a game, ya know. You're a starter; you average 30 minutes a game."

Kennedy said. "It's a done deal, Coach."

"Good. Tonight you should all relax, read the newspaper, a magazine, play checkers or cards."

Turner said, "How about some chess. You wanna come to the dorm tonight, play some chess?"

Andy looked at Turner and said, "No thanks, Eric. I'll be playing chess tomorrow night with the legend himself. Before we break up, does anybody have any suggestions, opinions, or questions on our game plan?" Half of them raised their hands.

The group and their leader and his assistants talked for an additional 35 minutes, discussing strategy and game plan scenarios for the upcoming foe. From afar. within the gymnasium, they looked like a small platoon deciding where they should set up camp for the night. Actually, they were a single-minded platoon with a purpose and not one to decide where to dig the next fox hole. They were on a mission not from God, but for themselves.

FIFTY-SEVEN

Philip, Winthrop, and Bart were over at Andrew's apartment once again. They had already eaten an early lunch together and were forced into waiting for game time still six hours away. In a little less than an hour, Biggerman would be picking them up in the limousine, taking the four of them to the Rosemont Horizon. They were all trying to relax, a difficult task to accomplish when the most prevalent emotion was impatience. Each of them could not deny that no matter what they did or said at the moment, it couldn't possibly be as important or as meaningful as the big event that would be taking place that evening. They knew that the players were like zombies the previous night, pacing the hallways of the dormitories like the night of the living dead. National television would do that. Andy and his coaching buddies were talking to each other, commenting on how certain players handled the night. More than half of them had had a sleepless night.

Winthrop informed them that when they checked in on Washington, he was in his room hanging from a chin-up bar upside down, doing curl-ups at 2:30 in the morning. Most of the players spent the night walking back and forth to the soda machines, telephones, and bathrooms in the dormitory corridors.

A couple of them had just watched horror movie after horror movie into the wee hours. Andy asked Bart and Winthrop if they thought the players seemed nervous or just impatient.

Luckily, both Bart and Winthrop told Andy the answer he wanted to hear. They were not nervous, they were ready.

As the game was against Carolina and near the end of the regular season, it was being picked up and broadcast around the nation. The broadcasters themselves were nationally known college basketball experts Jimmy Tacker and Bill Black. If ever there was a time for Western Chicago University's basketball team to strike a big blow, this was certainly it. Except for possibly a win in the glorified March Madness Tournament, that would be euphorically better.

However, just before game time would roll around, Jimmy Tacker would put things into perspective before going into actual game analysis. On the air, he'd proclaim that there was a strong likelihood that it wouldn't be much of a contest, and that the Carolina Cougars were on a roll and could not be stopped by such an up and down inconsistent team. He would also give much of the weight of his opinion due to the strong imbalance of the opposing coaching staffs. Tacker reserved his opinion based strictly on the comparison of the coaches. It was clearly a David versus Goliath scenario. Andy Trella was too young, too inexperienced, too unknown, while his counterpart was truly a legend in his own time. Bobby O'Brien was the only college coach to win four national titles, all with the Carolina Cougars. The only one to win more than that was John Wooden of UCLA, whose teams had won it all an astounding twelve times. Bobby O'Brien was closing in on having four hundred victories to his credit. Andy Trella had three. Bobby O'Brien had four assistants who knew basketball as if they graduated from Yale with a law degree. Tacker suggested that this would be a major struggle for Western Chicago and its new young coach.

On the television in Andy's apartment, a studio host broadcaster, Gary Olson, was conducting an interview with none other than Bobby O'Brien himself. The room fell quiet as all eight ears paid strict attention to what the legendary coach had to say. Olson held his microphone in front of Bobby O'Brien's mouth and would become quite embarrassed being put on the spot by Coach O'Brien, who was being his usual arrogant old self.

Olson asked, "How's it feel, Coach, to be going to the Big Dance for the twenty-second year in a row?"

"That's a dumb question. Can't any of you guys ever ask intelligent questions? I'm getting tired of the same stupid questions over and over. Of course, it feels good. It doesn't feel great. I've been there twenty-something times already. Go ahead, ask me something vaguely intelligent."

Olson tried again, doing a great job of maintaining his composure. "Coach O'Brien, no matter what region the committee sends the Cougars to, do you think you'll be a number one seed?"

"Ah, see that? He asked a better question," O'Brien said. "I knew you could do it. Ah, well. There's four regions, so that means four number one seeds. Since we're tied for number three in the nation, I can't imagine us not getting one of the top four spots. After all, 30–3 would be one of the best records in the nation."

Olson corrected O'Brien. "I thought the Cougars were 27–3 at the moment with three games to play."

Coach O'Brien made a smirk and said, "They're in the win column, pal, I can assure you."

Bobby O'Brien left the reporter with such a swift move that it made him feel like he was a kid that just had his candy snatched from him.

In Andy's living room they looked at each other silently, waiting for someone to break it. Phil, in a retaliating manner said, "Always so calm, so cool. I'd like to see his feathers get ruffled just once."

"That's okay. That's just fine. That's exactly the perfect attitude we need from him," Andy said.

Winthrop and Bart were flabbergasted by Bobby O'Brien's remarks on television but remained silent and content with listening to Andy and Phil communicate.

Phil said, "Is he unbelievable, or what? He just assumed three more victories before being played. If he was really smart, he would have said, 'Don't forget, we still have three games left'."

Andy said, "Yeah, well, maybe Mr. O'Brien has been counting his chickens before they hatched." Andy sat back with a smile on his face and continued. "Remember what I was saying yesterday? Everyone favors Big Bad Carolina. They have all the experience, yet we outnumber their seniors five to one, their juniors four to three. I'll tell ya something else. I've been watching his teams play for eight years. We know how Carolina plays their game. We know what they are going to try and do to us. I'll tell ya, O'Brien has no idea what type of game we're going to play. He doesn't know jack shit about us, and he can't even guess. We're a nobody team to him. If we're nobody to him, then our players are nobody to his team. We're gonna change tempo and rhythm all night long. We'll employ multiple change defensive zones. Every time he tries to figure out what type of strategy we're using, we'll change it that quickly. By the time he substitutes and makes adjustments, we'll be in different sets of zones. This will confuse his players. It won't confuse him. Eventually, he'll figure it out, but he won't be able to convey to his team quick enough. The only thing we mustn't do is get into a walk 'em down straight up game. That's when Carolina's at its best, and they'd be too strong for us."

Phil said, "Wait till the brothers hear this."

"Hear what?" Winthrop asked.

Answering Winthrop, but looking right at Andy, Phil said, "He's gonna let them run and gun."

Andy added, "That's right. We're gonna turn 'em loose and maybe."

Winthrop and Bart were smiling like they received some incredible wisdom from a prophet.

Phil stood up, getting carried away, "Are you kidding? You're telling the brothers they can run and gun in a real game? They won't stop. They'll be relentless, not to mention happy as shit."

Andy said, "Screw it! We're pulling out all the stops on this one. We're gonna push Carolina to the limit."

"We're gonna beat their asses inside and out."

Phil was talking excitedly to himself.

They all looked around the room at each other and felt a rush of inspiration. A total, uncommon, extraordinary feeling, as if they were at a seance and a ghost of Christmas past had just given them a Christmas present.

Andrew stood up at the coffee table and looked at Winthrop, Bart and Phil and said, "We all might not be here next year. But tomorrow night, you guys are going to see the wildest war on a basketball court that you'll ever see in your life." Andy was not lying. It was his turn to be a prophet, and he would not be wrong.

CHAPTER

FIFTY-EIGHT

Andy, Phil, Winthrop, and Bart entered the Beta dormitory housing complex from the entrance at the side of the building. They walked together down the long, narrow corridor and headed to Alan Jefferson's room. On reaching their destination, they found the door to his room left open and Jefferson was lying down in his bed reading a sports magazine. Andrew knocked on the door and entered with his buddy assistant coaches.

Jefferson got up and asked, "Coach, what's up."

"Jeff, get the guys. There's one important thing I forgot to tell you about."

Cooperating, Jefferson answered, "Sure thing. I'll be right back." Jefferson left the room, leaving the door wide open as it was occupied by the foursome. Andy sat down in an armchair near Jefferson's desk.

In a four-minute time span, Jefferson had the entire team in his small room, now holding fourteen people. The brothers were all standing barely within the doorway of the room. Jefferson said, "Coach, they're all here."

"Now," Andy said, "for the part you'll all be anxious to hear about. The offensive style and strategy we're going to employ against Carolina is that we're gonna play the brother's style of ball. Turn it loose, guys. We're gonna run and gun. First half only. Got it? Wait a minute. First half only."

The brothers were all dumbfounded. They were astounded at this, their preferred philosophy of play. They never expected to hear their greatest forte being employed as the style of play on a regimented college basketball level. They were clearly surprised, yet they couldn't have been happier. Phil, Winthrop, and Bart smiled as they watched the brothers whoop it up.

Andy then told them to settle down. "It's the only way to shake up this type of Carolina team. When they see you playing your type of game, they could panic.

The brothers were fully exploding with joy. They had their hands in the air, clapping and lifting each other up. Glenn Johnson, who never spoke a word in any team meeting said, "You know what? That means... it means we're all going pro."

The fellas all laughed and started tapping and hitting him in a fun way. They continued jiving and carrying on in the hallways. It was a brief party, then they broke off into small groups. They were high fiving it and informing one another of what kind of moves they were going to trick on the court.

Andy turned to Phil as they were still in the small dorm room while all the players were filtered into the hallway. "I want them to have as much confidence as humanly possible."

Phil shook his head affirmatively, looking right at Andy, acknowledging his understanding of Andrew's methods.

CHAPTER

FIFTY-NINE

Andy's three assistants sat in chairs opposite the desk in his office, rummaging through papers that were seasonal statistics on their upcoming opponent. Andy stood behind his desk looking out the window over the campus grounds. All of them were dressed in debonair fashion. Bart and Winthrop were wearing suits, as was Phil who also sported a walking shoe over his cast. Andy looked exceptionally handsome. He wore an exquisitely sharp-looking new black suit, and attached to his shirt was a beautiful red tie. He looked sophisticated and intelligent. He was ready. Andy, looking out at the present snow storm, asked, "Is this a blizzard we're having?"

Winthrop answered, "It certainly is."

"Seven to nine inches!" Phil exclaimed with obvious surprise.

Bart finalized the current conversation with, "That's what they're saying. We haven't had that in a couple of years!"

Andy circled his desk, poured some water in a glass from the white enamel pitcher, and sat in his desk chair. "That would be something. Imagine 9,000 people being snowed in for two days. All right! Tonight's assignments. Since Bobby O'Brien intimidates everyone including the referees, we could acquire a great deal of fouls against us. Bart, you keep track of all the foul trouble on our team. Winthrop, you keep track of everything against Carolina. The first guy that gets three fouls against him let me know right away. Same goes for you, Bart. Any one of our guys gets three, make sure I know about it. Phil, you're really gonna have to help me tonight. You keep track of the minutes for our guys, plus, also do the substitutions in the first half."

Philip's eyes opened up wide. He hadn't expected Andy to give him that responsibility and asked, "Are you sure?"

"Listen, in the first half, substitution is basically routine. You know the standard substitution patterns. After the five-minute mark, start subbing with two-minute intervals resting the starters. In the second half, you do all regular substitutions. I'll sub only for key critical situations. All four of us are gonna do nothing but boost the confidence of our players all night long. If something goes wrong, that's okay."

There was a sudden knock at the door. "Bart, see who that is," Andy said.

Bart followed the command and opened the door.

A man not known to anyone in the room walked in wearing a suit and carrying a black briefcase. He looked Italian. He was approximately six feet tall.

"Who the hell are you?" Phil asked.

Andrew looked at Phil with an expression that conveyed he was unknown, turned to the man, and asked, "Well, who are you, and what do you want?" The man walked to Andrew's desk, placed the briefcase on it, swiveled it around so that only Andy's eyes could watch its opening.

"My name is Dominick Arbucci."

Andy's three assistants could not see what was in the briefcase, but Andy's eyes quickly looked over the contents. He then raised them equally as fast. Based on hid silence, they couldn't tell if it was a dead cat or cold hard cash. Surprisingly, it was the latter.

Bart said, "What is it?"

"It's green and lots of it," Phil answered.

Winthrop's eyes grew as large as saucers. He could buy a lot of hamburgers and gorge himself on munchies if they all, in fact, did get snowed in.

Andy never took his eyes off the newcomer. "How much is there?" He asked.

"Thirty thousand dollars," Dominick responded.

Both Bart and Winthrop could not control their emotions, which clearly showed in their facial expressions. They couldn't believe it. Phil was intent on paying strict attention to the situation, trying to determine what might happen. Andrew was gathering facts but had already made his decision.

Andy said to Dominick Arbucci, "How much do we have to lose by?"

"More than 25."

Phil was astonished. He tried to figure out why 25. The point spread in the paper was 16.

Mr. Arbucci said, "I know what you're thinking."

'What's that?" Andy asked.

'Why 25 when it's 16 everywhere else. Let me just say we have special clients who have special interests at very big stakes."

Andy sputtered, "I wasn't thinking that at all, and I've had enough of this. You can shut that briefcase and move on out of this office.

Winthrop and Bart's facial expressions made it clear that they definitely didn't want to say goodbye to all that beautiful money. But, like Andy, they'd never sell out their team for a second.

Arbucci looked over his shoulder at Phil, laughing as he remained sparked with confidence, even though his offer was refused. The next thing he knew, someone was all over him. Andy Trella stepped around his desk, grabbed Dominic's suit with both hands, and spun him around, throwing him out of the office. Arbucci did not defend himself. Instinctively, he held on to his briefcase. Before another thought could come to him, he was out the door and on the floor, with his back up against a hallway wall. The briefcase opened, and a considerable amount of green spilled out onto the floor. Fortunately for Dominick Arbucci, it was a Sunday. There was no one in the corridor to witness the attempted bribe.

Before Andy closed the door on Arbucci, he said, "Make sure I don't ever see you again."

Arbucci gathered the cash, shoveling it back into the case, and said, "You shoulda taken the money. You're probably gonna lose by 30 anyway."

"We're giving points on this one. We're not taking any," Andy said.

Arbucci began to laugh hysterically as Andy slammed the door on this insane fool.

"Where did that come from?" Phil asked.

"Who knows," responded Andy. He went back behind his desk and stood behind his chair. "Now we know why Carolina wins all the time."

"Really?" Winthrop asked as if he had just learned something.

Phil answered, "No, he didn't mean that."

Andrew was rubbing his hands together, looking out the office window, trying to dismiss the event that just occurred. Trying to change the subject back to the priority at hand, Andy asked, "Are the guys wearing their black armbands in memory of Willie?"

"They're going a step further," said Bart.

"What do you mean?" Andy asked.

Phil answered, "You haven't seen the jerseys yet, have you?"

"No."

"They came in yesterday. It was Al Perkins' idea. Great idea."

"Have you guys seen them yet?" Andy asked Winny and Bart.

They answered in unison, "Yeah, they're great!"

Curious, Andy asked, "What did they do?"

Bart answered, "All the numbers on the jerseys front and back are two-tone black and white in a diagonal pattern."

"Let me see one." Andy asked. "Bart, go get one. Winthrop, go with him. I have to talk to Phil for a little bit."

"Sure thing, we'll be right back."

"And let me know if you see that asshole hanging around," Andy added.

"You got it," said Winny.

They left the room, leaving Andy to have a private conversation with Phil.

Andy was now sitting behind his desk after pouring another large glass of water. He began to speak to Phil. "'Phil, how come this guy conducted that kind of business in front of four of us? Why didn't he make his offer to me alone? I can't understand that."

Confidently, Phil answered, "He's in the Mafia. They like to kill people. If we refuse, it gives them more people to kill."

Andy looked at Phil strangely. He was looking to Phil for a serious solution, and all he received was a humorous one, which made him sorry he asked. Phil had a special talent for being serious and facetious at the same time. Then he took control of himself and said to Andy, "Hey, you forget about that shit for now. You've got a job to do. Let it motivate you. Don't let it frustrate you."

"You're right. Listen, Phil, I really need you tonight. You're very important to this game. I'm gonna be very busy instructing the guys, and I'm gonna be all over the referees. Plus, I'll be playing chess with Mr. Bobby O'Brien. I may not see something. If you pick it up, inform me. We've got to cover all the bases if we're gonna pull this off."

Phil really appreciated that Andy was showing so much faith in him. He stood up and answered, "You got it," and shook Andy's hand. "We're gonna win tonight!"

"How come you're so sure?"

"I see it, I feel it in my cast." Andy gave him a facial reaction and began shaking his head. Phil continued, " These guys really play for you. I've never seen them so determined. Plus, they're motivated on behalf of Willie's memory. What you said, about how we know Carolina. They don't know us. The game plan you came up with is fantastic. They're not gonna have a clue what we're doing. And the senior thing you came up with is a big advantage. I didn't know that."

Andy replied, "We have more experienced players, not coaches."

Then he stretched back in the chair and said, "Well, it's time to get over to the locker room, have our last chat with the boys. Andrew began to reach for his glass of water.

Phil said, "There's only one thing I want you to do if we win tonight."

"What's that?" Andy asked as he drank his water.

"Don't let me drive home. I'm getting filthy stinking drunk."

Andy spit the water he was drinking right onto the floor. He thought that was so funny, remembering what had happened the last time he was in a car with Philip. He was trying to picture what it would be like to be in a cataclysmic car accident with Phil driving with a broken hoof. He didn't have to imagine, he already experienced that result.

PART THREE

CHAPTER

SIXTY

The Rosemont Horizon was operating at full capacity. Student fans had already shuffled into the basketball arena and were just waiting out the final seconds before the clash of the two teams. Everyone within the walls of this beautifully constructed sports edifice were about to witness a terrific contest of not only athletic ability but sheer determination of two opposing clubs.

The contest about to take place was going to be different from any other contest of any sporting event. It was not going to be a traditional cheerleading rah-rah, pom-pom type of game. Naturally, there would be shooting and dribbling of the basketball, which was the nature of the game in itself. But this particular basketball contest was going to take on a new entity. It was going to be a physical ballet. There would be heated passions of intense levels for every coach and player involved for two solid hours.

Mostly, however, this contest was going to be different in that it was going to be one coach versus the other. They would play out a classical game of chess with one another. One of constant move and counter move. They'd pull out all the stops, letting it all hang out. Tempers would be flaring at levels that permitted them to actually hate one another where they'd both violate basic conduct of the game.

Bobby O'Brien walked on to the host team's court with his four assistants anchoring in his wake. The intense-looking tall, blond, frenetic student fan who was giving Al Perkins a hard time a couple of weeks ago was standing in the first row leaning over a railing, yelling at O'Brien at the top of his lungs, "Hey, O'Brien! You suck, man! You're gonna lose. We're gonna kick the living shit out of you tonight."

Bobby O'Brien couldn't resist at least taking a gander at the young man, since the student fan had acquired so much attention around him. Usually, Mr. O'Brien would never pay attention to a bellowing fan who proclaimed his own self-deprecation at shouting levels. But he was only ten feet away and found it difficult to ignore, especially since 50 people in the immediate area were all quiet and couldn't help but hear the quite aggressive blond student. When O'Brien looked up at him, he noticed his bulging blue eyes and solid-red cheeks as he used everything he had in vocalizing in Mr. O'Brien's direction. He appeared out of breath on the verge of choking as he had used up every ounce of energy he had in shouting out at Bobby O'Brien.

Up in a partly concealed balcony attached to the upper mezzanine level was a young man with a beard and long hair by the name of Timmy. Timmy had a companion with him, who was his girlfriend, Karen. Timmy was wearing raggy shorts and had a slothy appearance, as did his girlfriend. Timmy was currently obsessed and convincingly immersed into hooking up a quite impressive stereo amplifier system. He was moving about quickly, changing directions, throwing wires around all over the place. His girlfriend, Karen said, "Timmy, "I don't understand you at all. You never watched a sports game of any kind in your entire life. Why are you so engrossed in this game tonight,?

"Hey Karen, I stopped doing lines for a week now, and last

night I had an epiphany. It was this basketball game I dreamed about."

"Yeah, so what?"

"Wait! Just wait and see. You're not gonna believe this. All I know is some real serious shit is gonna happen here tonight."

"You're whacked out!"

"No, I'm not. It's gonna be tremendous. I'm not missing it, and you're going to be a witness."

Karen asked, "To what, an assassination?

"Karen, you're doing too many lines lately."

"Am not."

"You're having your monthly." She looked at him and decided to turn away.

Karen watched Timmy as she sat on top of this huge stereo system with her arms crossed over her knees. She said, "You've flipped out. You're crazy. I think I liked you better when you were stoned out of your mind."

Timmy was still flapping wires around, trying to insert his amplifying system into the dozen or so speakers set up along the rafters of the building. He turned toward Karen, approached her, and said, "Eh, Karen. Just do me a favor and stay out of my way."

Karen realized she was fighting a losing battle, gave in, and decided to do exactly what Timmy had told her. Karen figured she'd become a spectator like everyone else.

Andy stood near the scorer's table as his team was shooting warm-up baskets. He looked great. He was dressed for the occasion. Later, when he removed his jacket, instead of the usual vest, he wore a pair of black suspenders that made the red tie color contrast perfectly. Andy shook hands with the announcers, Jimmy Tacker and Bill Black. The three referees were standing together also, near the scorer's table. Andy walked away from them as the ten very sexy and beautiful cheerleaders, dressed in hot red, skipped past him after doing a quick set of their dance routine. Andy clapped his hands and then motioned at Winthrop and Bart who were catching basketballs and passing them out to the players to bring them in for final instructions. Winny and Bart gave the players the signal and started collecting the basketballs, sending them to the sidelines for the final pep talk.

The public address announcer's voice came out over the PA system. "Good evening, ladies and gentleman, and student fans of Western Chicago University." A huge roar immediately followed this welcome. "Tonight's basketball contest faces our Western Chicago Eagles ..." The accolades began and continued at deafening levels for 15 seconds before the announcer could continue "...versus the Carolina Cougars." The boo's began and registered the same intensity that the cheering had for the upstart underdog host team.

The announcer went on to introduce the starting line-ups. Then it came time for him to introduce the respective coaches for each club. The boo's started again, naturally, for Bobby O'Brien and were followed by cheers for Andy Trella, who was riding the crest of the now unified endorsement.

Both coaches walked toward one another to take part in the customary handshake of good faith and traditional offering of good luck. When they did, Bobby O'Brien towered over Andrew Trella. Six-foot four vs. five-feet ten. While shaking hands O'Brien said, "Well, kid. I've come here tonight to give you your initiation into the losing side of college coaching. Believe me, your first loss will be a memorable and quite devastating one, one you'll never forget.

The intimidation tactics of Bobby O'Brien had already started and the national anthem hadn't even been sung yet. O'Brien relied on this feature tactic that was incorporated in his arsenal more than anything else. He knew if he could put a small degree of apprehension or fear into this young leader, that would be enough. It would be enough just causing some self-doubt to mingle around in Andy's head, and it would rub off in an intangible way to his players. Andy just looked at Coach O'Brien, shook his head, and gave a smirk, leading O'Brien to think he was agreeing with his prediction. As Andy moved away, O'Brien smiled, thinking a win tonight would be much easier than he anticipated. The neophyte coach was conceding, surrendering, knowing that he and his team were greatly outmatched.

As Andrew turned and walked away, he buttoned the lower button on his suit coat and smiled ever so slightly. He believed that he was successful in letting O'Brien think he was greatly intimidated, that Coach O'Brien was quite relaxed, which was what he precisely desired.

The referees went over to each bench and informed the coaches the game would begin in two minutes. Andy turned toward his team who were all sitting in their proper seats on the bench. Andy knelt on one knee and gave his last words of inspiration.

"Okay, guys. You only have one thing to do. Go after it! Go after it by going after them. Mind, body, and soul. Take 'em out! You can do it! So do it!" They clapped and broke their huddle. The five starters headed onto the court while the fans waited impatiently, anticipating the moment the game was to begin.

Tommy Dorsey was a white ball player for the Carolina Cougars. He was sitting on the bench talking to a fellow player who was seated right next to him. "Do you see that guy standing there coaching that club?"

"Yeah."

"His name is Andy Trella. We went to the same high school, Christ the King, in the city back east. He was a senior when I was a freshman. I didn't play much at all my first year because I sat on the bench behind him waiting for him to graduate. He holds the school record for most points scored by eight points over me. He did it in four years, I did it in three. If it wasn't for him, I'd have the all-time record. You know what else the scumbag did? He stole my girlfriend from me. After she dumped me for him, he dumped her."

"Wow! If I were you Dorsey, I'd stay completely away from that guy. He's bad news and bad luck for you."

"Oh yeah? That's what you think. Watch this!"

Tommy Dorsey got up off the bench and strode across the court's floor, heading directly toward Andy.

When Tommy reached within 20 feet of Andy, Andy noticed his presence and was surprised to see him. "Tommy, how are you? You're on the Carolina team. That's great." Andy stuck his arm out to shake his hand. Instead, Tommy Dorsey reciprocated by throwing a straight forward punch to Andy's head. He was caught off-guard and could barely react in time to avoid the power of the blow. This was one time that Andrew could not manifest the lightning-quick speed to avoid the dangerous punch. It had connected with its intended target, decking Andy to the floor immediately. All he could do was turn his head slightly. He did not have enough time to manufacture any other sort of self-defense. But by turning his head away, he received the blow at the same spot his head had hit the windshield in the traffic accident and also when Sheila had hit him with the blackboard in his apartment. The wound was naturally tender and had opened up, thus the side of his head began to bleed.

The Eagle players jumped off the bench and were pushing Tommy Dorsey away. They were about to grab him and pound his face in, but the three referees happened to be standing only five feet away when the incident occurred. They collectively broke up the development of a fist fight immediately. Any further fighting at this moment became fruitless, but the frenzied condition of this night's game with the chaos of additional fighting was in its primordial stage.

On the opposite end of the sidelines, Bobby O'Brien looked up to see what had happened. He was in a huddle with his four assistants giving instructions when he saw his player Tommy Dorsey, the focus of a not-too-favorable circle of considerable attention. Dorsey was surrounded by referees and opposing players whose passions were heated, registering a great degree of dislike for this individual. O'Brien sent all four of his assistants to run over there, protect Tommy, and report back to him on the occurrence and the outcome.

Al Perkins was sitting in the first row of box seats with Dean Thompson and Sam Hastings. They were all standing now due to the situation at hand. Al immediately left them. He needed to know the seriousness of Andy's injury. Sam Hastings looked at the dean and the dean returned the favor, knowing that Sam was about to say something.

"Mel," Sam said, "You got any more coaches lined up?"

"No."

"Maybe you should call Nolan Castwell?"

"No fucking way!" The dean's facial expression was one of exasperation.

Andy now sat in a chair at the player's bench. Al Perkins, the team trainer, and the referees were attending to Andrew's physical and mental condition. The team trainer, a silver-haired, obese, short man was applying a bandage to the same specific spot that had been covered by bandages twice before during recent weeks. Stitches would not be necessary, but a bandage was applied for the purpose of stopping the bleeding.

The head referee leaned over and asked, "Andy, you gonna be okay?"

"Just give me five minutes."

"You got it, but no longer than that. That snow storm is building. We wanna get this one started."

The crowd around Andy parted and left Bobby O'Brien standing right in front of Andrew. Before he began to speak, Andy said to him, "Was this part of your initiation process?"

Everyone looked around, wondering what the two head coaches were talking about.

"No, Sonny, I'm sorry and must apologize for the behavior of one of my players, but at least you'll get a little taste of what your boys will be receiving tonight."

O'Brien looked at the referees and Al Perkins eye-to-eye and said, "Of course, I'm speaking figuratively, not literally. I want that to be perfectly clear. Now let's get on with it." O'Brien left them and walked back to his coaching sideline.

Phil Conig stared at O'Brien as did everyone else. "He's truly an asshole," Phil said.

Jake Murphy, the head referee said to Andy, "Okay, Coach, let's have the starting five on the floor, and let's clear this area out."

CHAPTER

SIXTY-ONE

Sheila stood at the curb, having just collected her baggage from the plane that had arrived back at O'Hare International Airport. It was extremely windy, as usual, but it was also snowing incredibly hard. It was coming down relentlessly, the largest snowflakes she had ever seen. Each one was a bit shy of the size of a golf ball. In fact, Sheila thought that they were almost the size of a little butterfly. There were thousands upon thousands of them, swimming in unprecedented schools of congestion. The flakes were dancing in the air with the rhythm of their flight controlled distinctly by the wind as they fell gently to the ground. Each snowflake evaporated instantly as it fell to the ground, as if held up by a parachute, breaking the violent velocity of its descent.

Sheila looked up and down the pick-up/drop-off area, searching for a vacant taxi cab. Her eyes caught on a black man standing outside his yellow cab, leaning on it with his arms folded.

"Hey, lady! Are you looking for me?"

"No. I'm looking for a cab, and I need one right away."

"On the double. You got it."

The cab driver jumped into his seat and bolted the yellow

automobile over near the curb, cutting off several now very perturbed drivers, and parked his cab near where Sheila was standing. He hopped out, grabbed her bag, and planted it in the trunk of his cab. Every maneuver he made he did in a subservient class gentleman's manner, for if Sheila detected he was hustling her for other notions, she would have never gotten into the car. The cabby opened the back door, Sheila got in and slid over, and the cabby slid in after her.

He said, "Hey, lady, where do you need to go? Sorry, lady. I just needed to joke around a little bit. Liven up my client's and my day. Sometimes, I feel like a limo driver for a funeral home. Most all my passengers are dead and they don't even know it." He moved to the front seat.

"Can you please take me to the Rosemont Horizon right away?" The cabby did a double-take and faced her in an excitable manner.

"The Horizon! Are you going to the game tonight?"

"If you ever get this car in gear."

"Lady, why didn't you say so? You got it." He turned back, faced the steering wheel, put the foot to the pedal, and continued his conversation. "Big, big game tonight; Carolina's in town."

"You a Cougar fan?" Sheila asked.

"No way, lady. The Eagles and that new young kid coach they got. Honey, I played basketball for Western Chicago Eagles 16 years ago."

"Really?"

"Yes, ma'am. We was good then, but now we're contenders. You know, lady, the game started already. We're about an hour and fifteen minutes out. With this storm brewing, I don't know if I can get you there before the game's over with."

"You got a radio in this car?"

"Hell, yeah. You want to listen to the game, lady?"

"Hell, yeah." Sheila said sarcastically. The cab driver laughed and immediately pulled a compact radio out of the glove compartment and hooked it up to the dashboard. He then began to adjust the tuner to the proper station to channel in the broad-cast for their mutual listening pleasure.

The radio announcer was going berserk. "I can't believe what we just saw, Hank. The basketball game hasn't even started yet, and one of the Carolina players, I don't know who it was, walked across the court, approached Coach Andy Trella, clocked him, hammering out a straight forward punch to the right side of his head, decking him."

Sheila jumped up, leaned forward in the back seat of the cab and said, "Oh, no!"

The cab driver looked to get a glimpse of Sheila's expression through the rearview mirror and wondered why she seemed to care so much. They both listened intently.

The broadcaster's voice channeled out into the taxi cab continuing on, "I've never seen anything like that ever before, when the game hasn't even started yet. No fist fights have started, as the referees were right on top of it. Hank, I wish we were over with Jimmy Tacker and Billy Black, looking at the teleprompter. I'd like to see that on tape.

The commentator Hank, working with the radio broadcaster said, "That was unbelievable! Why would he do such a stupid thing? Well, I'm sure Coach O'Brien is definitely upset, although he's not showing it as Tommy Dorsey, a player for Carolina is being escorted off the floor. He's been thrown out of this one before we even start."

The broadcaster said, "Well, Hank, I believe that doesn't hurt Carolina too much. I don't believe Tommy Dorsey played very much. Still, Coach O'Brien is down one player already.

Sheila's face reflected her alarm. The cabbie said, "Did you hear that?"

"Yes, I wonder what in the hell caused it."

"The bastard Carolina players always did play dirty. They nailed the goddamn coach before the goddamn game even started. They must be afraid of something."

Sheila gave the cab driver a look, intently trying to read

between the lines of his real meaning. "I hope Andy's okay!" she said.

The cab driver again looked into his rear view mirror, trying to decipher something about why she particularly cared about the coach or this game so much. Then the cab driver decided to turn around completely to face her while he was driving. "Uh, lady, you know this new coach personally, don't you?"

Sheila didn't respond as she looked at him, but a slow smile began to show on her face. The cabbie smiled, showing his white, glaring teeth. "Jesus, Christ!" He's your goddamn boyfriend, ain't he?"

"Yes, sir."

"Goddamn it! I knew it! Why didn't you say so, lady. Your man's hurt. We got to get you there. Well, just have to put this cab here into overdrive. Hold on to your hat, lady, we're making tracks."

As the cab kicked into higher gear, Sheila fell back toward the back of the seat and her hat came flying off. Yet they were still about one and a half hours away from the Rosemont Horizon, considering the snowfall..

The television announcers, Jimmy Tacker and Billy Black, were watching the incident between Tommy Dorsey and Andrew Trella. They showed it over and over on the television monitor. Billy Black said to Jimmy Tacker, "Jim, this is unbelievable. Why would this kid have done something like that for no apparent reason?"

"Well, Bill, I'm sure that these two must have known each other at one time or another, and it is obvious that Tommy Dorsey had a serious grudge and a score to settle–and that's exactly what he did. But he's paying an expensive price, as not only was he ejected from this game by the referees, but we've just learned that Coach Bobby O'Brien has proclaimed that due to that incident, not only has he suspended Mr. Dorsey, but he's thrown him off the Carolina team permanently."

"Wow! Looks like we're going to be in on a very interesting game," Bill Black said.

In the locker room, Tommy Dorsey was throwing clothing all over the place.

He was quite upset, as one of Bobby O'Brien's assistants was trying to calm him down. "Bullshit! He can't do that! I got a scholarship. I made a mistake. It shouldn't cost me that much. That's an expensive penalty, Roy."

"Sorry, kid, You're history. Get changed and stay in this locker room."

"Son of a bitch!" Dorsey kept repeating, "Son of a bitch." Then he began to think that, somehow, Andy Trella always seemed to get the best of him. He was thinking that he should have listened to his fellow player, who specifically told him to stay away from Andrew Trella, as only the mention of his name was bad luck for him.

Up in the partition on the mezzanine level, Timmy said to Karen, "Did you see that?"

"Yeah, that was wild!"

"I told you so. Serious, serious shit gonna happen here tonight. I know it." Karen looked at Timmy as she still sat on top of the huge stereo amplifier, believing he knew what he was talking about.

The public address announcer stated over the system that Carolina's Tommy Dorsey had been thrown out of the game and also that Coach O'Brien publicly announced that he has been terminated from the Carolina Cougars team effective immediately. The crowd in the Rosemont Horizon roared with approval.

CHAPTER

SIXTY-TWO

The five starting players for each team began moving out to center court. The Western Chicago Eagles had their usual president's row, while Carolina had four white ball players and their only black starter, Rayford Williamson, who was considered the best player in the entire country. He was a relentless non-tiring scorer, averaging thirty six points a game, ranking him as the number one scorer in college basketball.

Everyone was now seated in the arena, including all the coaches and players. "Are you okay?" asked Phil who was sitting next to Andy.

"Are you kidding? Of course, I'm fine."

"You ready?"

"Hell, yes!"

"Well, it's time to go to work."

Andrew got up off the bench and stood in the parameters of the coach's boxed-off area and shouted out encouragement to his starting five. The Eagle players were ready, and what had just happened to their coach had put fire in their eyes.

The head referee, Jake, threw the jump ball up in the air and a simple basketball contest that now began would run like an endless marathon. The Eagle players were so primed, so prepared and pumped as a result of the incredible chanting from the home-team crowd, that they started the game off like gangbusters. The Eagles jumped out to an 8–0 lead on a couple of baskets by Alan Jefferson, a steal by Calvin Kennedy, and a slam dunk by Chris Washington. The crowd of fans couldn't have been wilder or happier.

Bobby O'Brien was in shock. He had been thinking before the game that he'd be handing over the full throttle of the management of this game to his first assistant, Roy Hendley at the five-minute mark. Instead, he'd have to hold the reins all night. He usually sat on the bench next to his assistants for ninety five percent of any contest. Tonight, he'd be standing on his feet in the coach's box for ninety five percent of the time. Bobby O'Brien gave the appropriate gesture, signaling for the first time-out of the game. The early time-out was to hopefully curtail the current roll by Western Chicago and also get the kinks out of the Cougar players.

As the Eagle players engaged in a slow jog off the court, the Eagle reserves were pumping their arms in the air. Andy was on his feet, as Phil, Winthrop, and Bart were slapping hands with the players. Encouragement was everywhere as even the crowd followed suit. There was no let-up anywhere, that's how Andrew wanted it to be. Bobby O'Brien and his Carolina Cougars were in for the fight of their lives, and they didn't even know about it.

The television announcer, Bill Black, facetiously commented to Jimmy Tacker, "Well, Jim, this game's starting out just like you thought it would."

Jimmy Tacker was even more surprised than Bobby O'Brien. "I'm shocked at this opening, but aside from it being very early in the game, I feel confident Carolina will rebound. They're just too good a team. But the Western Chicago Eagles have definitely sent a message, and in a big way, that they will not be taken lightly, and this crowd is in ecstasy.

As the time-out period drew to its conclusion, Andrew

shouted out instructions to his five players, as they pranced back onto the court. Andy grabbed Alan Jefferson's arm and held him back a moment he said, "Alan, leave your cape off here tonight, no Superman tactics. You got four other players out there with you."

"You got it, Coach."

"And remind Kennedy, I want him to stick with Rayford like grease on glue."

"Say what?"

"Like white on rice. I didn't want to get you offended."

"I'm always offended."

"Exactly, like white on rice, tell him."

"Copy that."

Play had commenced, and both teams were at full tilt. Carolina was resorting to playing very physical basketball. They began to use their muscle to intimidate the Eagle squad, but Western Chicago had too much fight in them tonight. Carolina managed to get its offense straightened out and began scoring some points. They obviously weren't about to be blown out by a supposedly mediocre team and were going to make a game of it. However, Western Chicago also managed to keep its composure and led eighteen to twelve after seven minutes of play. The players of both teams were really beginning to bang the crap out of one another. Both coaches were yelling at the referees as hard as they could continuously and shouted out instructions at their respective players with unrelenting enthusiasm.

One of the white players for Carolina, who also happened to be the tallest man on the entire playing court, threw an elbow that caught Skin Head across his nose and broke it. He went down to the floor in instant pain. Shockingly, none of the three referees had seen it. Because it was unnoticed, it became one of the several non-calls that went in Carolina's favor.

Andrew was voraciously yelling at the three referees, registering his complaint emphatically. Suddenly, he turned away from the referees and marched over to the official scorer's table.

He approached one of the scorekeepers. "Chet," he said, "give me your fake eye."

Chet replied, "I know that one ref needs my eye more than I do. Don't worry about it. I've got plenty of them." Chet then reached his hand up toward his forehead, took his glasses off, and covered his left eye with the palm of his hand, proceeding to pull his glass eye out of his head. He handed it over to Andrew, who took it in the palm of his hand. Chet covered his vacant eye socket with a black patch, and sat back down at the scorer's table.

Andrew marched out to the crowd of people assisting Skin Head off the playing court, approached the referee named Marv, and stuck the contents of his palm into the top pocket of Marv's striped shirt, saying, "Marv, this is for you. You need it more than anybody." Andrew then assisted his injured player off the court.

Marv searched through the shirt pocket with his two fingers, wondering what the hell it was the kid coach had dropped in his pocket. When he saw it, his mouth opened up wide, and he was mortified.

By this time, Andrew turned back toward him, he began a tirade against Marv. "You need a third eye, Marv. You've been missing everything. You're supposed to be refereeing the game tonight, not the one you did last week. Get with it! He practically hit him with a sledgehammer. What's he got to do, hit 'em with a baseball bat before you call it? Wake up, man."

The head referee, Jake, came over to Marv, who was much younger than he was and said, "Don't worry about it. We all miss 'em sometimes. Happens to the best of us. Jake never saw the fake eye Andy had inserted into Marv's pocket. Marv was so shaken that he just dropped it back into his pocket as soon as he saw it and left it there. He was so concerned and preoccupied with it that he didn't look where he was walking and collided with a much taller person, a player from Carolina. There was a crunch and his face registered a squeamish expression. Then he hustled over to the scorer's table and asked for some tape, proceeding to tape the opening of the pocket, sealing it shut so that he wouldn't have to deal with it any further.

Then Jake approached the Western Chicago Eagle bench and said to Andrew, "You better cool it, Coach. I don't wanna hit you with a technical foul. Stay off the court! You're not allowed on it."

"What are you talking about, Jake? I have an injured player; his goddamn nose is broken. He's out of the game, and no foul was called."

"Just cool it!"

"Don't worry about it, Jake. It's our night."

Andy was certainly not overwhelmed by the governing forces of authority for this game. He knew the referees would not throw him out of the game since he was at a supposed disadvantage, going up against the great Bobby O'Brien. Throwing Andy Trella out of this game would be like taking the gun out of an infant's hand with a ferocious lion charging when the infant would be incapable of pulling the trigger to begin with.

Bobby O'Brien was shouting out at Jake, "Get him off the court, Jake!"

When Jake approached Bobby O'Brien, he said, "I just gave him a warning, and I'm giving one to you, too. Get off our backs and stay off the court." O'Brien just turned away from Jake and walked back to his bench area.

Andy came back to the sidelines and squatted down before his players in front of the bench.

Washington said, "Referees are gonna do us in."

Andy immediately scolded Washington, "Hey, you don't worry about the refereeing. That's my problem. You just concentrate on one thing–your assignments. Don't let their inadequacy affect your game. You got it, Washington?"

"Yes, sir."

"Okay, Bennett, you're in for Turner. Skin Brain, you're in for your brother. You guys are doing great. Just don't let up. This Carolina team is breakable. Remember that. Go get 'em!"

The players started out for the floor. The score at the moment was 25–17, the Eagles were still on top. As the players walked onto the court, Andy took a look at the Carolina bench area and noticed Bobby O'Brien smiling. Immediately, he became concerned as to why O'Brien felt a sudden surge of confidence. Clearly, O'Brien had something up his sleeve and had just inserted it. Andy swiveled his head back and forth, looking at the five players O'Brien was sending in. He noticed he was sending in five substitute players instead of his starters. O'Brien even kept Rayford on the bench. Andy was curious, searching with his eyes and brain, trying to figure why he would decide on a complete sudden overhaul swap of all players at one time. Usually, substitution procedures were inserting only a few at a time, keeping some of your best players on the floor while the others got a rest. Andy stared O'Brien down and observed that he was still wearing that legendary snickering smile. Andy suddenly reacted as if he had just been hit by a lightning bolt. He figured it out. Quickly, he turned to the closest referee signaling for a time-out just as the current time-out was concluding. O'Brien's smile disappeared instantly, and his facial expression turned to bewilderment. First, O'Brien couldn't believe the young kid would pull such a maneuver as a back-to-back time-out so early in the game. Andy motioned with his hands and arms for the players to come back to the bench area. They were surprised but followed his instructions obediently.

Andy sat them down and said, "Guys, remember what I told you about the pushing, the shoving, and the fighting?"

They answered in unison, "Yeah! Don't take shit!"

Jefferson said, "Yeah, if somebody hits us, hit the mother back."

Andy continued, "Yeah. That's right. That's how I want to play it, except for the next three minutes."

A couple of them said, "What?"

"If they push and shove or even throw a punch, don't retaliate, just for the next three minutes only. He's putting in all his substitutes at one time. They're gonna play very physical and try to fight to get some of you thrown out of the game. They're the scrubs; he doesn't care if one of two of them gets thrown out. So you know what we're gonna do?" He paused and they were all listening intently. "Those are his scrub players; we're going with our best. Our lead is seven points. Go out and increase it." They all smiled and knew that they were on the same wavelength as their coach. They put aside their personal feelings and stuck to Andrew's cue.

As they began to return to the court, Andy grabbed one of his players and submerged himself in the center of his five players. "Take the punishment for three minutes; after that, we'll dish out some of our own."

"Ten-four," Chris Washington said.

Andrew had hit the nail right on the head. The substitutes for O'Brien's squad were going to play just barely three minutes, long enough so they could afford to give fouls, push, shove, hit, and possibly get things really out of control. Since they were not nearly as valuable to the degree of O'Brien's original starting five, they were expendable. Bobby O'Brien figured he'd try to entice the Eagle players into fighting, taking the edge off their great basketball play thus far, especially since Skin Head had just gotten clocked. This would be the time that the Western Chicago Eagles would be most vulnerable. If O'Brien's current five could instigate enough trouble, a few Eagle players would retaliate and be more concerned about fighting rather than basketball. O'Brien was hoping that maybe one or two of Western Chicago's best players would get thrown out of the contest in exchange for one or two of his scrub players. Then O'Brien would come back with Rayford and his other four best players against a much weaker Eagle team. O'Brien also figured he had already lost Tommy Dorsey so it was reasonable to think that the referees would not eject more than one person from his team. With not even half the game over, he knew he wasn't going to have three players out of the game. So he was gambling, rolling dice, using his intimidation tactics ten-fold in attainment of putting fear into the Eagle team.

Bobby O'Brien was playing chess with this game. He was gambling. He was converting it into a Lacrosse, football, boxing match type of game. To Andy, it was a basketball game pure, and simple. He was managing it just that way.

Bobby O'Brien stood up. He smiled again when he saw Andrew send in his best starting five players. O'Brien thought, *Here is where the tables will turn on this game.*

For three minutes, the Eagle players refrained from pushing, shoving, fighting, and retaliating. They bitched and complained to the referees as Andy did, but they did not fight back. Meanwhile, the referees did their job in calling a fair game. The fouls by Carolina were quite obvious and accumulating quickly. During this time frame of the game, the referees had called seven fouls against Carolina and none against Western Chicago, and the Eagle players took the punishment like sentenced slaves. With Bobby O'Brien also taking out his best player during this interval of the game, Carolina managed only four points on two baskets. The Western Chicago Eagles also scored only two baskets, but they also shot nine free throws and managed to score on seven of them as a result of the free shots awarded from the Carolina fouls.

The Eagle lead was in double digits, and the fans were loudly ecstatic. The Western Chicago Eagles had put up 36 points thus far and led by 15 over the Carolina Cougars.

Bobby O'Brien's strange strategic implementation backfired, and it was costly, but it was still only the first half of the game. Andy Trella thought it was a good move by O'Brien to do something to shake up his team, but he thought he could have camouflaged it better by sending in two or three new players and keeping Rayford in there. When he had pulled five to insert five, he tipped his hand, and Andrew recognized it and countered.

Andy took a quick glance at O'Brien across the court and witnessed his opponent in a livid frenzy. He was pacing and ranting along the sidelines with great disgust and frustration. Coach O'Brien then grabbed a large broom from a passing custodian and flung it out across the basketball playing court. The head referee, Jake, stopped play and viciously called a technical foul on Coach O'Brien. The student fans were in an uproar. They were clapping, laughing, shouting, and jumping to the point of edging upon dancing. Winthrop and Bart were clapping their hands. Phil was standing next to them smiling and said, "This is really great. Can you believe this is happening?" They both shook their heads negatively. Dean Thompson looked at Al Perkins and they both made impressive facial expressions.

Alan Jefferson sank both ends of the free throws, and Western Chicago was up over Carolina by seventeen points with the half time approaching. Bobby O'Brien naturally did the only thing he could, he sent Rayford back in and the original four starters, and it was a good thing he did. Rayford Williamson started to heat up, hitting from all over the court right away. He sunk three baskets inside of a minute's time and cut the lead to eleven with only two minutes and thirteen seconds left in the first half.

When Alan Jefferson went up to score on a lay-in opportunity, he was practically pulled down, being pushed into the column of the basketball hoops stanchion extremely hard. Chris Washington then pushed the Carolina player, knocking him down. Two Carolina players then immediately gang-tackled Washington, and the game's first free-for-all fight ensued. Both benches emptied out onto the floor. All coaches were also now on the floor trying to separate fighting players from one another. They were wrestling on the floor and punches were being thrown. Several small groups of fights broke out apart from each other. Andy was immersed smack in the middle of one pile. He was at the core of the brawl, grabbing and pulling people off of each other. He was shouting at his players, instructing them to go to their designated bench area. Still, he was having a difficult time separating his troops from their targeted counterparts. If ever a ball game was out of control, this particular game certainly was.

Bobby O'Brien and his assistants were also out on the floor. He was reprimanding players of his own squad when he was able to get their attention. He was sending players one by one back to their respective bench areas. Even though both head coaches reacted like they wished to dissolve the brawl, both Andy T and Bobby O, deep down inside, were advocating this current fiasco. They both intended to send a message to their opponent, hoping that the other might now back down in their confident conviction. Thus, a simple fight for the struggle of power and domination. However, there would be no domination tonight.

The several small fights were beginning to break up. Even Winthrop was out on the basketball court's floor, and he was lying on top of a Carolina player with his hugely obese body, preventing the player from getting up off the floor.

"Get up off of me, you fat tub of shit," the player said. Winthrop looked around, his eyes rolling, to see if anyone was watching. When he felt secure that no one was, he sent it in a punch to the side of the player's abdomen. Winthrop smiled contentedly at the action he had taken. The player was momentarily hurt by the punch, but he was more surprised that Winthrop went ahead, slyly punching him and getting away with it.

The entire crowd was on their feet enjoying the full-out ruckus. Several of the fans were acting like they were fighters, throwing jabs and punches into the air, displaying their emotional ties to their team against their opponents. The referees finally seemed to get a handle on things and were able to simmer tempers down. The players were all sent to the benches, and Andy Trella and Bobby O'Brien stood at center court receiving a reprimand by Jake. Both coaches remained quiet and refrained from registering any point of rebuttal. Jake was hot, and this was his moment. This would not be the time to attempt to deny his authoritative role. Both coaches were merely riding out the scolding. Jake could not throw anyone out since so many were involved. However, the next ruckus that erupted was certainly going to resort to ejections, and he warned them both he might even suspend the ball game. Jake concluded by saying, "Enough with the muscle. You're not gangsters, you're basketball coaches. Let's play ball!"

Both coaches left one another, but they both managed to give each other brief looks before separating. A coach's mind never stopped. They each figured they might pick up on something by just looking the other one down, as Andrew demonstrated earlier at the expense of Bobby O'Brien.

Once play continued, both head coaches picked up where they left off, eternally working the referees over without as much as a pause. The shouting levels of these two head coaches was astounding. They both were complaining about the refereeing of the game. They complained about each other and the play of their opponents.

The two teams swapped baskets back and forth with fifty seconds left before half-time. The Cougar team was holding the ball in an attempt to take the last shot of the half. They passed and dribbled the basketball, getting the clock down to only eight seconds. They initiated their offensive play, but the Eagle squad was playing incredibly tough tight defense. Once the shot went up, it missed the basket, and the ball came off the glass into Glen Johnson's hands. Glen knew there was only about three seconds before the clock ran out. So he flung the ball the length of the floor in an attempt to hit the hoop. Just as he released the hook-type javelin throw, Rayford of Carolina gave him a close elbow to his neck and leveled him. Glen Johnson fell to the court floor instantly, and Marv called the appropriate foul against Rayford.

Suddenly, there was a thunderous, roaring cheer that echoed through the building. The Western Chicago players were smiling and the Carolina Cougars were not. Andy grinned, and O'Brien was disgusted. The lead was now 43–29, and Glen Johnson had a free foul shot coming. The Hail Mary prayer that he threw up was answered as the ball went right through the hoop. The student fans and everyone else in the building were stifled. The shot he made he hadn't even aimed for. He just threw it the length of the full court in the direction and it curved squarely, hitting its target like a homing missile. Glen Johnson didn't even know he had scored it, neither did the players. He was on the floor trying to get his wind back. Andrew was on the floor assisting Glen up, with all his players jubilantly satisfied with the outcome of the play, but concerned as to Glen's condition.

The Carolina team just walked off the floor with their coaches and Bobby O'Brien, their heads were down, not because they were losing but because the development of the last play before the half was discouraging. When Glen Johnson was able to, he shot the free throw, and the Eagles led Carolina by 15 points at half-time.

SIXTY-THREE

Timmy and Karen, still up in the rafters secluded in the mezzanine balcony, were laughing and jumping up and down at the tremendous play before the half. Karen had a big, wide smile as she was, by now, thoroughly convinced that this was the place to be.

Sheila and the cab driver were situated in a complete standstill of a traffic jam with the snowstorm reaching new heights and still gaining fortitude. Inside the cab, Sheila had a great big grin and the cabby was banging his feet and hands saying, "Yes, Yes, Yes and a foul. Up by fifteen over big bad Carolina." Then, just as enthused and excited as he was, he changed his emotional wave, opened the window, and yelled out at the traffic, "Let's go, Chicago! Move it! Move it! Let's rock! Got the president of the United States' mistress here." Sheila smiled as the cab driver was also at the top of his game tonight. Just as he finished shouting at the Chicago traffic, it opened up as if he parted it by just saying it. Both his and Sheila's eyes opened, and they laughed more. He hit the gas pedal, and Sheila and her hat flew back in the cab once again.

Bill Black was uncontrollable. "What a wild unbelievable first half, Jimmy. I can't believe what we've seen here tonight, and we still have another full half to go."

"Unbelievable is a total understatement, Billy," Jimmy Tacker said. "Absolutely, totally unbelievable. We had a knock down of Coach Andy Trella at the start, a full out brawl, just minutes ago. The Western Chicago Eagles are playing with a tremendous amount of heart and conviction, taking it right to Carolina. Bobby O'Brien, the master of strategy and mind games, has been held in check. I can't believe I'm saying this, but the young kid coach, Andy Trella, is actually playing a masterful game of chess against the legend himself."

Bill Black continued, "Well, Jimmy, the locker rooms of each team should be something to see as both teams are surely searching and plotting courses for the rest of the way. Bobby O'Brien searching for resiliency and Andy Trella hoping to maintain the belief and the execution."

"Well, Billy, the lead can be made up by this Carolina team, or perhaps the Eagle team could falter and squander it. I look for Bobby O'Brien and Carolina to implement some adjustments and take hold of this Eagle team. But that's not to say if the Eagles continue that type of play they could very well pull off a big upset in college basketball."

"Jimmy," Bill Black asked, "Do you think we'll have an exciting second half like we did in the first?"

"Frankly, I can't imagine it being as eventful as the first half. So much has happened. It's like we had a full game already. Sometimes what happens, Billy, is the first half of a game can be so thunderous and great that the second half is completely different, becoming a slow, lackluster affair. Don't be surprised if we have a totally different game here in the second half."

Billy Black said, "And sometimes the specialness continues right throughout, which is my guess. I think it's going to unfold as a truly classical contest. You can just feel the intensity and aura here at the Rosemont Horizon. It's like this university is on a mission not to be denied by anyone, including Bobby O'Brien and the Carolina Cougars."

In the locker room, O'Brien was in the midst of an ugly tirade. He was balling out everyone, all his assistants, and all his players. "We're supposed to be contending for the National Title in four weeks, and we're personally letting a mediocre, nationally unrated team grab hold of us and strangle us." He looked across the room, and saw Tommy Dorsey standing in a corner fully dressed in civilian clothes. He proceeded to take the moment and scold Tommy. "It's your fault, Mr. Dorsey." Tommy Dorsey was appalled as the head coach continued. "You put a hex on us right from the beginning with that stunt you pulled. You gave that team, that crowd, tremendous desire by laying into that kid coach of theirs. Division One college basketball is not about personal vendettas."

"Hey," Tommy retaliated, "I'm not even on this team anymore, remember? You can't say shit to me now." Bobby O'Brien threw his hands out and said, "Never mind, I got bigger problems to solve right now. I do have another question, though. Who is this guy? Where did he come from? All the assistants and players looked around the room, trying to decipher who Bobby O'Brien was referring to. They had all thought he meant one of the Eagle players. But there wasn't one particular Eagle player that was standing out as a brilliant performer. They were all playing solidly as a team. Finally, one of the assistants asked, "Who?"

"Who? Who?" Bobby O'Brien asked. "That young, punk coach they have, that's who. He's brilliant, he has vision, foresight, deceptiveness, not to mention motivation."

One of the assistants said, "He's from the East Coast–New York, an Ivy Leaguer."

"That figures. I should have guessed it. I should send you all back there for an education in basketball. I'd trade half this team for an assistant like him. And you, Billings, can I ask you what you're doing out there tonight? It looks like you're walking around looking for a bus stop. If I should have a heart attack, I just want you to know that it's your fault."

Roy, the top-notch assistant interjected, "Bobby, let's forget about it and get on with our adjustments and strategy for the second half. Let's not waste any more time."

"Yes, you're right. Okay. Second half. Let's talk about it." The four assistant coaches closed in around Bobby O'Brien, forming a small huddled circle and began their discussion.

O'Brien said, "We have to find something to combat the multiple changing zones that they're employing."

The remainder of their discussion seemed very secretive. The Carolina players just sat in their seats in the classroom-type setting, and they all looked at one another in a dumbfounded manner trying to figure which end was up.

Andy was exuberantly loquacious in the Eagle locker room. "Okay! Okay! Hold it down guys. I know you're all excited. Great job! Fantastic! But it's not over. Don't screw it up now." A couple of the players were still carrying on, jiving it up big time. Andy bellowed out, "Oh! Oh! You didn't win yet. You guys are celebrating, and Carolina is in their locker room plotting on how to come back and steal this game from you. If you think you've won, go hit the showers, get dressed, and go party. Go ahead. You've beaten Carolina." Andy paused and then continued, "You guys are relaxing, and they're going to come on strong. You won't be ready, and they're gonna kick your asses all over the goddamn gym. Now keep your enthusiasm, but don't get cocky."

Winthrop and Bart were handing out towels and water bottles and oranges as Phil entered the locker room. He was moving about pretty good with the walking shoe over his cast and no longer in need of the stilting crutches. "I got the stat sheet, Drew."

"Good. Fellas, eat your oranges and relax for a minute." They tore the oranges apart in every way possible, absorbing the nourishment and quenching their thirst. The enthusiasm was still embedded, but they were no longer bouncing off the walls with uncontrollable emotional behavior.

Andy looked over the stat sheet for a few seconds and finally said, "Excellent." Everyone was paying attention to him, wondering what he could be referring to. He then said, "Guys, you see this. This is a piece of paper of the past. It means nothing. Only what happens next matters. Okay. For strategy number one, no more fighting. Two, we've got to get Rayford fouled out of this game. He's got three, two more and he's out. On defense, I changed my mind, we're changing over, we're switching."

The players listened carefully for the new defense they were implementing. They wondered what Andy's new scheme would be, and they were confident no matter what he said for them to do, they'd do it.

"We're going straight up, man to man," Andy said. "We're gonna beat them at their best. No tricks."

Phil smiled, saying to himself, *This is a beautiful thing.* Phil was in total awe, for he knew that the opponents locker room was fiercely plotting out how to deal with the ever-changing zone defenses. It would be like a gag played fully on Coach O'Brien. Everyone in the stadium witnessed the beautiful changing zone defenses that stopped Carolina ice cold. So all observers, television, and radio people knew they were going to see more of the same, and the question remained, could Carolina figure out a way to break it. Andrew was not only a step ahead of Bobby O'Brien and big bad Carolina but also everyone else contained in the sold-out arena. In fact, not only did Bobby O'Brien and his assistants work on strategy to attack the zones, but even Billy Black and Jimmy Tacker discussed methods of how Carolina should approach it in the second half. They broadcasted their opinions on television on the half-time show. However, their efforts, and most importantly the time they spent on it at half time, were for naught.

Andy put the finishing touches on his half-time speech. "I

know you all got some bumps and bruises out there. Is anyone hurting badly?" No one voiced any major concerns. "If anyone gets tired, pull yourself out of the game immediately. Take your blow and I'll send you back in. Glen, you okay?"

Glen Johnson was sitting down rubbing his neck. "Hell, yeah, I'm okay. After tonight, I'm going pro." They all giggled and laughed for a moment.

Andy warned, "Guys, lose the cocky attitude right now. I don't want you to give Carolina even a fragment of a chance to get back into this game. If they're gonna do it, let them do it– don't give it to them."

Alan Jefferson stood up and said to Andy, "Coach, we got their number, we ain't let them off the hook."

Andy stared Jefferson down and appreciated his assurance and committed confidence. "That may be so, Jeff, but I'll tell you all right now. The present score of this game doesn't mean we're gonna go out there and walk all over Carolina. As sure as I'm standing here, Carolina didn't have one good run in the first half, and hopefully, they won't in the next half. If they do, we want them to only have one run and let it be as brief as possible. I'll tell you something else. Guaranteed, they're gonna play a lot harder and better the second half. We hit them from the blind side in the first half; now they'll be ready. They're capable of coming back and taking this victory away from you. You have to proclaim to yourselves that you're not about to let that happen. Guys, a win tonight will give us a bid to March Madness. Your basketball careers don't have to end when the season is over next week. Focus on that and make it happen. Now, are we going to the tournament or not?"

SkinHead, who was sitting in the back of the locker room with a huge towel wrapped around his head and completely covering one of his eyes, yelled out, "Yeah, we're going!"

Andy looked at them all hard and strong, and said softly, "Then do it!"

"Let's go warm up," Alan Jefferson said.

They all rolled out of the locker room leaving Andy and his assistant's behind. "Twenty minutes to go," Phil said as he walked over to Andy.

"Yeah, but it's gonna take an hour and a half to play it."

"After all you've been through in the last month, don't you think you could stand one more nerve wracking hour?"

Andy looked at Phil solemnly and replied, "Honestly?"

"Yes."

"No."

Philip slapped his arm around Andy's shoulder while Winthrop and Bart stood in the wings smiling at Andy's joke.

Suddenly, there was a knock at the locker room door. The door opened and the head referee, Jake, was standing at its entrance. He popped his head inside and said, "Coach Trella, can I talk to you for a minute?"

Andrew walked toward the door and stepped outside the locker room to listen to what Jake had to say.

"Listen, I just spoke to the athletic director, Al Perkins, and informed him that we're deciding that we might have to call the rest of this game."

Instantly startled, Andy asked, "What in the hell for?" He thought Jake was going to convey to him that there was too much fighting and foul play and that this particular game was out of control. Personally, Jake would never concede as much, for the NCAA committee would undoubtedly question the ability of the referee who was presiding over any basketball contest. If a referee canceled, postponed, or suspended any ball game, that referee would surely be watched closely, thus jeopardizing his own job. To Jake, no game would be out of control that he was governing over, even though this one was surely close to it.

Jake said, "There's four inches of snow on the ground as we speak. It's the biggest snowstorm in Chicago in more than eight years. There's 9,000 people in this building; we can't afford to have that many people snowed in. We can't have all these people stranded here."

Andrew looked down at the floor in front of him, even though his heart was dead-set against calling the game. But he knew he had no point of rebuttal. It definitely wouldn't be desirable to have nine thousand people trapped in a building, packed in like sardines for anything over a couple of hours or more.

"Have you informed O'Brien yet?"

"What? Are you kidding? First, I'm telling you. You know what the ruling is if half the ball game is over, which this one is, and the ball game is not completed."

"Yeah. It goes in the books as is, which is why you chose to tell me before you inform Bobby O'Brien."

"Precisely."

"He hasn't lost a game in six weeks. He's gonna hit the roof."

"Tell me about it."

"Jake, for whatever it's worth, I want you to know for the record that my team and myself are totally against this. We want to finish this one out. We don't want any short cuts. We got another hour or so to go. A couple more inches isn't going to make a difference at this point."

"Well, your opinion is purely academic at this juncture."

"Jake, he's not gonna let you call it."

"He doesn't have a choice."

"Tell O'Brien I said it doesn't matter. Either way, his Cougars are going down tonight."

Jake was quite astonished. He couldn't believe this young whippersnapper had the gall to relay such a message to a man of Bobby O'Brien's stature. Jake pulled away from Andrew to approach the opposite locker room and inform Andy's counterpart of this latest development. Jake knew exactly how O'Brien would react.

He'd be livid and shell out belligerent dissatisfaction to the point that he would register a formal protest of complaint.

Just as suddenly, Al Perkins and Dean Thompson came marching down the tunnel to the locker room. They were about to inform Jake of the latest developments. With a 15-point lead against the powerful Carolina Cougars, it was more than a fair bet they'd come up with something substantial to prevent this contest from being called off, even though it would be to their benefit to let things ride and take the win as is. But both Al and the Dean knew that the committee could reverse its selection of Western Chicago as being automatically qualified for the national tournament based on the fact that it wasn't a truly completed victory. They especially did not desire any complexities concerning this issue.

Both Al and the dean placed their hands on Jake's forearms, impeding his approach to the visitor's locker room. They had stopped Jake dead in his tracks, and Andrew kept a watchful eye, wondering what this discussion would entail. Andy walked slowly toward the three-man conference. He overheard Al Perkins' voice.

"I just spoke to Paul Wainwright over at WGNB television station. WGNB is paying the city of Chicago to send eight snow plow bulldozers to the Rosemont Horizon right away."

Jake's eyes almost popped out of his head.

Dean Thompson said confidently, "The snow plows are on the move as we speak. They'll be here within twenty minutes, so I take it this contest will not be suspended and will be finished to the end."

Jake looked at both Al and Dean Thompson, shook his head affirmatively, and said, "Yeah, sure. We'll finish it." Jake gave out a sigh of relief; he really didn't care to enter Bobby O'Brien's locker room with the legend's team having a double-digit deficit and proclaim that the Carolina Cougars weren't even going to get a fighting chance of coming back in the second half. He'd rather go swimming with a crocodile than have a quarrel with Mr. Bobby O'Brien.

Andrew came out of nowhere, slapped Al on the shoulder, and said, "All right, Al. That's excellent!" Jake left them and went about his business out on the basketball court. Al looked at Andy and said, "Listen, kid, the dean here is solely responsible by rolling the dice on you. We had to pull some strings to get this game fully completed. Somehow, we keep on gambling on you, and you keep coming through."

"Yeah, well, gambling successfully is usually a short-lived thing, you know that."

"Don't tell us that now at this point."

"Al, I'm not referring to tonight. I don't gamble. But tonight, bet the ranch."

Phil tugged on Andy's suit coat and said, "C'mon, let's go." Al and the dean watched as the two buddies walked out of the tunnel toward the arena.

Dean Thompson called, "Wait a minute! I forgot to tell you something."

Al stuck his arm out, preventing the dean from pursuit. "Mel, let him do what he's got to do. I don't think we should interrupt him. We've made our moves, let him make his."

"You're right. Al."

"Ya know, due to this snowstorm, everyone in Chicago is inside tonight. Wainwright just told me that this game has had a twenty nine point rating on the first half alone."

Dean Thompson's eyebrow arched and he smiled. He could smell a financial deal with WGNB television network. There were thousands of people awaiting the second half. None were more enthused and interested in the final outcome than Dean Thompson.

As Andrew and Phil walked out to the court floor, a riveting, standing ovation by the partisan crowd erupted for the outstanding job Andrew Trella had done with this Eagle team thus far. Phil still had his hand draped around Andy's shoulder, while Winthrop and Bart followed behind them. "Phil," Andy said, "I think they're cheering for you."

Phil laughed loudly, knowing everyone was cheering for Andrew.

"They must know your leg's getting better." As Phil smiled, Andrew continued, "Personally, I hope your leg stays broken forever. It only seems to give this team good luck."

"You know something, Trella? You are too much, pal. You are too much. Now go finish the job and knock this dinosaur down." Philip veered away from Andy to stop by the scorer's table and left Andrew alone to complete his walk to the appropriate bench across the court floor. The student fans did not let up. They really let Andy know he was doing a phenomenal job with this team as the bellowing crowd stayed on its feet, solely to cheer.

The Western Chicago Eagles ran to the hoop doing their lay-up routine warm-ups. The clapping student fans were all standing, giving their team the royal ovation that they deserved. The Cougar players noticed that the Eagle team looked incredibly confident.

SIXTY-FOUR

When the second half of the basketball game began, Bobby O'Brien's jaw could have fallen to the floor. It appeared as if he was going to have a stroke right then and there. His four assistants were all equally appalled at what they were witnessing with their own eyes, along with everyone else in the Rosemont Horizon. The Western Chicago Eagles had sized up to play a man-to-man defensive coverage. Bobby O'Brien and his admirals, captains, and troops were caught by surprise and were in awe of the ever-changing adjustments made by the Kid Coach, Andy Trella. At the intermission break, O'Brien and his assistants spent seventy percent of their time addressing ways to combat the multiple changing zones that the Eagle team implemented. Now that O'Brien and his team worked out a strategy to dissolve that problem, the problem wasn't there to be solved.

Andy Trella had instructed his team to go straight up against the Cougar players, which was Carolina's strength. But the players were so baffled, combined with the fact that they were prepared to attack multiple zone defenses, they couldn't adjust. The Carolina players were so bewildered and psyched out that the effect caused them to be just a tad out of sync. Carolina always played well when pitted against man-to-man coverage.

But the element of surprise threw them off rhythm just enough that they'd overthrow the basketball, drop it, kick it, and squander opportunity after opportunity in an attempt to get the game back to the break-even point.

The adjustment attack of strategy implemented by O'Brien at the half-time intermission was consummately thwarted by the strategy change made by Andy Trella. It showed in the faces of the Cougar players that they were frustrated at not even being able to execute against the zones. The zone defenses had vanished and were sent off to another time zone altogether. Thus, the Carolina Cougars felt that they were playing perhaps in the twilight zone. This made Bobby O'Brien, of all people, seem like a fool, and that's all that his Cougar players could think about. They needed to concentrate on basketball a hundred percent of the time, but they couldn't. A small percentage of that concentration was thinking that the young novice coach was coaching his pants off, and Coach O'Brien was caught with his pants down. It was not as if they had just fallen off for a moment. It was as if they fell off, and Andy Trella had stapled them to the ground where he couldn't pick them up.

Sheila and the cab driver were in a jubilant mood. The radio announcer was broadcasting the second half of the game. "Hank, this is absolutely unbelievable. I don't know if the Eagles will win this game, although it sure looks like it. But the whole college basketball world will be talking about this one for a long time. Andy Trella, who hasn't been a head coach for even a month, who hasn't even coached a half a dozen games, is completely astonishingly, out-coaching Bobby O'Brien and psyching out the Cougar players. Most importantly, it's reflected in the score of this game."

Hank said, "This is amazing! The Carolina players are in a state of turmoil, inner dissension, and could self-destruct. He, the kid coach, Trella, has foiled every move and countermove that Bobby O'Brien has tried."

The radio announcer said, "We have six and a half minutes gone by in the second half, with thirteen and one-half to go, and the Eagles are ahead 62–44, an 18-point lead, and Bobby O'Brien is searching frantically for answers and solutions, and he can't seem to come up with any."

Sheila had a smile on her face–a very proud smile. The cab driver was pumping his fist in the air, waving his arm so much that he almost forgot he was driving a cab. He was totally captivated, and Sheila understood.

"Gonna take 'em! Gonna take 'em!" he said. "Gonna do in Carolina tonight in my hometown Chicago. Watch out! There's a new sheriff in town, and his name is Andy T." Sheila was laughing at the carried-away tirade that the cab driver was letting loose. He turned around quickly and said to Sheila, "Shit, lady. Where did he learn to coach like that?"

"Don't ask me. I don't know how he does half the stuff he does."

"Well, lady, he's got the brother's playing like the brothers. I think you got yourself a golden boy. lady."

"I know." Sheila was quite happy, feeling thrilled at the judgment the cab driver made that left her content with her new-found boy friend.

Jimmy Tacker, on the television side of the broadcast, was becoming a believer. "I'm shocked. I'm stunned, Billy. I keep waiting for Carolina to get off on a roll, but it hasn't happened to this point. The Western Chicago Eagles are cutting them off every step of the way. There's still plenty of time left, but Carolina better start putting a dent into this lead, or it'll be over with even as much as seven to eight minutes left to play. The only good thing for Carolina is Rayford Williamson seems to be heating up and is doing all the scoring for the Cougars in the last four-and-a-half minutes. Without him, they'd be done for already. He now has twenty three points and is on the way to getting his thirty or more."

Billy Black took over the microphone and injected, "This game, for lack of a better word is just unreal, Jimmy. These student fans are as high as can be, up on their feet giving the Eagle squad an incredible amount of support. And Jimmy, I can't remember any basketball game where I've seen two coaches yelling, screaming at the refs, the players, and at each other to the degree with intensity that these two have here tonight. You have here the most experienced coach in all of college basketball against the youngest and most inexperienced coach in the entire country. And the young kid coach is taking the Carolina Cougars to school."

Jimmy Tacker said, "If you look at it on paper Billy, you say no way, it's impossible. But Andy Trella is eating Bobby O'Brien's lunch. This crowd really believes and that's helped tremendously. And the Eagle players really seem to love playing for Andy Trella, and that's so important for the players to respect and like their head coach. There has to be that something special between the players and the head coach, and when you have that, this is what can happen. And I'll tell ya, Billy, more than half the battle is believing you can. If you do, you will, and I think that's what we're seeing from Western Chicago University tonight."

SIXTY-FIVE

Even though the second half was a tight-fisted affair, the Carolina offensive attack was stifled, and so was the Western Chicago Eagles. The Cougars had to play tough, tight defense to even have a chance to get back in and they managed to do that. As a result, the two head coaches were exhibiting great degrees of frustration. The second half progressed, and both teams were merely matching basket for basket until the ten minute mark. Carolina chipped away at the lead slightly, getting the deficit reduced from eighteen to ten. The only reason was Rayford Williamson. For the most part, things were going well all night for Western Chicago University, but the student fans, the players, and Andy Trella only had one problem, and his name was Rayford Williamson.

He was on fire, uncorking two more shots in two-and-a-half minutes, hitting nothing but net. When play resumed, Rayford hit another shot, making him nine for his last eleven. The Eagle lead was now merely four points. However, Rayford did manage to acquire his fourth personal foul during that stretch.

O'Brien wasn't too alarmed with that. The Big C was now on the move at the most crucial part of the contest. It was like a heavyweight boxing match with the lightweight contender underdog beginning to fade, with the endurance and stamina of the champion surfacing to the top.

Andy called a time-out, hopefully to suppress the timely stint the Cougar players had put together. He massaged his palms into his face as if he were pounding pizza dough at a local town pizza shop on a Friday night, as if he had 30 large pies to make. He was boiling over with thoughts of strategy, but nothing seemed like the right choice. At this point, it was like a grab bag. He was certainly running out of weapons and strategy alternatives. He had used everything he could think of. He juggled players all night long, like musical chairs. He made adjustments, moves, countermoves, multiple defenses, perfectly executed plays, motivated players, disguised weaknesses, and exploited the Eagles' strengths. He used every trick he could think of. Yet, the lead was a measly four points. The crowd even began to simmer down considerably, compared to their consistent performance throughout the evening. They had sensed Carolina could be exactly where they wanted to be at this juncture.

Andy brushed his hair back off his forehead and said to the players and assistants, "We got to stop Rayford somehow."

Philip responded, "There's only one way."

"How?"

"Need a machine gun."

"That won't work, he's bulletproof. Okay Jefferson, you take Rayford the rest of the game. Turner, you're in. Kennedy, you're in for Skin Brain. For now, I want you to work extra hard on defense. We don't want to totally fall apart at this point and suddenly get blown out. If we got to play a close game to the wire, that's what we'll do. You guys played terrific tonight. You deserve a victory. Go get it!"

The players broke their huddle, and the fans started to clap in hopes of encouraging their confidence.

Billy Black said to Jimmy Tacker, "Well, Jimmy, here it is, just like you said. Sooner or later, we'd see a Carolina charge, and they're right in the middle of a run at a most critical point in the game."

"Billy," Tacker said, "Rayford Williamson has taken over this game completely. The momentum has swung over to Carolina, and we still have 6:45 left to play. I would not be surprised if Carolina didn't only catch Western Chicago, but even pulled away."

When play continued Rayford resumed his totally unconscious play. Alan Jefferson couldn't stop him at all. He hit three more jump shots–was twelve for his last fifteen and now had accumulated thirty-eight points for the game, which was more than half of his team's total output. The Carolina Cougars now led for the first time in the entire game, 74–72. They had wiped out an 18-point deficit.

The entire arena was not only sitting in their chairs, they were ungodly quiet, unlike the frenzy they had been in all night long.

Phil stood up off the bench and said, "Son of a bitch! We played great all night, and we're losing."

Up in the rafters, Timmy was smoking a cigarette and had a twisted pissed-off expression on his face. His girlfriend, Karen, was studying him, observing how upset he was, when he suddenly burst out, "Mother fucker!"

The cab driver stopped at a traffic light, turned around facing Sheila, and said, "Can you believe this shit!" Sheila had remained silent, hoping for the best. Then he punched the glass-framed box containing his photo identification card and smashed it.

Andy was immersed in calling out a play on the offensive scheme of things. He was shouting out numbers and gesturing with his hands to convey the particular play he had wanted them to run. The Eagle players were working the basketball up court, passing, and dribbling their way through the pressing Carolina defense. Chris Washington had received the ball in a favorable post-position, close to the basket, for a much needed easy two-points, but he shot the ball poorly, missing a relatively simple basket. When the rebound came off the backboard, Rayford Williamson was the one who had grabbed it. However, since Rayford was shot up with so much adrenalin from his outstanding performance, thus riding the crest of his confidence, he swung his elbows around in a loose and wild manner, accidentally hitting Alan Jefferson across his right eye extremely hard.

Jefferson immediately went down to the floor clutching his head with his huge hands. The crowd stood up and unanimously voiced their displeasure. Coach O'Brien's eyes dropped to the floor, and Andy moved closer to the referees, yelling and gesturing. The head referee, Jake, blew the whistle and stopped play. Rayford took the basketball and bounced it hard off the court. Then he caught it and threw the ball high into the crowd as he walked off the floor. Jake called the personal foul on Number 10.

The public address announcer broadcast over the system, "Personal foul number five on Number 10, Rayford Williamson." Rayford was now officially proclaimed out of the game for the remainder.

The crowd roared with approval as Rayford marched off the court and sat down. Bobby O'Brien gave him a big slap on his behind as he passed by, symbolizing his admiration for his fantastic performance. The student fans had now awakened from their reprieve and felt that this could be the pendulum that would push momentum back on their side.

Meanwhile, Andy Trella was on the court, leaning over the top of a teammate who was concerned with Alan Jefferson's condition. Alan turned his head to the side, revealing his previously concealed injury. Andy saw that Alan's eye was completely closed and that the hit he took swelled up to monumental size incredibly fast. Andy called for a towel to drape over Alan's head to shield the light from his eye; they then picked him up and assisted him off the court. Even though the eye was closed, he would experience further stinging sensations and tearing of the eye when sharp light penetrated it. Andy was no team trainer, but he wanted to make some small contribution to ease Alan Jefferson's pain. Within thirty seconds after they'd get Alan to the locker room, the team trainer would be applying ice packs to Alan's head.

Two of the team's players ducked their heads in under each of Alan Jefferson's armpits to begin assisting him off the playing area. When they began their escort, the trainer said, "Take him to the locker room."

Alan instinctively rebutted, "No man. Take me to the bench. I can't see, but I wanna at least hear this one out." He had given too much to this game and felt it unfair to be expected to sign off from it as if he was punching a time clock. So they did as he requested. They changed their course and walked him to the bench. The student fans offered the standard claps of the hands, which was the customary tribute when a player was able to walk off the court under his own power after a serious physical injury. Once Jefferson was sitting, the ice packs were torn open and applied immediately to Alan's face.

Andy stood with one hand on his hip and the other scratching his forehead briefly while looking at Alan Jefferson's injury. He was brainstorming and couldn't really decide what he wanted to do. Five minutes to go, down by two, and he just lost his best player for the remainder of the game, as did Bobby O'Brien. Andy thought that his team was extremely fortunate to get Rayford Williamson out of the game with a good five minutes left to play. But he never expected that he would lose his best player at the same time. It still was a great advantage to get Rayford out since he was purely playing in a God-like fashion tonight. Rayford had 38 points, which was his highest single game performance of the year, and he would have scored more had he not been eliminated for the last five minutes of play. Alan Jefferson was the second highest scorer of the game, with eighteen points, which wasn't even half of what Rayford had supplied. However, it still was a great loss for Western Chicago. They needed Alan Jefferson's offensive skill. Andy did not have enough time to think of what line-up he wanted out there, nor the right strategy to insert. It was do or die time now. He had to make the right selections, but late in the game, he was becoming a bit unsure of himself. He was procrastinating, not wanting to make a committed decision, especially since the pressure was certainly on him to make the right move. The injury time-out for Alan Jefferson had just concluded. He sensed panic, possibly even choke time. If Andy were a boxer, he was on the ropes and he knew it. He needed an idea. A lightning bolt. Divine intervention. Anything, but not just anything. A big anything. A light bulb went off. It came to him.

Andy looked over to Jake and signaled the appropriate gesture for a time-out. Jake awarded it, and the ballplayers were waiting for him to inform them of instructions on how to play the rest of the game. They were anxious. Both teams were huddling around the benches, and the crowd was on their feet. The arena was not loud at this point, since they were all stifled by the injury to their star player.

Suddenly, Andrew began walking away from his team's bench area. Phil, Winthrop, Bart, and the players were expecting Andy to go down on one knee and discuss strategy. As would Al Perkins, Dean Thompson, and the arena of student fans. As would television announcers, the radio people, the security people, the newspaper people, and all the people working the scorer's table, as well as the opponents.

O'Brien, while in a huddle, was being extremely talkative with his team. Suddenly, he became distracted as he had seen out of the corner of his eye his counterpart pacing along the court, appearing like he was walking off of it. O'Brien focused his attention, based on his curiousness, as to what in the hell this young kid was up to now. By now, everyone in the Rosemont Horizon was wondering why he wasn't addressing his team during the crucial two-minute time-out, and where he was off to.

The Eagle players couldn't figure out what was on his mind. Alan Jefferson, with the ice packs and towel wrapped around his head, couldn't see, said, "What's happening? What's going down? How come I don't hear Coach talking?"

"Don't know," Chris Washington answered. "He's walking away."

"What!"

For a moment, the Eagle bench was not only confused, they were distressed. There was no coach governing over them, no leader huddled before them. Their star player was injured and out of the game. There were five minutes to go, they were losing for the first time, and time was running out. Everyone was increasingly skeptical at Coach Andy Trella's antics. For they all knew he should undoubtedly be with his players for the few critical minutes he could talk to them.

All 18,000 eyes were focused on him, including the host team's cheerleaders. Even they were curiously alarmed at his sudden abandonment. When Andrew reached the center aisle of the court, juxtaposed from the scorer's table, he began to walk up the staircase of the center aisle into the crowd of fans.

In the taxi cab, Sheila and the cabby were paying the strictest attention to the radio broadcaster's words. "Folks, Andy Trella has called a time-out and he is not with his players at the Western Chicago Eagle bench. He is, amazingly, up in the stands, about ten rows up into the crowd, and he appears to be talking to someone. I don't know who, though. There's too many people standing up, and we can't see who it is, because whoever it is, is sitting down. Hank, do you know who he's speaking with?"

"Sid, I haven't the foggiest idea what he's up to or who he's talking to. Too many people are standing up in that area, impeding our vision. We'll just have to wait till we can see."

Andy was talking a mile a minute, his hands gesturing all over the place. Whomever he was speaking to was quiet and listening. Andy was informing the person that he and his team were finally running out of gas. He wasn't quite sure what strategy to use at this crucial juncture of the contest. He and his Eagle players had come too far, and he didn't want to blow this game, especially after his team played with incredible heart, desire, guts, and passion all night.

Andy Trella stepped aside in the aisle, and a man rose from his seated position and started to walk down the aisle, headed courtside. The immediate crowd started applauding tremendously, and the approval spread like a rapid wildfire throughout the entire Rosemont Horizon Stadium.

SIXTY-SIX

John Connors buttoned his suit coat as he came down from the stands headed courtside. Andy Trella was six to eight feet behind him, coming down the steps. John Connors altered his direction when his feet hit the court, turning and heading for the Western Chicago Eagle bench.

The fans were deliriously applauding with approval. The ball players were clapping themselves when they saw Big John Connors coming their way, only to aid their cause. Andy Trella had asked John Connors to take over the ball game.

Bobby O'Brien was in the middle of the basketball court, yelling and shouting at Jake Murphy in an unbelievably hostile manner. He was hot and had his face right in the head referee's jaw. O'Brien was yapping away, expressing his disfavor for what Andy Trella had just done. O'Brien was pissed off and began using obscenities. "This is bullshit! He can't do that! What kind of game are we running here, Jake? What are you fucking kidding me?"

Just because John Connors was going to coach the rest of the basketball game didn't mean the Eagles would automatically win. Their work was certainly cut out for them. But Bobby

O'Brien had had enough. Even though it was a perfectly legal maneuver, young Andy Trella had out-coached him all night long. This latest grab bag of tricks infuriated him because now he took it personally. Whether it would work or not didn't matter at the moment. He had enough with the young neophyte coach showing him up all night, felt incredible frustration, and so reacted.

Since his general reaction was so uncontrollable and the livid attitude so forcefully exhibited, Jake hit him with his second technical foul, which meant he was now thrown out of the game. The crowd went berserk. They knew O'Brien had one technical foul against him already. By being on the playing court illegally, combined with the tactless manner and choice of words he used, Jake Murphy had easily enough evidence to peg him with a second technical foul, and he did. Two technical fouls committed against any one person or coach was an automatic ejection from the game. Bobby O'Brien was gone. Done for the rest of the evening from managing his club. The crowd roared, hitting a new decibel level.

On the television side of the scorer's table, Jimmy Tacker was more excited than he had been all night while broadcasting. "Billy, Andy Trella has, without question, pulled a rabbit out of the hat. What a shocking set of developments. Listen to this. Do you realize that as a result of that last play with the injury to Alan Jefferson on the accidental foul by Rayford Williamson, both teams have lost not only their best two players, but both teams have lost their head coaches, as well."

"That's right, Jimmy," Billy said. "I didn't realize that. The four most important people to both teams are no longer in control of what happens in the last few minutes of this game. That's amazing! Of course, John Connors is at the helm, and Andy Trella is still going to be involved. But he has given this game over to John Connors who will undoubtedly be calling the shots the rest of the way for the Eagle team."

Jimmy Tacker added, "Bobby O'Brien has been thrown out of this game for being on the court and his excessive use of profanity against head referee, Jake Murphy. Only the third time he's been ejected in twenty years. And young Andy Trella, using an incredible amount of unconventional resources, has abdicated his coaching position and handed it over to his mentor, John Connors."

"Jimmy, we tried to predict what was going to happen here tonight. This is unquestionably amazing!" Billy Black said.

"Ya know, Billy, it's in the rule book that a head coach of any team can step down during a ballgame at any time and hand over the authority and management of a basketball contest in question, as long as the person is an employee of the university. And John Connors is certainly that. I have never seen it done before, here, or in the pro's. I've only seen when a coach was thrown out, as Bobby O'Brien was, and now Roy Hendley will take over the reins for the Cougar club. The resurgence of John Connors will allow him to run the show for the Eagles."

John Connors approached the Eagle bench there was an instant overwhelming divine aura in the air. In the box seat area, Al Perkins and Dean Thompson were smiling. Everyone was glad to see John Connors, but the manner in which he came back was spellbinding to everyone. He was the recipient of a standing ovation. The Eagle players formed a tight huddle around John Connors. He got down on one knee and addressed the team.

"Rayford Williamson is officially gone from this game. They only have one other real scorer, Kurt Timorson, so go with the box and one defense on him. Calvin Kennedy will play Timorson. The rest of you play a basic 2–2 zone."

Andy looked at John Connors as he spoke and smiled, realizing that John's strategy was exactly the correct move for this situation. It was so simple, but he'd never have thought of it. John Connors continued, "On offense, we'll go with the three quickest players, and Chris and Calvin playing down low on the post positions." Phil, Winthrop, and Bart smiled as the enthusiasm rose.

Across the court, Roy Hendley was governing his players and said, "Okay, without Ray, I want to go with specifically designed offensive plays for Timorson. Work the ball to his side of the court and pound it inside. Nobody else shoots the basketball unless you're wide open." The huddles on both sides broke. The players moved to the court, and the crowd egged the Eagle team on.

When play resumed, Calvin Kennedy hit both free shots as a result of the technical fouls acquired by Bobby O'Brien. They were also awarded possession of the ball after the foul shots were made. The Eagles inbounded the ball to Calvin Kennedy, who immediately put up a long-distance three-point shot that connected. The Eagles had scored five points in less than five seconds, up by three: 77–74.

On defense, the Eagles thwarted Carolina's plan to exploit Kurt Timorson each and every time. They blocked his shots, stole the ball from him; he bounced the ball off his foot and out of bounds. He missed a shot at the hoop by more than six feet. Each time he messed up, the Eagles got the ball and a different Eagle player came through by scoring. Calvin Kennedy was red hot. Chris Washington jammed one through the net as if his arm were a jack hammer. Bennett stole the ball and passed it up to Skin Brain, who finished it off. Eric Turner hit a lay-up and the Eagles astonishingly had a thirteen-point lead with one minute to play.

Once Carolina had scored their seventy-fourth point to take the lead for the first time, it was like a jinx. The Cougars did not score a single point since Rayford Williamson fouled out and Bobby O'Brien was thrown out. Andy Trella had demoted himself voluntarily and entreated John Connors to come to the forefront and assume control the rest of the way. All in a single swift moment, the wind was taken right out of the sails of the Cougar players and the Western Chicago players were revamped with adrenalin as if it was administered intravenously. Thus, the Eagle team went on a torrid scoring rampage that iced the game's victory, sending the fans into a jubilant frenzy.

With less than fifty seconds to play, the game was all but over, and the Western Chicago Eagle bench was loving it. The crowd was ecstatic. The tall, intense-looking, blonde student fan screamed his lungs out, stomped his feet, and waved his fist in the air.

Billy Black blurted out over the television microphone, "Well, folks, feast your eyes. The Western Chicago Eagles, a heavy underdog, are about to have knocked off the mighty Carolina Cougars. This certainly proves that in college sports, anything can happen. A team that is, at best, mediocre with, let's face it, an inexperienced young head coach has brought a giant university to its knees. Just incredible, Jimmy. By Andy Trella not going the distance, his team goes the distance. What a move."

Tacker said, "And it also throws a monkey wrench into the committee, as well. Knocking a chip off of Carolina's foothold for a top seed position, forcing the committee to recognize Western Chicago and its vibrant, obviously credible program as an attendee.

Billy Black then asked Jimmy Tacker, "What did you think of Andy Trella's game plan against Carolina?"

"Incredibly terrific, resourceful, all night long." He started to laugh and continued, "Are you kidding me? Just when it looks like he's on the ropes, desperate not to fall apart, he comes up with an ace in the hole. He summons John Connors back from total obscurity, which ultimately leads to Bobby O'Brien's ejection, and the momentum that had just been controlled by Carolina was instantly transferred right back to Western Chicago. I'd say you couldn't possibly ask for a better strategy or game plan than we saw here tonight on behalf of Andrew Trella."

Sheila's cab had just pulled to the curb outside the front entrance to the Rosemont Horizon. The snow plows were spread out all over the parking lot with their bright lights shining everywhere Sheila could see. She opened the cab door herself, not waiting for the cabbie's assistance. She bolted out of the car and started trudging through the snow. When she reached the cleared pavement, she began to run as the snow was still coming down violently.

The cab driver had the trunk of the car open and yelled out, "Hey, lady, don't you want your luggage?" Sheila never even turned around to respond. She began to open the entrance door to the arena with difficulty, as snow was tucked in at the base of the door on the ground. A huge snow drift fell off the overhang and fell right on her head, her hat now covered with snow. Sheila worked the door open and stepped inside. The cab driver started to walk the same pavement she had, only he was carrying her bag. Once Sheila was in the corridor she heard screaming, yelling, and cheering, and began to run toward the sounds she heard. She was able to get to the doors quickly, as her path was not impeded by the snow she had faced outside the building, nor by people, for there wasn't a soul in the corridors. When Sheila stepped into the arena, she was blocked by standing observers of the game. She saw people way up in the mezzanine level celebrating joyously. She looked in every direction around her, continuing to see people celebrating. She started to make her way through the crowd.

There were thirty seconds left in the contest and the Eagle bench was on its feet, jumping up and down waving their towels above their heads. They were ecstatic. The euphoric state of mind of each player was plainly fantastic. Sweet victory was never better than it was today. Today they were better than the powerhouse Carolina Cougars. The entire arena was standing on its feet cheering wildly.

Sheila had finally worked her way to the baseline under one of the basketball hoops. She spotted him instantly. Andrew was wearing a great big smile. He had both his arms pointed straight up in the air, and both his hands were clenched into tight fists.

He spun around one full time, a full 360 degrees, and pumped the chain three times with his arm. Sheila couldn't resist joining the over crowded gymnasium floor with a smile of her own. She then saw Winthrop, Bart, and Phil close toward Andy. They formed a tight circle and hugged each other all at once. The four of them raised their arms straight up in the air. The crowd was sensitized to the gathering taking place at the Eagle bench and loved it, especially when their huddle broke and their arms went climbing uninhibited into the air.

The contest was still not over. Only eleven seconds were left. In the corner, Bobby O'Brien appeared in an entrance. His arms were on his hips. He took it all in, wanting to observe for himself the incredible energy this university was uncommonly exhibiting. For the most part, he did not think of his stature, his reputation, or the legend that he was. Even though he was appalled by the events surrounding this night's game, he wanted to witness this university's celebration. He figured he might be able to learn something from this experience.

There were nine seconds left now, but it was clearly academic. For these last few seconds, the players on the court, all ten of them, played because they had to, not because they wanted to.

Sheila heard the crowd chant as everyone else did: "Nine! Eight! Seven! Six! Five! Four!" She was just admiring Andy, feeling so happy for him. She wished she had a camera at this particular moment. Then she thought, well you can't have everything. Having a boyfriend like Andrew, being loved by him and loving him was good enough. It was such a perfect moment that she felt privileged to just be an observer. She savored it in her heart and would tell him about it a million times over.

The student fans finished off the chant, like the finishing of a great song, "Three! Two! One!" Chris Washington, the tallest player for the Eagles, threw the basketball deep into the crowd in the upper mezzanine level. There was such a mighty roar in the Rosemont Horizon that it could have initiated an earthquake. The Eagle players and coaches ran onto the court, and the players who were playing were running off of it. They embraced, tackled, and hugged one another with the utmost conviction and sincerity.

Al Perkins, Dean Thompson, and John Connors were smiling big time, shaking hands and talking about the wildly intense basketball game they had witnessed and been part of.

SIXTY-SEVEN

Timmy King, who was still up in the rafters in the secluded section of the mezzanine level that was closed off to everyone else said to his girlfriend, "Okay, Karen, let 'em have it. Hit that power button, baby."

Karen followed his command and pressed the power button on the tremendous, elaborate stereo system that her boyfriend had put together. The music that came out of it was channeled through all twelve speakers that had been set up for the New Year's Eve party in just two weeks time. The music that bellowed out through the high-powered amplifying system descended over everyone.

The Western Chicago Eagle cheerleaders, who were underneath one of the basketball hoops, heard the music and recognized the song right off the bat. Without being told, they immediately dropped their pom poms to the floor and, in unison, went into a routine dance right then and there. The twelve cheerleaders were instantly hypnotized by this particular song, captivating their hearts and minds. The cheerleaders performed a magnificent, captivating routine as they danced to the beat and rhythm of the song perfectly.

The first ones to notice were the Eagle basketball players

themselves. They were much taller than everyone else, and several of them had girlfriends on the cheerleading team. When they saw the girls dancing away, they could not resist jumping in and joining the outrageous celebration about to take place. Many of the Eagle players had towels that they were waving high above their heads.

Mrs. Schmidt, the cheerleading instructor, had an expression on her face that was angry and confused. She called out to them, "Get back here! All of you! I want every last one of you to come back here right now and stop doing that dance!" Mrs. Schmidt meant what she said, but the problem was not one single person had heard her and even if they had, they would surely have ignored her. They were all having too much fun at the present time.

The players themselves joined the dance routine; not only was it charismatic, but the song was gaining momentum, as well as gaining membership by the dozens, as the student fans began to funnel down through the stands to the courtside's floor. The outstanding underdog's victory, combined with the especially perfect music that was cast out over the gymnasium of the Rosemont Horizon, indisputably converted the basketball arena into a widespread dance floor.

The entire crowd was in a standing ovation, clapping their hands, and swaying back and forth to the music. The dance routine that they were witnessing was mesmerizing. It had heart, charisma, emotion, and the uplifting spirit of human victory that catapulted everyone's adrenalin.

Timmy King was smoking a joint, bopping to the music, and his girlfriend, Karen, was quite happy in doing the same.

Andy was standing on the court and could see this unusual development on the other end of the room. He was quite captivated by it, especially since he noticed it was working its way toward him. Suddenly, the words of the song sprang out. "Life is a mystery, everyone must stand alone. I hear you call my name and it feels like home." Andy found himself standing in the middle of the floor all by himself. He then turned completely around in a fast, swivel motion, as he heard his name called by someone who was very close to him. There she was. Sheila was standing on the court ten feet behind him with a hat full of snow. She could not put it off any longer and ran toward him with the biggest smile she could possibly have had. She jumped into his waiting arms, and he caught her wholly and hugged her tightly. Within a few seconds, he had to put her down because he just had to look at that beautiful, happy face.

"Sheila, you missed the game."

She looked into his eyes deeply, strongly. "No, I missed you." Andy squinted his eyes and savored what she said. Sheila then said, while pointing to his head, "You can't stay out of trouble while I'm gone I see." He couldn't figure out what she meant for a second or two, and then touched the side of his face where the bandage covered his eye.

He smirked and said, "No, I guess not."

"Andy, what's going on?"

"I don't know. Come on."

He held his hand out for her to grab and she did so immediately. He led her into the stands and walked up six or seven rows in order to see the basketball court better and what was happening there. As they proceeded through the stands, Andy was shaking hands with the student fans who were clapping, dancing, and swaying back and forth. Sheila was watching people dancing on the court and on the opposite side, they were singing and swaying just as they were on the side she was on. Andrew could not turn around to watch as Sheila could, he was too busy shaking hands with people.

A little kid with a cute face and only one tooth up front held out a little notebook and pen. The kid didn't have to say a word. Andy knew what he wanted and obliged him with an autograph. A mother came over with her two-year-old child in her arms and said to Andy, "This is my son. He has the same name as you."

"Is that right?" Andy asked. "Well, when you have more kids, make sure you name them the same." The woman laughed out loud then moved on.

An elderly black man in a green uniform, the university's maintenance man, walked in front of the gymnasium's doors which were all open. He was pushing a mop bucket with a mop in hand. His heart could have fallen out of his mouth when he saw all those people dancing on the gym's floor, knowing he would be the only one to clean it up. That would be quite a job with millions of scuff marks on the parquet floor. The very next moment, the black cab driver appeared next to him with Sheila's luggage in hand. Simultaneously, they both recognized one another and pointed their fingers at each other. The maintenance man dropped his mop and put on a huge grin. The cab driver dropped the luggage and did the same as they hugged each other.

Just then, the men who had been manning the snow plows in the parking lots appeared next to the two black men. They were curious to find out what the hell was happening. One of the men asked, "What the hell's going on in here?"

The thin-looking janitor answered him, "We just beat Carolina."

"Bullshit!" the plow driver said.

"Kicked their ass all night long, beat 'em good," the janitor responded.

As the snow plow guys looked bewildered, one of them said, "Holy Shit."

Bobby O'Brien was below Andy with his four assistants at his side. He climbed up two or three steps and Andrew jumped down three or four to meet him. O'Brien extended his hand and shook Andrew's and said, "I don't know who the hell you are or where you came from, but you did a phenomenal job here tonight."

"Thanks."

"Listen, kid, there's one thing I want you to know while

you're having the time of your life and that's that you're getting real popular very quickly, and I don't like it. I'm the MAN of college basketball out here in the Midwest. I've had five books written about me, my own television show, million-dollar endorsements. I don't like the idea of you threatening my fame."

"Well, you know what?"

"I'm listening."

"You better get used to it."

O'Brien was shocked at the young kid's response. "I'll be back."

"We'll be here," Andy concluded.

Bobby O'Brien departed with his four sidekicks. If he had a tail, he would be walking out with it pointed down between his legs. He then observed one of his assistants tapping his foot to the music. He gave him a hard stare and the assistant immediately became a statue. When O'Brien walked on, he stepped on the assistant's shoe that had been tapping away. The assistant yelled, "Ouch" and O'Brien walked on without apologizing.

Al Perkins stepped up onto the bleachers, shook Andy's hand, and said, "How you doing, kid?"

"Pretty damn good, to tell you the truth."

Al then looked at the young woman who was holding hands with Andrew and said, "Hello."

"Hi!"

"You know something? You're something else."

"What do you mean?"

"You never told me you were a magician?"

"You never asked."

Both the man and the young adult laughed.

Al said, "You know what else you did tonight?"

Confidently Andy said, "Yeah. Just about finalized the deal with WGNB for $3. 7 million for television next year."

"How did you know that?" Al asked with great surprise.

"Don't you think I hear things?" Andy then steered away from Al, taking Sheila with him, holding her hand.

Al said aloud to himself, "No, I don't."

A very pretty girl came up to Andy as he was still shaking hands. She stopped him then kissed him on the cheek. She smiled and walked away. Andy looked at Sheila and she made a face, making him think she was jealous and didn't care for that sort of thing. Of course, she did it in a manner that let him know that she was mature and understanding. Sheila was not being insecure.

"Tonight you can get away with that. But next time watch out!"

Just then, Sheila tapped Andy on his shoulder. He turned to her and his face, if it could talk, would have asked, what? She pointed down at the court for him to get a look. He turned around to face the arena. The song was building up to its greatest climax. The cheerleaders were leading the way, and it seemed that they were at the pinnacle of their dance sequence. There were easily three hundred people out on the basketball court dancing behind the girls and the players. The only thing that was peculiar was they were now heading up the side of the stands, targeted toward Andy Trella. Andrew saw this right away and reached out for Sheila's hand and jerked it closer to himself. He wanted her closer to him since he was momentarily insecure. But he also wanted her next to him for selfish reasons. Andy was quite consciously aware that soon he was to be the center of attention, for something.

This dance was meant to be a tribute to him. The cheerleaders and basketball players were now dancing their way up into the crowd toward Sheila and Andrew.

At the scorer's table, a couple of wildly excited students stole the headsets from Bill Black and Jimmy Tacker. They were screaming and yelling with joy as both Tacker and Black were smiling at the crazy antics they were seeing.

Alan Jefferson was dancing on the bleacher's seats, doing the moonwalk with the towel wrapped as a blindfold over both his eyes. He was astonishingly impressive, since it was so dangerous to be doing what he was–and blindfolded. People were really enjoying Alan Jefferson's talented footwork, especially since he had been injured.

The whole stadium was rocking. If ever there was a night the Rosemont Horizon would come down, this was certainly it. The core of the Rosemont was like a nuclear power plant reactor ready for major explosion and final meltdown.

The cheerleaders formed a circle that was hardly perfect, but a circle it was, and Andrew was in the middle of it with Sheila right at his side. There were many fans within close proximity to this gathering. Two of the basketball players, while waving their towels high and hard, reached up with their free hands and each grabbed both Andy's wrists and raised their long arms upward. Naturally, Andrew's arms followed their flight as his fists were clenched tightly. Sheila moved one bleacher step below Andrew and was now facing him with her head equal to his chest. She had a big grin on her face as she looked up at him and saw him smile quite charmingly as the basketball players danced with their feet while keeping their arms up stationery to signify that they had beaten the best. Magnificent, letter-perfect victory would never be more glorious than this.

There were perhaps 500 students out on the court, dancing out on the wooden floor behind the cheerleaders. The song was nearing its conclusion. Andy and Sheila saw people across from them swaying back and forth as happy as hell. Just then, everyone on the dance floor threw their hands up high into the air to symbolize glorious victory and the ultimate in happiness. Then they suddenly clapped, dropped their arms down, turned and clapped, turned and clapped, and turned, and clapped again. It was a grand sight. They all threw their hands up high in the air again and clapped, turned the opposite way, and clapped, and turned, clapped and turned, and clapped and turned again.

It was 10:47 p.m., and outside the Rosemont Horizon it was dark, a frigid 12 degrees as the great gusts of the windy city pushed the accumulations everywhere. There was no sign of life anywhere. Everything seemed to be either dead or dormant or inside. Only sounds of exuberant singing and dancing could be heard in the loneliness of the night. For these privileged ones on the inside were singing and dancing with vivacious contentment. The court was a COURT OF DREAMS. For the members of Western Chicago University, it was the greatest dance party they had ever seen or participated in. For the players, they were the champions of the city of Chicago for a single night that no one could dispute.

For the fans, the players, the coaches, for the athletic department, for Al Perkins, Dean Thompson and John Connors, for the entire University of Western Chicago, it was an epic night for the history of the school's annuals. Nothing could be better than this. It was the best. For Andy Trella and Sheila Collins, it wasn't the best, but it was damn near close. The best for them was yet to come their way.

Andy dropped his arms and hands down from the players who were holding them up. He grabbed Sheila and drew her close to him. Andrew said, "I love you, Sheila."

Sheila moved into his mass and said, "I love you, Andy." They kissed each other passionately.

And so on a snowy night in December in downtown Chicago at the Rosemont Horizon, they both were consumed by a perfectly mesmerizing evening as the fans sang and danced the night away, on a night that anyone who was there would remember for a long, long time.

THE END

ACKNOWLEDGMENTS

Special thanks to Barbara Spinelli, Carl Sabatino, Christian Lee, Nancy Koch, Ray Stallone, Joe Stallone, Mary Stallone, Mike Shershenovich, Irina Babushkina, Joe Garcia Jr., Robert Youngren, The Freeport Memorial Library, the team of Red Penguin, especially Stephanie Larkin, Janet Larkin, and Katherine Abraham for contributing to *Court of Dreams*.

ABOUT THE AUTHOR

Frank Michael Stallone is a scriptwriter with half a dozen screenplays completed. He has written and produced several short films. In recent years he thrown his hat into the acting environment securing a principle character in the feature film *Skid Row*. *Court of Dreams* is his very first novel and is currently working on his second novel, *The Duplicate*.